Happily Ever After
Everyone Else

She Said He Said Series
The Morins Book 1

Happily Ever After
Everyone Else

Mary Becker
Diane St.Cyr Janelle

MOUNTAIN ARBOR
PRESS

MOUNTAIN ARBOR
PRESS
Alpharetta, GA

ISBN: 978-1-63183-086-0

Library of Congress Control Number: 2017931297

10 9 8 7 6 5 4 3 2   0 9 1 1 1 7

Printed in the United States of America

∞This paper meets the requirements of ANSI/NISO Z39.48-1992 (Permanence of Paper)

This book is dedicated to women everywhere who are part of the sandwich generation, always trying to balance raising children and caring for aging parents, while deeply longing for that romance with your significant other. Be encouraged—you can make it happen!

—Mary

For my husband, Marc, and our children, Emilie and Mathieu, whose generous love and support help to make my dreams possible; for my parents, Arthur and Lorraine St.Cyr, who gave me so much and made my education possible; and for God, who makes all things possible.

—Diane

One advantage of marriage, it seems to me, is that when you fall out of love with each other, it keeps you together until maybe you fall in love again.
—Judith Viorst

Acknowledgments

We, the coauthors, would like to practice what we've always preached to our children, which is to generously show gratitude to others. First and foremost, we would like to thank God for all that we have, all that we are, and the blessing of being able to share our mutual passion for writing. It's always wonderful when God provides us the opportunity to work with a friend and a P.I.M.P. (Pea in My Pod)! A close second on the list are our husbands for always being there to listen, to laugh, and to love us unconditionally in spite of ourselves! We would then like to acknowledge our children for bringing to our lives the lightheartedness of youth and their friendships as adults. Both of us would also like to honor our parents, who have all since passed, for the privilege of caring for them at the end of their lives the way they did for us at the beginning of ours; the faith and values we hold in our hearts today, we owe to them. Our in-laws also deserve our gratitude for raising the remarkable sons who became our husbands. Merci mille fois!

We acknowledge the rest of our families as well—our siblings and their spouses, other in-laws, and our nieces, nephews, aunts, uncles, cousins, and grandchildren—for their love, humor, and encouragement while writing this book. A big thank-you goes to our friends, coworkers, and those in our networks for their suggestions and inspirations, and for keeping us on task by repeatedly asking us, "When is that book going to come out?"

We feel blessed by the Mountain Arbor Press team for helping us to answer that question with their guidance, timelines, and expertise, not to mention those fun wolf-personality tests and mouthwatering bundtini moments we shared! Your staff rocks!

Lastly and most importantly, we are definitely grateful for our readers, who are taking this journey with us. The characters Julie and Mike Morin are family to us now, and so, all together, we'd like to welcome you to our crazy, funny, sometimes dysfunctional, but always loving gang!

Chapter 1

Sex? Definitely not. Self-improvement? No. Horror? Perhaps. Nothing seemed to fit the mood of the moment. Then she saw it—comedy. That was exactly what they needed!

Julie was standing in the middle of the audiobook aisle at the public library. It seemed humorous to her that choosing an audiobook for the trip to Wisconsin seemed more like naming the type of *marriage* that she and Mike had lately. Perhaps their marriage was like a mystery; they had started off young and clueless, and had ended up trying to figure out who did it to whom and with what weapon.

Yes, marriages could be compared to books. Some were total comedies, while others were filled with drama or romance. Which one described her and Mike? *Mr. and Mrs. Michael and Julie Morin . . . hmm.* She couldn't choose, but Julie was sure that she needed something funny to lighten the mood between her and Mike during this trip.

Julie chuckled to herself as her eyes fell upon the next title sitting on the shelf before her: *Weight Loss in Ten Easy Days.* All she could think of was how a divorce could help a woman lose 150 pounds or more in ten days, no matter what her spouse was named! The very next title brought her laughter to a noticeably louder level: *You Are What You*

Eat. The evil thought entered her head, *Mike must be eating the back end of a lot of horses lately!* Julie moved on to the next section, where she found several audio comedies. She finally found two CDs that fit her needs perfectly: a self-improvement one entitled *Sextraordinary! Putting Passion in Your Marriage* by Maggie Jones, and a comedy, *Until Death Do Us Part (Cyanide Mint, Anyone?)* by Thelma Bermback. On the cover of the second CD was a review written in bold letters stating that the book was "loved and laughed to by husbands and wives alike!" These words struck Julie like an arrow hitting a bull's-eye. Perhaps these audiobooks would lessen the grip of the stresses that wrapped themselves tightly around Julie and Mike. Heck, it might even get them to talk! Talk was that four-letter word that freaked out men a lot more than any four-letter "f" word ever had. *Well,* she thought, *if we don't talk, at least we'll laugh!* Laughter would, for sure, beat any cross-country silence that likely awaited them. Julie wasn't going to allow that to happen without a fight.

She took the two audiobooks with her and stopped by the children's section to find a fun pop-up book her granddaughter could enjoy in case she got bored during the wedding ceremony. Having raised five children herself, Julie knew the little tricks that her daughter Erin might not know yet in raising Grace. Julie loved being a helpful grandmother, especially when she could steal time to enjoy her grandchildren. She located a great pop-up filled with lots of classic children's songs. There were tabs that could make Jack and Jill slide up and down a hill. A finely detailed London Bridge majestically came to life when the page was turned, popping up to full attention. It could still be folded back down to look as if it had fallen. The book brought back to Julie the words of those classic children's songs she had grown up with, and she wore the hint of a smile while revisiting precious memories. She had sung them, her children had sung them, and now Grace would too. This would be one of those wonderful traditions passed down through time.

Time! Oh my goodness! What am I doing, browsing and daydreaming? Mike is waiting for me!

Julie abruptly shut the pop-up book, added it to her selections, and rushed to the library's checkout line. The line was really long for a Wednesday morning. Several mothers with children in tow were ahead of her. What was the delay, anyway? As she searched for her library card in the overstuffed purse that resembled her life, she found the packing list that she had written the previous day. It included all the items they would need for their oldest son William's wedding to his fiancée, Elizabeth, in Wisconsin.

First on the list were all the things their daughter, Erin, would need. She was two years younger than William and was happily married to Scott with their own two children, Grace and Alex. Being a young family with a preschooler and a newborn, they required the most items to be brought to Wisconsin. Traveling by air was just not conducive to dragging along all those items they would need along with a bridesmaid gown.

"Next? Next in line, please . . . ma'am?"

Julie found herself being nudged from behind and hurriedly approached the counter, checked out her items, and headed out of the library. The oppressive Georgia humidity hit her hard as she hurried outside. It felt like one of her hot flashes reaching out to embrace her. As she opened the car door, the high temperature from the interior of the car felt like the oppressive fumes from some invisible molten lava that must have been sizzling somewhere inside. Oh, yay! Just what her perspiring body needed right now.

She genuinely considered starting the car and waiting outside the vehicle until the air conditioner worked a miracle, but that would put her even more behind schedule. She knew time was a luxury she couldn't waste at this point.

There's just never enough time!

Julie started the engine and steered the car out of the parking lot and onto Dahlonega Highway. She checked her watch. Mike was not going to be happy with the length of time she had spent on this particular errand.

Suddenly, Julie was cut off by another driver who had quickly pulled out in front of her, only to slow down once he was on the roadway. "Just great," she muttered. "Just what I need . . . a rude moron who rushes out and then slows down." It felt like they were traveling at the speed of a slug attached to a snail on the back of a turtle. Oh, how that type of driver irritated her (and probably every other person in America)!

"*C'mon!*"

The rude driver finally turned after having led their little caravan to nowhere for half a mile. "YES!" Julie exclaimed with disbelief. She smiled as she congratulated herself on her new pretend telepathic skills. "Wish I could do that with other irritating drivers whenever I needed the ability," she said triumphantly as she accelerated to make up for the delay. She had just made it through the set of lights at Bethelview and Kelly Mill, cruising just a bit above the speed limit, when the hammer of the time gods slammed down upon her in the form of flashing blue lights in her rearview mirror. She pulled over to let the cruiser go by, but it pulled up behind her.

Mrs. Julie Morin, congratulations! We, the time gods, are here to award you your prize! You've won a traffic stop with a local deputized officer of the law and another delay in time. Crap.

Julie parked just past the exit lane from West Forsyth High School's parking lot. Why was she being pulled over by this officer? She quickly glanced toward the passenger seat to reassure herself that her purse was there. She would need her driver's license in her wallet if the officer asked. Next to her purse were her audio selections and the pop-up book with a picture of the London Bridge on it. The London Bridge rhyme popped into her mind as she watched the deputy exit his cruiser. Julie couldn't believe this was happening to her next to, of all places, the school where she taught! She hadn't run the light, her plate was current, she hadn't been speeding *that* much, and she didn't need more problems or stress in her life right now! The rhyme returned to haunt her with a twist on its original verse:

Julie Morin's falling down, falling down, falling down.
Julie Morin's falling down, poor ol' Julie!

As the officer approached the car, Julie pressed the button to lower her window. A loud car horn beeped; then there came another honk, a wave, and another beep. Her heart began to race and her palms became clammy. Why was she so nervous? Surely there was some mistake. She didn't think she had done anything to break the law. She kept her eyes cast downward. She was deeply embarrassed.

"Way to go, Mrs. M!" shouted a voice belonging to yet another driver leaving the high school's parking lot and zipping past the situation. How was she going to explain yet another delay to her husband?

"License and registration, please, ma'am," said the deputy in a businesslike manner. The car's manual and some papers tumbled onto the floor mat of the car as she opened the glove box.

Falling down, falling down, poor ol' Julie!

The deputy waited patiently as Julie retrieved the registration. Next, she dug down deep into her purse like a claw in a prize machine. She finally located her license and handed it over to the officer along with the car's registration. Julie forced herself not to burst out crying as humiliation painted her face a shameful shade of red. The officer thanked her and retreated to his vehicle with the necessary information.

Take the key and lock her up, lock her up, lock her up.

Take the key and lock her up, poor Julie Morin!

She brought her window up to preserve the air conditioning that she so desperately needed at this point, wanting something, anything, to keep herself busy — tapping her fingers on her steering wheel . . . glancing in the rearview mirror to see the deputy talking into the cruiser's mike . . . picking up the papers on the floor mat . . . then returning to tapping her fingers. She slowly returned her gaze to the rearview mirror to see him now looking down at something.

Is he reviewing my entire life? He's so-o-o slow . . . like that darn slug attached to a snail on the back of that turtle, only the turtle works for the government now. Oh, yay. He must be writing up a darn ticket; I just know it.

Beeping came from another exiting car. Julie was dying of humiliation. This was not going to do anything to help ease the stress at home right now, that was for sure! Julie's eyes once again returned to the rearview mirror to stare at the deputy. She tried her luck with her pretend telepathic powers. Using the strongest brain waves she could muster, Julie willed the cop to let her go. Her eyes widened as the deputy exited his cruiser right at that very moment.

Did my willful wishing actually work again? Could it be? Could it be?! Crap. He's holding a paper with my license and registration. I guess my telepathic skills are more like tele-pathetic.

Julie brought the window back down and was surprised to see a smirk on the deputy's face as he held out what she thought was a ticket for some awful offense that would surely push her marriage further into a stressful pit of demise. "Mrs. Morin, are you a teacher at this high school?" he asked.

"Yes, I am," Julie replied, surprised and a bit confused by his smirk.

"Well, good. The football players are all leaving from a summer practice session right now, and you are offering them a valuable lesson: no one is above the law. You were going a little bit too fast, and that is why I stopped you."

Falling down, falling down . . .

Then he continued. "However, seeing as you have no prior offenses and you've offered a great lesson to your students, I'm going to let you off with a written warning this time. But you need to either slow down or have your speedometer checked." He handed all the documents to her, wished her a good day, and returned to his vehicle to shut off the blue lights that welcomed everyone to the *Julie Morin Show*. She felt relieved for a few moments before a more painful thought occurred to her: *What show is waiting for me back home at this point? Cyanide mint, anyone?*

She continued down the road a bit before turning into the local pharmacy. Julie dashed into the store, found her target aisle, picked up the two bottles of antacid tabs that were listed on her errands list, and headed to the checkout counter. Even if it took a few more minutes of her precious time, these bottles were necessary items for the Morins' trip. They were vessels of comfort for Mike's and Julie's stomachs as they navigated the upset waters of the pressure-filled life they had come to know. Julie purchased the products, left the store, and returned to her car. She pulled out and came to the stop sign at the parking lot's exit. Julie was upset with Mike for pressuring rather than appreciating her. She was upset with herself for speeding and getting pulled over by the deputy. She was upset about her humiliation with the football players. She was even upset that she had allowed herself to become so upset about so many things! How she would love to scream out her frustration at the world right now! Julie changed her face to one of rebellion as she kept her left foot planted on the brake while her right foot floored the gas. She quickly tried to release the brake so that she could squeal her wheels out of the parking lot and scream at the world with her tires. The car lurched forward instead, and it sent Julie's head banging into the top of the steering wheel, causing her to yelp in pain. She quickly stopped the car to get it back under control. A driver approaching from behind beeped at her and yelled out, "Way to go, Mrs. Morin! Hey, I can show you how to really peel out if you want!"

Oh, for goodness' sake! It's another football player from school. Falling down, falling down.

Julie gave an embarrassed smile, waved politely, and continued to the left lane as she turned onto Post Road. She couldn't even get being upset right. Julie gave a quick look into the rearview mirror and noticed the start of a small, red circle in the very center of her forehead.

"Great! It will probably be a bruise by tomorrow. Well, now Mike can scratch it like a marital lottery card and see what prize he won. Oh, lucky us!"

Julie continued to make her way back to her neighborhood, and then drove slowly down the cul-de-sac that led to her house. When her kids were younger, they had referred to it as the cool-de-sac. Now it was more like a kill-de-sac with all the arguing and tensions brewing in their home. She could see Mike packing some of the last items into their practical Chevy Traverse. Once her floral suitcase was in place, he slammed the tailgate shut. That didn't make any sense to Julie; hadn't he remembered her last comment this morning as she had walked out of the master bath? "Be sure to pack the bridesmaid dress last so it doesn't get wrinkled!" He must have known she meant for it to be at the rear of the car so the skirt could be spread out and not get creased. She wondered how Mike had positioned the suitcases for three of their sons and the travel pack for her mother in relation to the dresses. It really wasn't feasible for them to navigate the world's busiest airport with all their luggage. It also wasn't practical to have to iron a wrinkled gown in a hotel room before the wedding. Lord knows that dress would probably get scorched, and where would they find the time to take it to be professionally ironed once they arrived in Madison?

Julie parked her car near a young magnolia tree at a curve in the street so that the tree could mask most of the car from Mike's vision should he look that way. She could feel her blood pressure rising, and she needed to calm down. After all, she knew there would already be a discussion about her being late, and she was determined not to stoke the flames of an argument in this sultry August heat. She planned to be the first one to speak and explain why she was late. Julie had learned from her sports-loving sons that the best defense is a good offense, so employing this strategy would hopefully control the conversation.

Pulling out from the shelter of the magnolia and continuing down the street, she maneuvered the car next to Mike and rolled down the window. But before she could even say anything, Mike began with a snap, "Where have you been and why are you so late? And by the way, where's the list?"

Julie started to say, "Well, I . . ."

Mike shot her a look of annoyance before she could finish. "Just park the car in the garage! It's time for lunch, and thank you, we're now behind schedule."

Wow! She had expected Mike to be upset with her for being so late, but she certainly hadn't mentally prepared herself for that much of a reaction. She was definitely getting home later than expected, but what had fueled his mini outburst? He made no comment about the bruise forming in the center of her forehead. If he did notice it, he didn't seem to care about its origin or her well-being. As far as that list was concerned, yes, she had absentmindedly picked it up when she grabbed her purse off the dresser, but so what? They had been married a very long time, long enough for her to know Mike was more than capable of remembering everything on that list and packing the car on his own. If he was that troubled by it being missing or if he had a question regarding the items, why hadn't he just called her cell phone? Julie had made sure that her phone was fully charged the night before, so she knew without a doubt that she would not and had not missed a call.

She bit her lip as she guided the car ever so slowly to the vacant spot in the three-car garage. She hated having to pull into the garage with any of her sons' vehicles already parked there. Brett's extended-cab truck usually occupied that space, but since the boys and GG would be taking that vehicle to the MARTA train station for their trip to the airport, it made sense for her to store her own car there instead. GG, her mother and the boys' grandmother, had this affectionate name because she was a great-grandmother now, thanks to Grace and Alex. Julie thought of their large family, their five cars, the three-car garage, and the wide driveway. In her mind, she could hear Mike complaining, "Why can't the boys share one vehicle? If the neighbors owned this street, they would want to set up a tollbooth and pocket a gazillion dollars off of us for all the times we are driving in and out of here, backing out to have someone drive in, or backing in to let someone get out."

Yes, Mike was right; she too wished that the boys could share one vehicle. That would save her the stress of hoping she did not ding one of their vehicles or put another dent in the extra refrigerator that was directly ahead of her. She backed up and made another attempt at turning the wheels a bit more sharply. If she did damage that old fridge, it wouldn't be such a great loss. After all, it wasn't currently stocked. She had made sure that anything perishable in that fridge had been used so that nothing would spoil while they were away.

Grabbing her purse and all the items from the library, she opened the car door and squeezed past the refrigerator. She thought Mike would still be standing in the driveway, but he was no longer there.

He probably already ran up to the shower and will be expecting his lunch by the time he comes back downstairs. I definitely need to hurry! What should I make?

Opening the door to the kitchen, she heard her son John say to his best friend, "Hey Zach, can you pass the dressing to my Gram?"

"Hi, guys. Hi, Mom," Julie said as she entered the kitchen and set everything in her arms down on the counter.

"Hey," the boys chimed in near unison as they turned toward Julie.

"Hello, dear. Glad you're home," added GG.

"We're having subs and salads for lunch. Want some?" asked John.

"Thanks, honey, but that's okay. I'm going to fix lunch for your dad and me."

"Say, what day are we flying out?" GG asked the group.

"That's Thursday, Gram," John replied.

"Well, go ahead and pour yourself something, honey, if you're thirsty," offered GG. "But you didn't answer my question. What day do we fly to Wisconsin?"

John looked confused. "I just did."

"You did? I don't see the glass, but that's nice."

Zach joined in the conversation. "No, GG. I think John is just saying that he already told you the day you're flying out."

"Oh? He does? Well, that's what I want to know too, Zach! Doesn't anybody here know? John and I are supposed to leave for Wisconsin on Thursday, I think."

John chuckled. "I think so too!"

"So do I!" Zach added.

"I know everyone has drinks! But I seriously think we are supposed to fly out on Thursday!" GG's frustration was growing.

"WE KNOW!" Zach and John half shouted together with smiles on their faces.

"RENO? NO! John and I are going to WISCONSIN! You boys need to listen better when someone is telling you something! Good thing my hearing and my memory are as solid as the day I was born! One of us needs to know what's happening on this trip! I can't wait to see William get married to that lovely girl—*in Wisconsin!*"

The boys and Julie all looked at each other, suppressing smiles from their faces as GG continued, "Well, that lunch was great. Thanks, boys. All this fuss has made me tired. I'm going to head upstairs for a nap. See you in a bit."

"Okay, Gram," said John.

Julie added, "See you in a bit, Mom."

GG walked slowly out of the room and up the stairs to her bedroom. John was the first to speak again. "Well, I'm done too." He brought his and GG's dishes to the counter and then placed them in the dishwasher. Zach got up from the table with his glass and plate and walked over next to his friend at the counter. Zach placed his glass in the dishwasher and the boys headed out. "Where are you headed?" Julie asked.

John replied, "Well right now I need to call and see how my football team's offense did this morning at practice."

Oh my goodness! Julie had already forgotten about that embarrassing scene with the deputy on Kelly Mill! She hoped that whichever football player it was that John was calling hadn't been in one of cars that had passed her and the flashing blue lights! Maybe Mike already knew about the scenario and that's why he had snapped at her. Julie bent down and lifted the panini maker from underneath the counter. She plugged it in and retrieved the leftover roast beef, sautéed onions, and remaining cheese slices from the refrigerator. As she was slicing the ciabatta bread for their lunch, the house phone rang. She picked up their land line and answered it.

"Hello? Can you speak up, please? I can barely hear you. Brett? Brett, is that you?" There was a very long pause before Julie exclaimed, "Oh, my goodness! Are you all right, honey?"

It was then that John reentered the room, obviously thinking the phone call was for him. "Hurry! Get Dad," whispered Julie.

"What happened?" asked John.

"It doesn't matter, John, just get Dad!" Julie scolded him. It was at that moment that Mike entered the kitchen from outside on the deck. Julie was surprised to see him—she had thought he was in the shower. "Here. Take the phone. It's Brett."

By the end of Mike's conversation with Brett, he had a captive audience. "Brett had an accident on Highway 9, but he's okay. Truck is totaled, though, so John, I need you to go get him. Take your time and drive carefully."

"But what happened, Dad?"

"Brett will fill you in, John. Right now, I just need you to take your vehicle and go pick up your brother."

John and Zach left quickly, and Julie found herself still standing in front of the panini maker, holding the knife in her hand.

"What happened, Mike? All Brett told me was that there'd been an accident, but he was all right."

"Brett was on his way home from work for lunch. He was coming down the hill on Highway 9 just past the Baptist church. His windows were rolled down because the interior of the truck was so hot that the air conditioning couldn't cool the inside quickly enough all by itself. He figured the air movement would help. As he rounded the curve, a sparrow flew in through the open window and somehow flew up the leg of his cargo shorts."

"WHAT?" Julie couldn't believe what Mike was saying. "You have GOT to be joking!"

"That's what I thought at first too, but it really happened, according to Brett."

"Okay," said Julie, frozen with the knife in her hand. "Continue."

"Well, Brett thought it was a bee that had buzzed in and gotten lodged inside his pant leg, so he began swatting at his leg. Apparently, he was really surprised when a bird suddenly flew out. That's when his eyes left the road, he said, and he hit several trees and totaled the truck. Fortunately, there wasn't a lot of traffic in either lane, so no other people were involved. The good news is, if that's even possible, that there were good Samaritans who stopped to make sure Brett was all right. The fellow who saw it happen called the sheriff, so assistance came very quickly."

"Wow," said Julie. "That's almost unbelievable!"

"Sure is," said Mike. "And you know what else is unbelievable?" Julie couldn't imagine there being anything more to this wild tale. "When Brett gave the responding deputy his full name, that deputy asked Brett if he wouldn't happen to be the son of a Julie Morin. Brett asked me why the deputy would ask him that. Care to explain *that one*?"

"No, not really, but I will," Julie replied with dread.

"Oh! Don't bother!" said Mike. "I already got the explanation from Brett, who got it from the deputy. Were you not going to tell me about your speeding fiasco? Did you think that since you were given a verbal warning I wouldn't find out and you wouldn't have to tell me?"

Julie stiffened her body with her response. "Mike, I never got the chance to tell you! You practically bit off my head when I pulled into the driveway! Then you cut off my explanation and told me to park the car and that you wanted lunch! So I stopped—and I parked when you barked! Then I came inside to make lunch." Julie felt like she was being grilled, endlessly pressed, and filled with unappreciated resentment. Yes, she was being grilled, filled, and pressed! She closed her eyes and whispered, "I feel like a panini."

"Really? A panini?" Mike jumped in. "I took the time this morning to make two perfectly fine hamburger patties for us, and they are apparently still sitting in the refrigerator, just waiting to be grilled for lunch so there is no muss, fuss, or clean-up, but no-o-o, Julie bypasses the quick and easy plan because she feels like having a panini!"

Julie could feel her face becoming pink. Just once, couldn't he listen closely to what she was saying? "I didn't say I felt like *having* a panini. I said *I felt like a panini*! I am getting melted and fused together from all sides here. Haven't you heard of our generation being referred to as the sandwich generation? Sandwiched between kids and aging parents who need our assistance? If it's not my mother who needs my help, one of our children needs me. And if I don't have an obligation with one of them, I have an obligation to do something for you!" She immediately realized she shouldn't have phrased it in that exact manner. "Well, I mean . . . I mean . . . like make lunch! I'm just saying that my to-do list never ends!"

Mike launched in with his retort. "Oh yes, let's talk about lists, shall we? Or maybe just one list—the list that disappeared! The list you were supposed to leave with me so I wouldn't miss anything, right? Like say, for instance, loading a walker, a baby monitor, or *a bedpan*? Come on Julie, really? A bedpan? What in the world were you thinking? The hotel we are staying at does indeed have indoor plumbing, you know!"

"I'll tell you what I was thinking!" countered Julie. "Remember last month when we had that torrid night of passion together? We had decided to turn off the baby monitor for GG's room. Remember? 'No hanky-panky makes a man cranky,' is what you said. We had to make sure there was no *In-law-ous interrupt-us*, so off the machine went! And believe me, as fantastic as that night of sex might have been for me to remember, what I think of first is that next morning when I had to clean up a mess in my mother's bedroom! And once I was done with that, I got to listen to your monologue about how much it was going to cost to purchase a new mattress! That could have been avoided with the bedpan, and that is why I thought we should pack it, Mike. Just in case it could prevent you from having to pay for another mattress, Mike, and this time at a hotel! It's miraculous what a bedpan can do for you— Mike!"

"Yeah, a bedpan is miraculous, all right! Wait till you get a load of what a difference a bedpan can make in the life of your husband! In the interim, I think I'll go take an extra-cold shower to unload a ton of sweat, a heaping amount of frustration with this morning's events, and the promise of embarrassment, I'm sure, from the neighborhood grapevine! Oh, and by the way, I hope it's not asking too much for you to do a few more things for me: put the panini machine away, turn off the grill that was supposed to cook hamburgers, and check that wonderful list that I haven't seen since yesterday. Then make sure everything that your sweet little heart desires to take to Wisconsin is packed in the car according to your wishes. I will be in the car in exactly thirty minutes for us to leave on this magnificent trip. Now, I hope that's not too much of an obligation for you! I know you're probably tired from speeding and all the pressure that apparently you alone are feeling around here."

"I'm all set and I'll take care of it," Julie sighed with defeat. She just stood there as Mike marched up the stairs to take his shower. *Correction. Two bedpans. We definitely need two. One to help my mom, and one to catch our marriage. And if there's enough room left, I'll throw my man-ini in the bedpan-ini, and I'll make sure it's well organized to boot! No fuss. No muss. Boy, those audiobooks had better entertain us on this trip or it's going to be a really long one!*

Julie left the bottom of the stairs to go take care of the itemized list that had been dictated to her. As she walked away, she reminded herself not to forget to put the antacid tabs and the books on CD in the car. Was she forgetting anything else? Was there anything to add that could improve this trip?

Perhaps a cyanide mint or two!

Men! Take a key and lock them up!

Chapter 2

Julie closed the passenger door of the Traverse and glanced at the clock. She had accomplished the challenge Mike had presented to her with four minutes to spare. If only she could feel the smallest smidgeon of satisfaction in beating the thirty-minute time frame. It just seemed that it didn't matter what she did anymore; there was no pleasing that man, whether it was achieving a major accomplishment or fulfilling his smallest request. Julie turned her focus toward the closing garage door as Mike strode to the car. Fresh from his obviously invigorating shower, Mike hurried to the car with what appeared to be a sense of urgency. He looked like a man on a mission, and they were indeed behind schedule. Julie just knew that he would be pleasantly surprised by her being in the car ahead of the given time. She herself certainly didn't feel refreshed, having rushed like a cheetah on crack to clean the kitchen from the panini fiasco, to turn off the gas grill as instructed, and to recheck the list. Thanks to that list, she confirmed her observation that Mike had indeed forgotten to place the bridesmaid gown in the car! Once Julie had carefully hung the dress so as not to get wrinkled, she had run back upstairs to check on her napping mother. John hadn't returned yet from getting Brett, so she had scribbled a couple last-minute instructions in a note for them as well, sticking the paper to the refrigerator door where any one of them would be sure to see it. Before getting into the car, she had worried that she had forgotten to tell "somebody something" but now attempted to alleviate that concern with the knowledge that everybody had smartphones and could be reached with any possibly forgotten "something for somebody"!

Julie hoped Mike would compliment her promptness, regardless of how small it might be, so that she could feel anything better than what she had been feeling all morning. Mike opened the door and smiled. *Yes! A smile! My knight in shining armor has arrived to save the day, and we're going to drive off into the sunset happily in love once again!*

"Finally." He placed the key in the ignition.

Yes! He will now turn and look at me, his maiden and soul mate, with loving, passionate eyes. He will apologize for his earlier unkind words, and then my knight in shining armor will hold me passionately and . . .

"Wanna open one of those water bottles in the cooler for me?" Mike asked as he backed out of the driveway.

Nothing? Nothing at all? No compliment. Nothing. My knight in shining armor has definitely lost his shinola!

She opened the cooler that formed a wall between them and removed one of the water bottles. She closed the cooler, opened the bottle, and placed it in the cupholder closest to Mike. "Didn't, um, happen to bring any metal polish with you, did you?" she remarked.

"Metal polish? For what? I don't remember anything about any polish," Mike said as he drove up the cul-de-sac.

"Never mind," she sighed. "I was just kidding." *Definitely need some polish, lots and lots of polish—or a new knight!*

Julie shifted her position so she could pretend to gaze out her window at their neighbor's newly painted home.

She sat in such a way that she could check to see if he was looking and noticing that she was not looking at or noticing him. She didn't feel like talking, either. Although she didn't really feel like looking at her neighbor's pretty home with the perfectly manicured lawn, almost anything to divert a possible conversation was a better option. She continued to gaze out her window while Mike drove. Julie wondered how long she could keep up the pretense that the scenery really did hold her interest. She knew it was way too early to slip one of her library rentals into the CD player. Besides, at the moment, she just wanted to feel invisible—and she wanted Mike to notice her being invisible. She wanted him to feel as bothered as she did and then offer to do something about it.

Julie was usually busy from sunup till sundown and, oftentimes, later than that. Her mother called it "burning the midnight oil," and it appeared that Julie had inherited that gene. However, that industrious, diligent mindset eluded her as she sat watching the scenery roll past them. It was extremely upsetting to Julie to think that she just couldn't measure up to the type of wife Mike seemed to desire. Over the years, she had truly tried to mold herself into the person she thought Mike wanted her to be. It was becoming more obvious to her that it appeared she had failed. They were drifting away from each other, and while Julie had read articles on the subject, she had never expected anything like that to happen to them. She knew there was plenty of stress for Mike with his job, and now, with her mother needing her assistance, well, that all played a role, but she held herself most responsible.

Mike broke the silence. "Quite a setup he's got over there."

"Mmhm," she replied as she continued to pretend to stare at the scenery while her thoughts rolled by in the forefront of her mind. She truly missed what they once had.

Their daily lives were now filled with such predictability: jobs, chores at home, being parents of teenagers and young adults, and being a caregiver to an aging parent. Where was there any room for spontaneity? Would there ever be any passion between them again? That thought, along with a surprisingly loud growl of hunger from her stomach, almost made Julie blush.

"Hey Julie, are you getting hungry? We didn't end up having lunch before we left. Would you like to stop at Canton Marketplace before we get on 575?" Julie realized Mike must have heard the growl.

She made eye contact with him but didn't dare look at him for very long, for fear that he would read her thoughts. "No, thanks, I'm not hungry," she said and turned back to look out her window. She was hungry, but she was too stubborn to admit it. After all, he had been the one who had assigned her duties to complete, which is why she never did get to eat lunch. *Feel my hunger you caused, and suffer from the guilt of it!*

Her stomach started growling again, and she could smell the aroma of roasting pork drifting from the chimney at a favorite barbecue restaurant. She had eaten there once with John's lacrosse team after a victory. The memory of it brought a smile to her face. The aroma waned as they drove on, but her stomach continued to banter. As it rumbled off and on, she wondered if Mike was hungry at all. Then Mike turned into the entrance for a Sip and Soup. *Well, that answers that question! Boy, our family loves this place—and I'm starving! Yes!*

Julie let out a smile and then quickly corrected it to its original somber position. *Do not let him see the points he just scored, girl!*

Chapter 3

The wooden rocking chairs that graced the front porch of Sip and Soup were a welcoming sign to Julie. Even though it was past the normal lunch rush for most restaurants, she secretly hoped that there would be a waiting list delaying her and Mike from being seated. Sitting and rocking to whatever rhythm she wanted would be a soothing way to unwind from the tension she had felt during the drive, and besides, there was something mysteriously medicinal about rocking chairs to Julie; she absolutely loved to sit in them! Maybe it was the rigidness of the spokes against her back, or perhaps it was the memories of rocking their babies that soothed her psyche, but whatever the secret ingredient was didn't matter; she knew that it would be time well spent even if "Bustlin' Mike" and his road-map agenda were detoured. As they stepped onto the covered front porch, Julie heard a comment regarding having to wait for a table, so she turned and said to Mike, "I bet there's a waiting list. I'll just grab us a couple of rockers in case we can't get a table right away." She sat down, placing her hand on the arm of the adjacent rocker in order to reserve it for Mike. Julie sighed as she positioned herself in the oak rocker with the army medallion that crested the header. She closed her eyes, and her mind began to wander.

"Excuse us, darlin', but are these chairs taken?" Julie opened her eyes and saw two very attractive elderly ladies standing in front of her. They appeared to be in their early seventies but acted (and definitely dressed) younger than their years.

"This chair is taken," Julie said, patting the arm of the neighboring rocker, "but I believe the two over there are available."

"Why thank you ever so much," replied the other woman. "My name is Ginger and this here is Rosemary."

"I'm Julie."

"Well, we certainly didn't mean to wake you. You didn't sleep through your name being called for a table, did you, dear? I didn't hear the name Julie being called. Did you, Rosemary?"

"Oh, I am sure I didn't miss being called for a table," Julie intervened. "Besides, my husband is already inside the restaurant, and I am sure he would have come to get me if that were the case."

"That's good to know, dear. Tables can be difficult to come by at this fine place. We always sit at the same table by the oversized kitchen windows. Absolutely worth the extra waiting time to sit there at our favorite spot, right, Rosemary?"

Ginger and Rosemary looked at each other and exchanged what seemed to be an expression that only those two would understand. Julie didn't care. She wasn't the type to take interest in the frivolities and idiosyncrasies of her fellow rockers. She just wanted to have a nice, quiet lunch that would silence the rumblings holding her stomach hostage.

"It will be about a twenty-minute wait," Mike said to Julie as he sat down next to her. "Maybe we should decide now what we are going to order so we don't get further behind schedule. See that sidewalk chalkboard? What do you want to have?"

"I don't know," Julie whispered. "I can't read it without my glasses, and besides, Ginger and Rosemary are blocking my view. Why don't you just read it to me?"

"Who are Ginger and Rosemary?" Mike asked.

"Why, hello there," said Ginger, standing up after obviously overhearing her name. She extended her arm and shook hands with Mike in a way that matched her smile. Her eyes were being quenched by the tall, cool drink standing in front of her. "Ah, you're the kind gentleman who held the door open for us. How nice of Julie to introduce us to you. I'm Ginger and this is my sister, Rosemary, and your name is . . .?"

"Mike. Just Mike."

"Well, it is a pleasure to make your acquaintance on this hot, *very* hot, summer afternoon. But then, we do like it hot, don't we, Rosemary?"

"Oh yes, Ginger, we do love it when it sizzles!" the other replied, grinning back to her. Julie thought for a very fleeting moment that there was something unusual about these two . . . but then, she really wasn't one to explore the quirks of others.

Mike turned his attention back to Julie. "Would you like me to read the chalkboard to you?" Julie nodded. Mike turned back to face the entrance. "It says, 'In a hurry? Want a quickie? Try rosemary chicken, meatloaf, barbeque, beef stew, vegetable plate, or beans 'n greens.' I think I'm going to get the chicken. Do you know what you want?"

Julie knew what she wanted to eat, but never heard Mike ask her. She had become fully distracted by the sideshow going on behind Mike's back. Ginger and Rosemary had become quite animated and were whispering back and forth in great excitement.

"Well, Julie?" asked Mike. "*Do* you know what you want?"

"Yes," replied Julie. "I'm going to have the vegetable plate."

Mike continued. "Want to stay out here till they call us, or do you want to go inside to the gift shop? It's air conditioned." She knew he wanted to go inside. He didn't like the heat and he didn't like to "just sit," but she didn't want to give up the therapy of her rocking chair so soon.

"Just give me five more minutes to rock," she said and closed her eyes. Julie's five minutes seemed more like thirty seconds to her as she felt Mike tapping her hand.

"Time's up," said Mike as he conscientiously took her hand in his—as if she were once again his princess. *This is nice; I can't remember the last time Mike took me by the hand.*

They walked in to the air-conditioned comfort that Julie knew Mike had wanted. Julie found herself actually happy to have had her rocking time cut short. It could be fun walking hand in hand through the gift shop, browsing the unusual decorative items the restaurant chain was known to sell on a regular basis.

She paused to look at the Halloween costumes on display. There were more costumes for infants than she ever imagined: a lion with an adorable mane of ringlets, a puppy with the cutest curly tail, a magical-looking dragon with metallic wings, and more. The girls' costumes were just as charming: a princess, a ballerina, a butterfly—all equally lovely, frilly, and girly! "Wouldn't Grace look adorable in this witch costume? Oh! And Alex could be this baby ghost for trick-or-treating."

"Sure," replied Mike. The tone of Mike's response caused Julie to turn away from the mesmerizing Halloween display.

"Mike, you aren't paying attention to what I am saying! What's going on?" she asked.

"It's those two older women from outside on the porch. I think they're following us around."

"Don't be silly, Mike! Come on, let's walk over to the other side of the store." This time Julie led the way, meandering past a never-ending display of candies. She was happy to see they still carried the pecan log rolls that were Mike's favorite, along with the colorful array of old-fashioned candy sticks that her kids loved. They stopped at the display of decorative kitchen items.

"Ha! Look at this!" Mike said, challenging the writing on a sign. "'The rooster crows but the hen delivers.' I'm sure the rooster knows how to deliver too. Well, at least this rooster can!" Mike heard a snicker followed by a loud whisper and turned to see Ginger peeking at him from behind a tall display. She then walked by him quickly and murmured, "Don't worry, Mike! We got your vibe. We'll think about it!"

Julie felt herself suddenly being pulled in the opposite direction. "Mike, what are you doing?"

"C'mon! We need to get away from here, Julie. I swear those two ladies from the porch are following me."

"Oh, please! You're a legend in your own mind!"

"Morons? Morons . . . Table for two Morons!" blared over the loudspeaker.

"Oh, good grief! Now that's embarrassing! Doesn't she know how to pronounce our last name?" Julie asked. "Or maybe she can't read her own writing."

"All I know," said Mike, "is that I just want a nice, quiet, uninterrupted lunch."

Julie and Mike followed the hostess into the dining room. From the fieldstone fireplace to the old-time photos and advertisements decorating the walls, there was a cozy, comfortable, homey feeling in this place that Julie adored.

They were led past families, couples, and unaccompanied individuals; it was as busy as a lunch-hour rush, and Julie could only imagine what was going through Mike's methodical mind as he calculated how long this was going to take. The hostess seated them at a table that backed up to a lattice-work partition, decorated with photos of farmers in their fields. Julie was glad that the only occupied neighboring table looked to be finishing up their lunch. The three muscular fellows sitting diagonally one table away were wearing T-shirts advertising a moving company. Pretty safe bet that they wouldn't be having dessert, and hopefully Mike and she could eat in seclusion.

Handing menus to both Mike and Julie, the hostess said, "Your server's name is Bernice, and she'll be right with y'all." She faintly smiled at them before turning on the charm as she paused to chat with the finely chiseled young hunks. Julie listened in on their conversation and realized that they might be muscular and fairly good looking, but those qualities totally disappeared when they opened their mouths. Having to listen to the grammar chosen by Jimmy James, Bubba, and Junior was almost unbearable to Mrs. Morin, who was a true high school English teacher around the clock.

While looking around instead of at his menu, Mike spoke up. "Thank goodness she didn't say our name again. I don't want Ginger and Rosemary to know anything more about us than they already do!"

"I'm sorry, Mike, what did you say?"

"I said that I didn't want Ginger and Rosemary to know anything more about me than they already know!"

"Oh, Mike, get over it. Those two old ladies are as harmless as my mother! Either your imagination is out of control or the heat is getting to you," Julie replied while rolling her eyes.

Their server greeted them with a heavy Southern drawl as she finished setting the table just beyond them. "Hey there! Just give me a minute, okay? Not gonna leave all y'all hanging! My name's Bernice, and I'll be right with ya." They each gave her a small, polite smile of acknowledgement.

Julie set the menu down. "Honey, when Bernice is ready for us, please order the vegetable plate and a sweet tea for me. I'm going to go wash my hands."

"All right," Mike replied without lowering the menu, which was now shielding the front of his face like the wall of a fort. Julie couldn't figure out if he was undecided on what to order or if he was trying to hide from his imaginary cougars!

As Julie made her way past the hostess station, she heard the hostess announce, "Spice sisters? Table for our two Spicy sisters: Ginger and Rosemary . . . Now seating a table for the spicy two."

Oh my goodness, are Ginger and Rosemary such regulars here that they would be called to their table like that? And I thought "table for two Morons" was horrible! The line for the ladies' restroom was a little long, and as Julie waited, she continued to wonder. *Spicy sisters? Really? Maybe they were a little TOO much. Maybe they were TOO interested in Mike as well? MY Mike? Crap! I hate it when he's right. They better not be interested in him!* Julie suddenly felt the urge to hurry and get back to keep her man. He could be a real pain sometimes, but he was HER pain!

It was now Julie's turn to enter the bathroom. There were three stalls, and the door to the middle one was open for Julie's use. As she closed the stall door, she suddenly heard a kind, elderly voice. "Julie? Julie Moron, are you in here?"

"Yes, I am," Julie replied hesitantly, "and it's Morin, Julie Morin."

"I thought I saw you in line here! It's me, Ginger Spice! Would you be a dear and help me out for just a shake of a second?"

"Uh, sure," replied Julie. "What do you need?"

"Well, I've got my belt all twisted up behind me on my dress, and it's not comfortable at all. If you could just untwist it for me, I would be ever so grateful."

Julie exited the stall and washed her hands as Ginger waited for her. While drying her hands, Julie inquired, "Wouldn't you want your sister to help instead? Where is she?"

"Ah . . . ah . . . well, she's busy checking on a . . . a rooster delivery."

"A rooster delivery? You two sisters sure are interesting," Julie remarked as she began untwisting the belt from behind Ginger's dress. "Hey, why are you twisting the belt in the front as I'm untwisting it?"

"Oh, ah," Ginger searched for an answer, "I thought I was helping to untwist the belt WITH you. Well, anyway, that's all the twisting it needed, I guess." Ginger adjusted her belt one last time. "See? All set, feels wonderful. Thank you, and gotta go!"

Julie watched as the elderly but spry woman hurried out of the restroom and then followed her back to their seats. *What was THAT all about? Pretty strange, those sisters. Hey! Why was Rosemary just at our table?*

Julie watched the two Spice sisters return to their table at the same time but from different paths. She arrived back at the table as the good ol' boys next to them chanted, "Bubba wants jugs! Bubba wants jugs!" Julie looked at the young men, wondering why they found so much humor in that chant. Then she looked over at Rosemary and Ginger and wondered why they were giggling and why Mike was looking at them.

After Bernice appeased Bubba and his buddies with a refilled jug of soda, she arrived to take the Morins' orders. Julie placed her order for the vegetable plate and sweet tea. Mike ordered the same meal for himself but with a glass of water.

Bernice added before leaving their table, "I'm downright sorry y'all had to wait. I've been busier today than a one-legged man in a butt-kickin' contest! I'll git yer order to ya, though, faster than a superhero and a speeding bullet combined!"

Just then one of the movers, named Jimmy James, belched and announced, "My friends, that there's a sign that the tank is full!"

"Hush your cute self, Jimmy James, and mind your manners!" Bernice chided him, after which she commented to the Morins, "I hope these three boys ain't botherin' you none. Course, they're about as harmless as a gang 'o gators running around with their three left legs in boots made from their three right legs, God bless their hearts!"

"We're fine, thank you," replied Mike. "If you can just get our order in, it would be greatly appreciated. We are trying to hurry." Julie smiled at Bernice without adding any words to Mike's comment.

"Sure thing, folks! I'm on it," Bernice said as she hurried off to the kitchen with their order.

"I thought you were getting the rosemary chicken special. You changed your mind?" Julie inquired.

Mike gave a quick look around and said in a lowered voice, "I don't want any plate involving anything to do with the spices rosemary or ginger! I just want to eat and leave. I'll tell you too that, even though I get very little appreciation for all that I do, I still love you and you alone. Okay? So let's just eat and get out of here."

"Uh, sure," replied Julie. "But what do you mean you're not appreciated? I do more than anyone in our house and I don't get even half of the appreciation you get!"

Mike countered, "I don't have just home to worry about, you know. I have stresses at work as well. Not to mention the fact that I can't even relax with you after a long day. When we're in bed it's either 'I'm not in the mood, Mike,' or worse, you *are* in the mood and it gets interrupted by the monitor. Then it ends with you rushing to the next room to take care of your mom. God forbid she should wait a few seconds or we should shut off the mom-itor."

"Mike," Julie defended herself, "I would do the same for you. As for work, I stress too when you're on the road, because that means I'm running everything alone, without your help. As for my mother, you know I would do the same for your mom if it was her! I do my best for everyone— you, our children, my mom, the dog, everyone—from the moment I wake up to the moment I go to sleep. The only person I don't take care of enough is me!"

"Okay, so fine. We both do way too much for everyone else and are way too stressed and don't get enough appreciation apparently. Agreed?" asked Mike.

"Agreed," replied Julie.

She knew Mike loved solving problems in an analytical and logical way.

"Look, I don't want to fight. So let's make this easy," Mike offered. "It's obvious we need to find a way to get others to do more so we have less to do, which will probably help with the stress. Then we both have to figure out a way we can feel more appreciated, especially me."

"See? There you go again," Julie retaliated. "Just when I think you're going to say something nice, you go around and twist it or slam it down."

"I didn't twist or slam anything down. I just want to fix whatever it is that is keeping us from being the great team we used to be," Mike said, "and I don't think the solution is impossible."

"I want the same thing you do," replied Julie, "but I think our needs should be considered equally."

Their orders arrived. As she placed their plates in front of them, Bernice added, "Both the sweet tea and the ice water come with refill jugs, if y'all want."

Mike spoke to Bernice politely. "Thank you. I don't think we'll be needing any extra jugs."

The movers at the next table snickered at Mike's answer until Bernice shooed them with her hand before she walked away toward the kitchen. Julie shot a quick glance toward the elderly ladies and saw they were busily eating their meals.

Mike began again. "Look, we're both tired and obviously still frustrated. At least we have some time to ourselves the next couple of days to figure out our problems. So let's just eat and lose those two looney ladies! We can finish talking and sorting all of this out while we're on the road, agreed?"

"Agreed again," answered Julie as they ate the food placed in front of them.

They continued to eat their meals quickly as each contemplated their thoughts and the points they would bring up in the privacy of their car. The movers left their table among one-liners and teasing comments with Bernice. "See all y'all tomorrow, boys," she called to them with a smile as they exited to the gift shop to pay their bills.

"By the way," Julie inquired, "what was Rosemary doing at this table while I was in the ladies' room?"

Mike's eyes became animated as he exclaimed, "That lady is bold and outrageous! Do you know what she said to me? And her intent is no imagination on my part either! She said . . ."

His words trailed off to Julie as she noticed and picked up a slip of paper that was sitting on the table next to Mike's elbow. "What's this slip of paper for? Why does it have the names Rosemary and Ginger Spice written on it with a phone number and the words 'How about tonight, Rooster Mike-olicious'?"

"I know! That's what I'm trying to tell you," Mike stated indignantly. "Rosemary came on to me! She handed me that slip of paper. Said that she and her sister want me to join them in some crazy threesome. I told you they were nuts! See? I told you!"

Julie looked over at the ladies, placed her napkin down on the table, and informed Mike that it was time for them to leave. "Mike, please pay the bill while I have a word with Rosemary and Ginger." She rose from the table and didn't wait for an approval or any other answer from him. Actually, what Julie did next probably surprised Mike, and would have surprised herself as well if she weren't so busy being brave in defending her claim.

She approached the two sisters as they were just finishing their meals. "Look, Ginger and Rosemary, or whoever you two are," she began as they looked up at her in surprise. "I don't like this little game that you have decided to play with my husband. Are either of you hookers? Because if either of you are, this whole charade is over and I am personally calling the authorities right now!"

The sisters exchanged a look of repugnance. "No, we are not hookers!" declared Ginger. "I am seventy-two and

Rosemary is seventy-one, and if we were in that business, we would certainly be madams by now!"

What? What kind of an answer was that? Weren't they ashamed to even have been asked that question?

Somewhere from deep inside, Julie found the nerve to say, "Well, if neither of you is a hooker or a madam, who are you two? And what's more important, what are you trying to do with my husband?" Julie felt empowered by asking such a bold question, considering she never wanted to push the envelope.

"Geez, just having a little fun in life," Rosemary explained. "Yeah, we thought your husband was interested too, especially with his rooster comment in the gift shop."

"That," Julie proclaimed, "was just my husband's comment to a sign we were reading at the time. You old hens can chase after someone else's rooster. This one is staying in *my* barnyard and he is *not* 'Mike-olicious'! He's like he said—Mike, just Mike! Come near him again and I'll shake the spice right out of you! Good day and goodbye, Rosemary and Ginger!" Julie left their table without looking back, probably afraid that she'd lose her gumption and apologize for her words if she did. She then hooked her arm through Mike's, glad that the bill was paid and that his timing was perfect. It definitely wouldn't have had the same great effect if, after telling someone off, she was stuck there waiting and standing around. Together they headed to the exit.

As they stepped into the parking lot, they heard the stalker sisters call out to Mike from the door, "You know where our barnyard is if you're ever ready to deliver, 'Mike, just Mike'!"

"That barnyard has two cracked eggs!" Mike said as he opened the passenger door to the car for Julie. He closed her door and then got in the car himself. After starting the engine, Mike left the parking lot with a wind that would stop any "spice" from collecting upon them or their marriage. At least they now had food in their stomachs and they were back on the road in their car, which was overpacked with luggage, wedding items, and personal issues that needed discussion.

Chapter 4

Julie double-checked her seat belt to make sure it was secure. Mike had driven out of the Sip and Soup's parking lot like a biker on adrenaline and they were now being surrounded by huge tractor trailers on I-75. At this point, she just wanted to feel safe from any potential accidents. After all, there would be plenty of worrying for her to do in about ninety minutes when they approached the curvy roads of Monteagle Mountain. That was the one part of the road trip she consistently dreaded. Julie believed that section of Interstate 24 was absolutely treacherous. Although she had never seen a runaway truck, fear still gripped her every time they were on any portion of that roadway. At least this time they would be driving it during sunny, daylight hours. Julie sure didn't want a repeat of previous years' trips, navigating through rainstorms or in the black of night. She drew a deep breath and exhaled slowly.

Relax; just breathe!

Julie turned her attention to the countryside as huge semi-trailers sped past them. Signs for Vidalia onions, pecans, peaches, and pralines played peek-a-boo between the trucks. The items seemed to be available at every exit, and Julie wondered if they should stop and buy something to take to Wisconsin. Their car was already packed tight, but she was confident there was always room for something more. She turned to Mike to ask him but decided against saying anything. He appeared to be thinking intently about something and she didn't want to interrupt his concentration. Besides, the peace and quiet that surrounded them in the car was a welcome respite from the craziness of their lunch location and its clientele! Turning to look out the window, she noticed there were still signs of the tornado that had ripped through Adairsville. A tornado in January was almost unheard of and had caught a lot of people by surprise. Julie wondered if Barnsley Resort was, for the most part, left unharmed. It served as a sweet and tender memory of their twentieth anniversary, especially the moment when the resident fairy godmother had offered a wave of her wand to bring magic to all their romantic wishes. Julie sighed. She could see that the debris from tossed vehicles had long disappeared, but the sheared treetops and holes in several road signs still remained almost seven months later.

Boy, a few minutes in time for those folks became a big moment that quickly changed everything.

Julie could sympathize. The Morins' lives had definitely changed since her mother had come to live with them a few months ago. Julie wondered what that would mean for them in the future—would they continue to disagree and behave like two roommates who shared little other than the same address and bills? She thought they had truly considered all the aspects of every possible scenario; however, in retrospect, it was obvious that they had not been fully prepared. Julie didn't think that her mother was an overly demanding individual, but she did need some help with the basics of everyday living. Add that to a semichaotic summertime household with teenage boys, and there were bound to be a few "bumps in the road" for them. Julie hated to admit it to herself, but her life together with Mike had been transformed into two people with separate priorities and almost no time for any spontaneity or passion. What they had had at Barnsley Resort that weekend felt like a fairy tale from a lifetime ago.

Julie turned to remove a bottle of water from the cooler wedged between them and glanced at Mike. He was still the most attractive man she had ever met, and even though they were currently going through some "marital challenges," as Julie referred to them, she really couldn't picture her life without him. She had first noticed him while walking the high school hallways early one morning before the start of classes; he was a mighty senior, looking preppy with a tucked-in shirt and crisply pressed slacks. His pants had a crease so unyielding that they could have stood on their own! His curly, blonde hair was neatly trimmed, and when he passed her, she caught the faint scent of English Leather. Several days later, a mutual friend had paved the way for her to invite Mike to the Sadie Hawkins dance, and they had been pretty much inseparable since that memorable February 13.

It's funny, but what I remember most about getting to know him during those high school days was the incredible blueness of his eyes and how my heart melted when I would look at him. Then in college, my favorite memory was walking up Bascom Hill after a Badger football game, sitting in Old Abe's shadow, and watching the rotunda of the capital light up. We shared our dreams and hopes for the future—it was so romantic. Oh, how I want to feel like that again!

Mike's voice broke the silence. "A penny for your thoughts?" That was a key phrase from their early dating days, and Julie was surprised to hear it.

"Actually, I was just thinking about when we were in high school and college."

"What about it?"

"I was just thinking how we met . . . the fun times we had at the UW . . . friends . . . that's about it."

"Yup." Mike paused for a long moment, and Julie wasn't quite sure what he was thinking.

I hope he's thinking about me. How much fun we would have together on dates and how we would laugh . . . I hope he's remembering how we fell in love. Maybe we can rekindle that feeling this weekend!

"Hey, I didn't get a chance to tell you, but I spoke with Larry yesterday," Mike said.

Larry was one of Mike's best friends in college and had been in their wedding party. Mike and Julie had double-dated with him and his "flavor-of-the-month girlfriend" pretty regularly. "Wow, we haven't heard from him since his wedding announcement arrived in the mail. How is he?" asked Julie.

"He's doing great! In fact, he said he and his new 'gorgeous-gorgeous' wife are enjoying their newlywed life. Did you know they also took six weeks off for a honeymoon in Europe? Then, as soon as they got back into town, guess what happened? He got promoted to vice president of the bank! Seems everything he touches turns to gold."

"Well, I'm happy for him," said Julie.

"Yeah, me too. Considering all that's been going on in his life, I'm surprised he even had a free moment to answer my phone call! Then he offered some time in his busy schedule to get together tomorrow. It sure will be good to see Larry again, won't it?"

"We're seeing Larry tomorrow? I didn't know that!"

"Well, what am I supposed to say, Julie? Yesterday I gave him a call. He answered his phone. We brought each other up to date on what's happening in our lives, and when he heard that we are heading to Wisconsin, he said he would love for us to meet his wife. He invited us to stop for a quick lunch on our way through Illinois. I mean, really, Julie? Do I need to ask permission from my wife first?"

Wonderful! He's not thinking about us at all; he's thinking about getting to see his old buddy tomorrow. We have a chance to get away alone, *spend time together* alone, *and without asking me, he just lines up a man meeting.*

"Gee whiz, Mike, I don't know," Julie said sarcastically. "What would have been wrong with saying something like 'Wow, we'd sure like to see you and meet your wife; it would be great for the four of us to get together. Let me double-check with Julie and make sure there hasn't been any change in our schedule. You know how things can come up before a wedding!' What would have been wrong with that?" Julie folded her arms across her chest and glared.

"I'll tell you what's wrong with that. It either makes me look clueless, like I don't know what's happening at all, or, even worse, like I have to ask permission from my wife before I can accept a simple invitation. C'mon, Julie! He's my best friend from college and it's been a really long time since I've seen him. We have all day tomorrow to travel through the entire state of Illinois. What's wrong with taking time to have lunch with an old friend?"

"I'll tell you what's wrong with having lunch with your college buddy and his new gorgeous-gorgeous wife: absolutely nothing. What *is* wrong with this playdate is that you didn't have the courtesy to mention it to me before now! I remember how you two were when we all got together.

There was never anything that the two of you did together that didn't broaden in scope and extend in duration. This won't be a lunch with a buddy and his wife, Mike; this will be an afternoon marathon. Did you not stop to think about anyone else but yourself?"

"Congratulations, Julie, you are exactly right! I thought about myself. I didn't put my 'Julie cap' on and think of everyone else's needs before my own. I didn't martyr myself on some pyre of kindness and torch away my personal happiness for the sake of others, which, by the way, is exactly what you seem to do at my expense. Your actions proclaim it morning, afternoon, and night! You seem to have plenty of time for everyone else but me. Trust me, Julie, our toilet bowl gets more attention than I do!"

Julie could feel her eyes beginning to well up, and she tried to fight back the tears.

Do I really make time for everyone but Mike? I don't think so; I make time for him . . . probably just not as much as he wants, but there's time with him once my other obligations are fulfilled. And am I upset about this lunch with Larry because our roles are reversed? After all, Mike made the plans, and I'm the one who usually does that. I'm used to being the one who knows what's going on right away. Did our previous conversation back at the restaurant about finding a way to feel more appreciated just fly out the window now? This road trip is for us to have time alone together, and Mike is not taking advantage of this opportunity at all!

Without looking to her left, Julie was convinced that Mike had somehow miraculously fixed his eyes in her direction, even though he was driving. He was now waiting for her reply. "Honestly, Mike, did you hear what I said? Here is the problem: you forget that I know you both from college days. Like I said before, this won't be a lunch with a buddy and his wife, this will be an afternoon marathon. That is what I said, Mike. I guess maybe you men just don't listen! Talk about paying attention!"

Julie turned away from the man in the driver's seat. She felt exhausted from their recurring squabbles, and once again the thought of taking a nap to escape beckoned her. She closed her eyes and hoped that she could close her mind from recurring thoughts of today's visit with the sheriff, the spice sisters, and tomorrow's lunch with Larry. She was just drifting off when she heard, "Well, isn't that just great!" Julie opened her eyes ever so slightly; if she really was awake, she didn't want Mike to know it. She must have been dreaming because everything seemed the same, so she closed her eyes. Mike continued, "How much more behind schedule can this make us?" Julie reopened her eyes but still didn't see anything different and wondered if she truly was dreaming. As they rounded a curve in the road, Julie saw a sign that read, "Repaving Project I-24 to Monteagle. Exit Ahead for Detour. Expect Delays." Julie wasn't dreaming; there was a detour and Mike was correct that this would put them more behind schedule.

What a shame. Wouldn't that be something if we're so far behind schedule that tomorrow's lunch with Larry is cancelled! Ha!

Julie closed her eyes again and thought about the happy possibility that their lunch date might be erased; she then hoped that sleep would return to her. It did—until the two-lane road became so bumpy it would be impossible for even a narcoleptic to catch forty winks.

"Boy, this road is terrible!" Julie opened her eyes but said nothing in reply to Mike's complaint. She wasn't in the mood for conversation and certainly didn't want to revisit their previous discussion. Mike continued. "Why in the world would they detour traffic to such an awful two-lane highway? I-24 couldn't possibly be worse than this!"

Mike's statement was correct. There seemed to be more cracks and potholes in this particular road than she had ever experienced in the past. The jarring effect reminded her of past times spent on old, bumpy country roads that they would take when Julie had had enough of being pregnant and desperately wanted to go into labor. Unfortunately, that age-old advice never did work for them. The sign on the back flap of the truck in front of them at that moment grabbed Julie's attention: Stay Back 300 Feet. Mike certainly wasn't adhering to the sign's instruction, but Julie knew better than to give him any driving advice. *Ping*. She realized it was a time to keep silent, but something had just happened; she just couldn't be quiet now. "Hey, Mike? I think a piece of gravel just dinged our windshield."

"Really? Where?"

"There's a little spot between the windshield wipers. It's probably about an inch above the bottom part of the glass, and more toward my side but still kinda in the middle. Can you see it?"

Julie watched as Mike tried to locate it. "Julie, I can't see any crack, and I didn't hear anything hit the car."

"I thought I maybe heard a little ping, Mike, and I wonder if something came out of that gravel truck that's in front of us. Some little piece could have bounced and hit our car."

"Bounced and hit us?" Julie saw Mike roll his eyes. Why couldn't he believe her? Mike continued. "I'm sure that if anything hit our windshield, I would have heard it, Julie. Don't worry about it."

"I'm not worried, just a bit concerned. Those kinds of things can happen. Then if you don't do anything about it, it can get worse, right? Don't you think that we should maybe take the next exit and just check it out to be sure?"

"No, I don't. I think you're overreacting. I really can't see anything there, and we need to keep going. We're already behind schedule if we are going to get to Paducah at a reasonable time."

He's just being plain stubborn!

Julie leaned forward and peered at the center area of the windshield again. "Mike, I really think there is a chip in the windshield. Look, I just think we should check this out. It should only take a moment. What's wrong with that? Why don't you just listen to me for a change?"

"Let it go, Julie. Why can't you just let it go?"

"If there really is a chip in the windshield and it gets bigger, it is going to drive you nuts knowing you could have prevented that. That's why!"

"Do you always have to tell me how I am going to feel? I'll determine how I'm going to feel, thank you very much!"

"Wow! You really don't listen," murmured Julie.

"YEAH! WOW! *WOW!*" Julie could tell by the look on Mike's face that their conversation had hit a raw nerve with him. "Want to know how big of a W-O-W it is, Julie?"

"Mike, you don't need to spell it. I get your drift."

"Really? Well, let me show you," he announced as he rolled down the window, craned his head as far as possible out the window, and screamed at the top of his lungs. "WOW!" Julie reached for her cell phone. She wasn't sure if she should google information regarding chips in windshields or erratic behavior in husbands. It was then she noticed that there was no cell service available.

Oh well, there might not be cell service but at least we could listen to the Cyanide Mint, Anyone? *CD. Maybe that will calm down this crazy moment.*

Julie put her cell phone away and took out the audio discs from their box. She decided to reread the back of the now empty box before putting it back. The truck exited onto a gravel road, leaving Mike and Julie to follow a squad car. Julie looked up and hoped Mike would not make any snide law-enforcement remarks; she did not want to be reminded of the encounter from earlier this morning. In fact, she did not want to be reminded of a lot of things. The list to her was quite long, but as she replayed their earlier debate, number one on her current list was labeled "innocent neglect."

Do I truly put everyone else's needs above my husband's?

Years ago, she had read a book about love language, and she had asked her family how they liked to be shown they were loved. Everyone, including Mike, had answered "quality time" in one way or another. She had begun a concerted effort to do just that for each one, but how could she possibly have enough time for everyone? Couldn't Mike be mature enough to understand? She had told Mike that her love language was words of affirmation, but that did not motivate him to write her a love letter or even a short note. She had come to the realization a long time ago that just wasn't going to happen; he wasn't even going to try. She understood that and had slowly grown to accept that fact. Why couldn't Mike do the same in regard to the time issue? Why couldn't he appreciate her being upset regarding the surprise lunch commitment? Didn't he understand that she was making a great effort to make this road trip one hundred percent just for them? That in itself was frustrating!

As they came to a four-way stop, the blaring sound of a honking horn grabbed Julie's attention. What she observed was bordering the comical. A very attractive young woman in a convertible was pointing behind her, wildly waving her arms and screaming, "Pig! Pig!" as she entered the intersection. Once through the intersection and alongside their car, she stopped her vehicle, and it appeared to Julie that she was going to offer advice to Mike. All Julie heard her say was "pig" as Mike pressed on the accelerator and continued through the intersection.

"How ridiculous!" muttered Mike. "Of course I can see there is a policeman in front of me! Stupid female!" Julie wondered what he was trying to convey with that comment. Whatever it was, it didn't work. All she had seen was a woman who was trying to get a point across, albeit in what appeared a humorous manner.

As they rounded the bend in the road, Julie understood the woman's bizarre behavior. There was a huge swine right in the middle of the road. It was a pig—a huge, *real*, four-legged pig! Mike swerved and barely missed colliding with it.

Julie whispered to herself, "Like I said, Mike, you men just don't listen."

Chapter 5

As Mike continued driving, Julie inserted the first of the Thelma Bermback's *Until Death Do Us Part (Cyanide Mint, Anyone?)* audio discs into the car's player. It was certainly better than sitting in the loud silence she had been enduring for the past thirty minutes since they had left the Monteagle area. In all the excitement with the pig in the road, she had forgotten about playing the CD. Perhaps it would be funny enough for Mike to actually want to listen to it, sharing in the humor with Julie while lightening the mood in the car. She was ready to shed their mutual cloak of competitive bitterness and hoped that Mike was too. Heck, for all she knew, Mike probably didn't even realize that they had competed to see who was suffering the most neglect in their marriage. The disc began, and Julie was thrilled that Mike wasn't spouting off any objections to it. She pressed the skip button to advance past the book's credits and introduction.

"Remember the old marital vow 'until death do us part'? I look back at it and it seems like it was more the closing terms on a contract instead of passionate words of love! Now how many of us spouses are thinking to ourselves that a quick cyanide mint would close out that contract sooner rather than later—doesn't even matter who takes it, as long as the separation occurs! No one ever fairly disclosed all the tiny little subclauses in that marital contract that could bring us to the edge of insanity. So, I present to you my list of the top five 'we are so done' marital annoyances that deserve a cyanide mint to help rush things along:

"Number 1: Snoring. If your spouse snores like a loud locomotive with dual air horns and a rocket-blasting-screaming engine that could set off a nuclear bomb while screeching on an old, rusty track . . . you need to be done sooner than later. Here's your cyanide mint!

"Number 2: TSP, also known as Toilet-Seat Positioning. If your husband leaves the seat up so that your toilet becomes a back-splashing water fountain waiting to baptize your behind in the middle of the night . . . you need to be done sooner than later. Here's your cyanide mint!

"Number 3: Clunker versus Keeper. Do you wish your hard-to-please wife did less nagging and more bragging where you're concerned? Do you wish she was a graduate of Praise U? If you are always the clunker she's pushing around instead of her knight in shining armor . . . you need to be done sooner than later. Here's your cyanide mint!

"Number 4: The Remote-Control Czar. Is your partner the Surfing Sultan of the Sofa? The Captain of Cable Control? The President of Programming Perusal? If you're at the brink of insanity and have had enough of your significant other surfing TV stations while you sit helplessly annoyed and frustrated because of indecisiveness . . . you need to be done sooner rather than later. But wait! You then think that a show has miraculously been chosen, you settle into the story, and suddenly more programs from other channels are parading across the screen. You want to scream because maybe, just maybe, you're ready to choke your Chief of Channel Chasing? Here's your cyanide mint!

"Number 5: Mood-Swing Mama. Watch out, Tarzan! Here comes Jane, and she's swinging back and forth on her estrogen vine through the scary, threatening, moody, call-of-the-wild, don't-say-a-word-because-we-don't-know-where-she's-landing-in-your-jungle adventures of I love you, hate you, now I'm going to kill you, let's make up, and I love you again. If your wife changes moods faster than you wish you could put your mother-in-law in a nursing home . . . here's your cyanide mint—or poison blow dart if you prefer the jungle theme."

Mike blurted, "Well, she nailed that last one. Number three was good too." Julie was surprised to see that Mike was truly listening to something she had chosen for the trip. Normally, she would defend all of those comments being read aloud, but she was just happy that the CD was serving its purpose; they were finally enjoying something alone together.

Julie's cell phone suddenly rang as if to counter her last thought. She was pleasantly surprised that there was reception again and picked the phone up from the drink holder next to her. She knew by the ringtone that it was their son Jake.

"Hi Jake! Glad you're calling. What's going on?"

"Hey, Mom. Didn't you get my text? I sent you a photo of some of the guys here at the fire academy. I had them pose as flaming matchsticks in the picture and I was wondering if you could think of a caption that I can put under it."

"What? Flaming matchsticks? What are you talking about?" Julie asked. "Oh. Wait a minute. I think there's something downloading right now. Oh. Okay. It's your picture. Oh my goodness, Jake! Is that fire on the brims of their caps? What the heck are you guys doing?"

"Mom, it's nothing dangerous. It's just a cotton ball with nail-polish remover that's been ignited. Look it up on

the Internet. I had the guys here help me make a congratulations picture for William and Elizabeth. This is so cool
to do, and we wanted to let Elizabeth know we thought
she was a real hottie. Now I need a great caption to go with
the photo."

"Oh my goodness, Jake! Are you kidding me? Your
hats are on fire!"

Julie saw Mike look over toward her phone with a
quizzical expression. She rolled her eyes toward him to
convey her feelings that one of their children was doing
something crazy again. His eyes shot her an even bigger
question mark. A different ringtone sounded and this time
Mike's cell phone beckoned him. As their son was filling
in the details behind the texted photo for Julie, she was
also now half listening to her husband talking to the
person at the other end of his phone. "I just don't know,
Erin. Your mom's the baby expert, not me. She can answer
you on that one. Huh? No. She can't; she's on her cell
phone right now . . . uh-huh . . . right . . . well, now you know
why it went straight to her voicemail. Yeah . . . okay . . . I'll
have her call you when she gets off with your brother. No,
it's Jake. Okay. She'll talk to you soon. Yup. Bye."

"Okay, Jake. Well, let's see. How about . . . what's wrong
with the baby?"

With precision timing Mike remarked, "Oh. You done
with Jake?" at the same time that Jake asked, "What the
heck does a baby have to do with flaming matchsticks,
Mom? Are you all right?"

Julie replied, "I was talking to Dad, Jake."

Mike knitted his brows. "Oh. So you're not done with
Jake then."

"What baby does Dad have?" asked a very confused
Jake.

"*Not Dad*, Erin's baby—Alex!"

Mike piped up, "How does Jake know about Alex? Did Erin call him too?"

"Stop! Everybody just stop! You're both getting mixed up and you're not letting me finish. Now, as I was trying to say—"

Mike's phone rang. "Oops. Hold on. I've got a call."

"Mom? You still there?" a voice called out from Julie's cellular.

Julie reassured her son. "Yes, Jake. I'm still here. I'm sorry but your sister, Erin, needs my help with something about Alex and I need to call her back. Let's take care of you first, though. Okay. So the caption. How about . . . congratulations on your upcoming wedding and . . ." Julie was searching for the second half of her idea for the caption.

Mike spoke loudly. "Well, Brett, if your buddy's car is old but you think it's big enough and the engine is safe enough to get all of you to the airport, I trust your judgment on this."

Julie looked over at Mike and added in a higher volume, "Just make sure you check under his hood first."

Jake replied sarcastically, "Yeah right. Ha-ha-ha, Mom. Congratulations on your upcoming wedding and just make sure you check under his hood first. I'm sure that message will go over like a ton of bricks with Elizabeth and William."

"Honey, I'm sorry. It's just that your dad is talking with Brett and since his truck got totaled today, they're trying to figure out how to get everyone to the airport tomorrow."

"Mom, you're supposed to be talking with me right now. Wait a minute! Totaled his truck? What happened? Is Brett okay? Why didn't anyone call me?"

"Look, Jake, it just happened today. I need to call Erin about her emergency right now. Let me think about your photo, and I'll send you a caption if I can think of one."

Jake sighed. "Mom, I need this now. I don't want to send it after the wedding, you know. Just . . . well, just hurry up and text me. Okay?"

Julie ended their conversation with a promise to her son that she would send him some kind of an idea for a caption under the flaming-knobs photo. She knew he was annoyed with her, but he would just have to remember that emergencies happen and that they need to be prioritized. It was always quite the emotional challenge for her to balance everyone's happiness on her family's scale of satisfaction.

Julie's eye caught sight of the window's slight crack once again. Was it just a smidge bigger now? Should she mention it to Mike again? She closed her eyes, debating her options for a few seconds, before coming to a decision. No. She had enough on her plate right now without adding another bout of bickering.

Mike's voice broke into his wife's thoughts. "Hello! Earth to Julie! Are you going to handle this phone call?"

Julie looked at Mike and asked, "Why am I handling Brett and airport transportation? You were doing fine."

Mike replied, "Why yes, I was, but it's not Brett now."

"Oh, good," Julie said matter-of-factly. "Erin called back, then?"

"Nope. It's John. I've got him on Bluetooth, and he's very upset with you!"

Julie cringed and half whispered, "Well, tell him to take a number and get in line. I am calling Erin."

"Oh, no you are not. You need to handle this!" Mike insisted firmly.

Julie stopped and then offered Mike a short, intense glare before speaking. "Hi John."

"Hi. You know, Dad has me on speaker phone and I will *not* take a number and get in line, and you can forget about blowing me off by promising to text me an explanation like you just did with Jake."

"Let's just cut to the chase, what's the problem," Julie stated more than asked, bracing herself in preparation for her son's ire.

"Well gee, Mom, you ought to know!" accused John.

"Know what?"

"A little heavy on the foot, were you?"

"Look, I'm sorry, but it's not like I woke up this morning planning on being stopped by the police. Don't you think I'll be just as embarrassed facing other teachers and my students? I'm sure that's going to get around the whole school."

"Whatever," John mumbled.

Before John could protest further, Julie cut the conversation short. "We can discuss this after the wedding. Right now I really need to call Erin. She has an emergency."

"What's wrong?"

"I don't know anything and I won't until I call her. So I have to go, and I *am* sorry. Goodbye."

Julie pressed the missed-call button for Erin and waited. Thank goodness they were getting closer to Nashville and the reception would be solid. Due to the delay in returning her daughter's phone call, Julie anticipated that Erin would be stressed, and she certainly didn't need a poor connection to fan the flames.

"Hi Mom. Glad you finally found time to return my call." Julie became cautious upon hearing the coolness of Erin's greeting.

"Hey, sweetheart. I am so sorry that it took a while to return your call. How can I help?"

"Well, you're a little late, and even if you had called back sooner, you probably wouldn't have been able to help me anyway. It was just such a mess . . ." Erin's voice trailed off and Julie thought she heard a slight sniffle, as though Erin were trying to disguise a small sob.

"I am so sorry, Erin! What happened, honey?" Julie asked.

Erin jumped in with her issue at hand. "Oh Mom, it's awful, just awful! It's Alex's poop! It explodes!"

Julie had to muffle a laugh. "Alex . . . explodes? That's the awful problem?"

"Yes. It was, like, exploding everywhere!"

"What do you mean by exploding everywhere? Explain it to me."

Mike tossed a look toward Julie that silently said, "Oh, please, give me a break!" as he rolled his eyes. She had come to understand that expression and often wished he was more empathetic; after all, it had been a mere six weeks since Erin had delivered, and her hormone levels were still definitely askew. At times like this, it just made the situation more problematic. Julie could tell that he was tired of not being the recipient of her attention, but how could she not help Erin when her daughter was in this frame of mind? Julie returned Mike's look of annoyance just as she heard Erin exclaim, "And that's when it happened!"

"When what happened?" Julie inquired.

"*Mom!* Have you *not* been listening? Great Mom; just great!"

"Honey, I lost contact with you. We must have gone through a spot with no cell towers. Could you just please repeat what you were saying?" She glanced at Mike, who mouthed, "You're lying. Shame on you." Julie shrugged and refocused on the phone conversation. She didn't dare miss the explanation a second time.

Erin let out an exasperated sigh before repeating herself. "I went to the mall with Grace and Alex to pick up Grace's flower-girl dress and to finish some other shopping. As we were walking back to the van, Alex started squirming in his carrier and I heard that rumbling sound that tells me he's going to need changing before we get home—what a mistake!"

Julie inserted a quick, "A mistake? Okay . . . go on."

Erin continued. "Scott's dry cleaning was already hanging on the crossbar in the back of the van. The kids' car seats were already fastened in the backseat, though, so I had no choice but to change Alex in the back of the van. Grace got into her car seat and started looking at a book. Then I closed her door, walked around to the back of the van, hung Grace's dress on the hanging bar alongside Scott's dry cleaning, and pulled a diaper, wipes, and a clean blanket out from the diaper bag for Alex. When I lifted Alex out of his carrier, I realized he had messed himself all over the place."

"All over?" Julie wondered aloud.

"Yes! Let's just say it didn't stay in the outfit. It was in the outfit, out of the outfit, around the outfit, way beyond the outfit, and everywhere in that carrier . . . like spin art gone wrong. It was everywhere!"

Julie tried to console her daughter. "Well, at least it's over and done."

Erin replied almost hysterically, "Is it, Mom, is it? Because there's more! That's right, more! I then laid him on the blanket and was in the middle of changing him when Alex let out another erupting geyser of poop. Mom, the force of it was shocking. It went everywhere except where it should have gone. It was on the carpet, the kids' sunshades, the cargo lights, and Scott's dry cleaning. Thank God the plastic bags covering the clothes held up on impact! The worst of it, Mom, was that, after I got the second round of cleanup done and stood up, baby poop started dripping down my legs. Mom, that is just so gross and embarrassing! There I am standing in the middle of the parking lot like that. It was a rough moment, and I just wish you had been there to help me through it."

Julie suddenly felt guilt dripping all over her motherhood. Then it struck her. She took a deep breath and decided to handle her emotions differently. Mike was right! Mike. Was. Right! She saw it now like a flashing neon light. It was indeed time for changes. They had their turn raising their family, and they had earned this new part of their lives. Julie wiped her guilt away and replaced it with a whole new outfit of motherly wisdom.

She offered Erin a small gift of enlightenment. "You know, honey, if I had been there, you would not have discovered just how capable you are. None of us can be everywhere all the time. I've learned that, my mother learned that in her time, and you're learning it now. There comes a moment for each us when it's time to learn the important life lesson of just how capable we are when the situation demands. Besides, Alex sent you that same message loud and clear."

Erin asked, "What message?"

Julie replied, "Crap happens, Erin, so deal with it the best you can." There was a short pause.

She could then hear Erin start out with a chuckle, which grew into a duet of laughter as Julie herself joined her daughter.

"I suppose now you're going to tell me that I'm going to laugh about this in the future?" Erin asked with a smirk in her voice.

"Absolutely! Probably even tomorrow," Julie replied. "Better yet, you'll probably start laughing tonight when you tell Scott. Most importantly, though, it's in the past."

Her daughter added, "Thank God, too! And, you know, afterward Grace was still happily looking at her book, and Alex was too exhausted from his major blowout to be fussy! But what if this happens to us when we are on the plane, Mom? What am I going to do?"

Julie chuckled.

"Mom? Mom? What is so funny?"

"Nothing, sweetie. You'll be prepared to handle the situation if it happens again. Pack several of those heavy-duty freezer bags for dirty clothes. At least that way they won't stink or leak onto other items in the diaper bag. And remember, you're not alone, honey. I had my share of diaper surprises, thanks to you and your siblings! Now it's your turn."

Erin snickered. "Sounds like we're two peas in a pod, huh, Mom?"

Julie laughed as she quipped, "Nah, we're more like two pees and a poop in a pod!" She smiled, glad that her daughter was already laughing about her life lesson.

"Oh. Gotta go, Mom! I just got home and Scott's car is here. Wait until he hears this one! And Mom? You're the best. Thanks. I love you. Bye."

"Bye, Erin. Love you too!"

Julie looked over at Mike and smiled to herself. She liked her new outfit of wisdom! It felt like a perfect fit for her. She looked down. With a quick press of a button, Julie gave another glance at the photo on her phone. She texted, "How about 'Congratulations on your upcoming wedding. William is a lucky man to gain a wife who can hold her hottie candle higher than all the other women around her.'"

Jake texted back, "Thanks, Mom. That's perfect! For her *and* you. You're the best!"

Her fingers tapped out a reply: "Thanks, sweetie."

Not bad! At least I'm at the top of Mount Appreciation with two of our kids. Now I just need to work a little more on the big kid next to me.

Julie was thankful the challenges had been resolved, and Mike seemed somewhat better as well. She smiled and closed her eyes.

"See that?" Mike piped up. "They can live without us fixing every one of their problems."

Julie reached out to hold Mike's hand. The best part was that Mike, in return, took her hand and held it tenderly, as if it were thirty years ago.

Her smile grew wider.

His smile grew wider.

The crack in the windshield grew wider.

This time, no one noticed.

Chapter 6

"What do you think, Julie? *Julie?* Honey? Are you there?" Mike asked louder and louder. The imprint of Julie's memories dissolved as she was pulled back to the present by her husband's voice. She had very slowly withdrawn from the awareness of sitting and holding hands with Mike as her mind tarried between the moments and lessons in their lives that had made them the couple they were today. Had she dozed off for a bit? Her focus clung a moment or two longer to her recollections before she dutifully responded to the words calling her.

"Hmm? Sorry, sweetie," Julie apologized. "Just floating around in my thoughts . . . or somewhere, anyway. Did you ask something?"

"Well, there's an exit coming up. Since we should probably stop soon, seeing the gas is just under a quarter tank, why don't we get a bite to eat as well? Two birds with one stone. You hungry?"

Julie thought for a moment. Her stomach hadn't been growling, and she really wanted to be able to slip into her gorgeous dress for the wedding without having to inhale excessively or exhale in short, shallow puffs. She weighed this thought against Mike's hinted desire to eat dinner.

"What time is it, anyway?"

"Do you want central time zone or eastern?"

"I'll go with my body clock and say eastern."

"Eight o'clock, then, my dear. So are you hungry?"

"Eight o'clock? I guess I am actually kind of hungry. So, yes, let's stop."

Mike took the next exit. After passing a quick car-loan place, a bank, and a mini plaza, he pulled into a large gas station aptly named Petrol Palace. It was a clean, oversized gas station, complete with towers displaying company logo flags and a full-service car wash. The station offered no fewer than three dozen pumps, an oversized convenience store with food islands and munchies galore, and a vacuum-hose center for those who needed the inside of their car as clean as the outside. The place was quite busy with customers coming and going, filling their tanks as well as their cravings, cleaning their cars, and hustling about in general before leaving out into the world that had brought them there in the first place.

Mike pulled up to one of the pumps, got out of the car, removed the hose from its holder, and squeezed its trigger, placing the tab in the hold position. While the gasoline flowed through the hose, Mike pulled out a handkerchief and wiped his brow. He replaced it in his pocket and walked back to his door, opening it momentarily to say, "It's so hot and humid, I feel like I'm wrapped in a wet rag hanging in an oven! And I've only been out here for a minute!"

Julie giggled and replied with a wink, "You just want me to think you're steaming hot!"

"Cute," Mike shot back before closing the door. He returned to the pump. Julie's head turned in various directions as she studied all the customers bustling about like speedy gerbils working separately yet in sync. Mike knocked on the window, grabbing Julie's attention, and pointed to a sign advertising the Petrol Palace special: Free car wash with every fill-up, minimum $30.00. She noticed it and then looked back at Mike as he gave her a thumbs-up and a "might as well" expression. She flashed him a quick smile and returned his gesture.

Julie watched Mike return the hose to its resting spot, close the gas latch, and return to his driver's seat. She turned up the air conditioning to maximum for him so he could cool off quickly. Mike thanked her and added, "It might be hot and sticky out there, but I'll tell you, it sure smells good! I think it's coming from a great barbecue place that should be pretty close to us."

Julie lowered her window and inhaled deeply to catch the barbecue smell. Masked behind a thin veil of gas fumes, she was rewarded with a sweet, savory aroma that whispered a tempting invitation to a feast. She closed the window. "Yeah, it's obviously close by with a strong aroma like that."

"I'm betting it's the barbecue place that was advertised for the last several miles on the highway. Didn't you see the signs for it? There were a bunch of them! It's owned by that celebrity chef Pete Wolfe. You know, 'The Big Wolfe— Nothing bad here, just good yummy good'!"

"I guess I missed it. I don't remember seeing any signs like that."

"Boy, you really were asleep for a while. You missed some clever signs! Oh well. At least you won't miss the experience. I say we eat there while we're so close to it."

"If it tastes like it smells, minus the gas fumes, I'm ready for that treat!"

Her husband began steering the car toward the car wash, getting his gas receipt ready to show to the attendant, stopping for a moment to let a small group of teenagers run across from their pump to the convenience center. "I'd sure love to walk through that car wash and refresh myself instead of our car. It was a nice surprise, though, to get the wash free with the fill-up. I'm glad I noticed the sign. It may have started badly, but I tell you, Julie, our luck is already turning for the better. The further we get away from all our stresses, except for those crazy old ladies, the better everything seems to be going. And tonight when we're in Paducah, maybe you'll let this old guy get even luckier!"

Get lucky? Does he not remember the heated argument we had earlier today? There are still issues and hurt feelings that need discussion! Sure we love each other, but I want assurance; I want romance. I want to know my opinion counts for something. I want to feel the same love I give. I want him to know that sex is not the solution to everything!

"Gettin' lucky in Kentucky! Love it!" Mike spouted as if to dispute Julie's thoughts.

Julie's small smile offered a weak acknowledgment. "You'll just have to wait and see, I guess."

Yuck! Lame response, girl! Surprise him instead with "Me Jane, you Tarzan, me the boss now. Hand over the vine!"

"Oh! A frisky response! Glad we're fixing everything, Jules. We always do!"

Where's that vine when I need it? "Let's just get the car washed, Mike, and head over to that barbecue. I'm definitely ready to eat." *More like eat my words.*

Mike retorted, "Your wish is my command."

Ha! Wouldn't that be nice for a change!

The Morins' car was processed through the car-wash line in a matter of minutes, and they were happily on their way in search of Big Wolfe's Barbecue. They pulled back out onto the two-lane road, drove just a quarter mile more, and spotted the restaurant. Mike turned into the shared entrance for two different eating establishments, one of them being Big Wolfe's. The parking lot was loaded, a testament to the place's popularity.

Their car slowed to a temporary idle while they tried to locate a place to park, hoping to grab a spot close to them before a few other arrivals could pounce on it. Drivers and pedestrians were trying to avoid each other as visitors flowed to and from the restaurant. After a long two minutes of visually canvassing the area and watching others claim their prized spaces, the Morins spoke up in unison when they spied a man in a nearby pickup truck carefully backing out of his spot. The driver barely had time to put his truck into drive and proceed past them. Mike quickly pulled forward and performed a two-step driving maneuver that allowed him to back into and claim ownership of their own parking spot.

"And voila! The master has outwitted the situation once again!" Mike proudly proclaimed. "See that? I didn't just park, I parked 'smart'! Not only was I able to grab this spot, but I was also able to back *in* so that we don't have to worry about having to back *out* and maybe hitting someone when we leave!"

"Great job, honey," Julie congratulated Mike. "Wow. That sun is still so strong at this hour." Julie squinted in the light that seemed to radiate its power right past the windshield and through her. "Too bad we didn't get one of the spots in the shade. The car is going to be so hot inside when we get back."

Mike replied, "Hey! You know we had to grab what we could. This place is so busy! Besides, we've had the air conditioning on and it's plenty cold in here. We'll just have to eat quickly and get back here before it has a chance to warm up too much." He let out a chuckle. "At least our seats aren't covered in plastic like the ones our parents used to have! Remember those? Ha! C'mon! Let's go eat!"

The Morins exited their car, locked the doors, walked past two rows of parked cars, and then crossed a wider area in front of the restaurant. One driver was dropping off its passengers by the door, and one group of happy eaters was exiting with oinking, plastic-pig-snout-wearing children in tow. Mike opened a big, red barn door for Julie at the entrance.

Once inside, Julie could feel a wave of refreshing cool air wash over and envelop her. She walked toward a large sign that greeted customers on their way toward an orchestrated line of people who were waiting to place their orders. Country music was playing in the background, the kind that sets a person's toes a-tappin' with the beat. Julie felt Mike come up behind her as he said, "Interesting place. Can't wait to try the food that I see on some of Chef Wolfe's cooking episodes."

Julie returned a small "mhmm" before she began reading the welcome sign aloud for the two of them.

"'Welcome to Big Wolfe's! No bad here, only good— real good! Please let us know what you're fixin' on eatin' and in which one of the three pigs' houses you would like to dine. We'll huff and puff and blooooow you away with our great food! Straw House has picnic-table dining with plenty of room for your little ones to play. Make sure they get to slide down the silo! Wood House has casual dining in a farmhouse-kitchen setting. Brick House has pub tables, bar service, and a dance floor. Adults only, please!'"

"Well, we're not here for a night of entertainment, and the last thing we need right now are kids. I say it's the Wood House for us," voted Mike. Julie agreed. They entered the line that moved them between metal, S-shaped railings before walking up to one of several order takers at a long counter.

The Morins stepped forward to place their order with a polite young man who matched the wall photo of the current employee of the month. Julie congratulated him upon his recent achievement. He thanked her as he flashed a proud smile and then asked, "Which house will you be dining in tonight, ma'am?"

Julie responded with their choice of the wooden house and began her order. "I'd like to try the small pork plate, please."

"Would you like that sliced, diced, pulled, or whole?"

"Sliced? Diced? Excuse me?" Julie asked.

"Would you like your pork sliced, diced, pulled, or whole?" the counterperson repeated.

Julie wanted to keep things neat and not get any sauce on herself, so she chose to have her pork diced.

"Diced it is," said the young man. "Now you get to have two sides with that. Which two would you like?"

She answered while looking up at the above menu on the wall. "I would love to try the black-eyed peas and . . . let's see . . . how are the collard greens?"

"Well, to be honest, ma'am, kinda stringy right now. We ran out of the fresh and actually had to use canned for the rest of this evening. Sorry about that."

"That's okay," Julie politely declined, "and thank you for your refreshing honesty. I'll have the coleslaw instead. I'd like to get a small drink also, please."

"Not a problem. All our meals come with drinks. It's included in the price. It's only extra if you order a la carte. And you, sir, what can we fix for you tonight?"

Mike eyed the menu one last time. "Does Chef Wolfe cook all these dishes here on these premises?"

"He'll pop in sometimes and just start cooking away! He is so awesome to watch. He's really nice too. And funny! He's not here tonight, unfortunately. All the chefs here have trained under him, though, and they cook all his recipes according to his directions."

"That's great! I've watched his show on TV several times. He's the big *good* wolf! Smart man. I'm sure he's a multimillionaire by now."

"Oh, and this restaurant is the cutest idea!" Julie added. "The big Wolfe and the three little pigs. Great theme. Just love it!"

"Yeah, like everything he touches turns to gold, right?" the young counter help chuckled in agreement.

"No, everything he touches turns into deliciousness!" Mike corrected with his "I'm so clever" grin. "And my delicious meal tonight is going to be barbecued ribs, fried okra, and you know what? The barbecue jalapeño cheese grits!" He clapped his hands together as he smiled, thinking about the Chef Wolfe meal he was sure he was about to enjoy. Then he added, "Oh, and I'll take a soda, please. And could I get extra sauce with that too?"

The server asked the Morins if this visit was their first, and they told him that it was indeed. He explained to them that the sauce and napkins were supplied on the tables and handed them the receipt, two soda cups, their table number, and a large coin. The employee next informed them that they could help themselves at the drink station at any time, and that there were electronic table toppers on the table should they want to add any extras to their meals. They could then pay for those electronically through the topper as well and have everything delivered to their table. The coin was for one of the two machines for them to enjoy on their way out.

"One last thing," the counterperson offered. "There's trivia and games on the toppers, too, if you folks like that, and I highly recommend the Wolf Personality Test that is on your table. It's free, and it's more fun if you do it before your meal comes—that's when you get the answers to it. Better to do it before you read all the answers, know what I mean?" The Morins thanked him and then turned around to explore the restaurant while on their way to the Wood House section.

Mike spoke first as they exited the ordering area. "I can't wait to try Wolfe's ribs and cheese grits. If they're anything like the other food I've seen him prepare for guests on his show, it's going to be fantastic."

"I can't wait to do the Wolf Personality Test and find out what kind of wolves we are!" Julie replied. "By the way, I'm surprised you didn't ask for any order of beans. You usually enjoy eating them with Southern dishes."

"I didn't order any because I plan on being a wolf tonight, and we don't need any body music while I blow your house down and get romantic!" Mike chuckled.

Julie rolled her eyes and complained to herself, *Why do men always equate sex with romance? Why don't they use their heads and hearts instead of their wild animal instincts?*

"Ah wooo . . ." Mike whispered next to Julie's ear, as if he knew what she was thinking.

Ah noooooo!

They continued walking and lingered for a few moments at a wall filled with autographed photos from visiting celebrities. There were local politicians as well as national personalities. There was one of the president with a written message scrawled across the bottom saying, "To Big Wolfe, thanks for feeding the troops! Barbecue was great. Our mission was a success thanks to your help!"

Mike tilted his head toward Julie as he stated through the side of his mouth, "Wow. Quite a few celebrities have been here, huh?"

"I wonder if this restaurant has a special place for them so, you know, people don't bother them."

"Mmm. Good point. They probably have something of some sort. There are quite a few here on the wall so, yeah, most likely," Mike agreed.

"This is sweet. Look at this next wall section. It's dedicated to people in the military and their families. Photos, letters, dedications . . . there's a POW/MIA flag . . . each branch of the service is here. Look at this. Oh! That's right. Fort Campbell is near here. They have a dedication written here to them and a section within a section here just for them, their families too. Isn't that wonderful?"

"It's more than wonderful. It's fantastic. People need to be aware that it's not just the service people who serve their country. Their families sacrifice so much as well on a daily basis."

"Well said, honey," Julie responded, reaching out for her husband's hand. "Been there ourselves, right? Worrying every day, praying every night that they make it back to us, holding our breaths when something is announced on the news."

Julie squeezed Mike's hand. He squeezed back and then quickly worked to keep his composure. "*But*, you have to do what has to be done and just have faith. Nice wall, very nice."

The Morins then strolled past a hanging quilted blanket with a pattern of flying geese beautifully appliquéd upon it. Mike and Julie arrived at the drink station to fill their cups while a server was busily catching up with the many spills from its spouts. They were careful not to come into contact with any of the remaining sticky soda pools and remnant rings of other beverages near their end. The server apologized to them, saying that they were arriving closer to the end of the dinner rush. Mike smiled politely, but Julie knew that he would not be returning for any refills if it meant a dirty or littered drink station. The overall untidiness of the thoughtless members of society was one of his pet peeves. Once their cups were filled, the Morins made their way to the Wood House room. They found a free table, settled into their seats, and placed their table number at the outer edge of the table's surface.

"Here's that table topper they mentioned," Mike stated as he reached for it. Julie looked around and smiled as she saw that all the tables had attractive red-and-white-checkered tablecloths that matched the curtains hanging in the windows. The attached trim at the bottom of each curtain had a farm scene. All the chairs in the room were mismatched—a perfect addition to the charming farmhouse character of their surroundings. The walls had tongue-in-groove wood panels at the bottom while the top half consisted of a thick glass pane. On the pane, there was a frosted pattern of three houses in a row, one made of straw, one of sticks, and then one of bricks, followed by a section of space. The pattern was repeated for the length of the wall, and each house had a cute frosted pig standing next to it. Through one of the spaces, Julie could see the Brick House room. It had a beautiful open fireplace, protected by a black-iron screen, with classic natural bricks and a gas fire that offered great ambiance to the pub-style setting and small dance floor. There was a variety of wine glasses hanging upside down above a well-polished bar and warmly lit shelves of liquor that served as its backdrop. It was obvious that the night scene was coming to life as adults began to fill that room. Julie watched for a moment as a couple of men tried to pick up a young lady and her friend sitting at one of the pub tables. Julie thought to herself, *Do I miss those days? Not by the hairs on that brick pig's chinny chin chin! It's kind of funny to see them in action, though, knowing that game from long ago!*

"Hey, Jules, are you up for a game? Do you want to try the Oink Blot Test? They have a bunch of games on this computer-topper thing we can try while we're waiting."

Julie had to catch herself at first because she thought he was asking about the pickup game she was witnessing in the brick room. "Not by the hairs on your—oh. The topper. Actually, I'm more interested in that Wolf Personality Test the counterperson mentioned."

"We already know what we're like. We don't need a wolf telling us that," Mike replied.

Julie countered, "Exactly. So we'll see how close it comes. It's just for fun."

"Okay," Mike surrendered, and they both picked up a pencil and paper from the middle of the table. Mike read the instructions aloud for both of them as Julie followed along. "Please turn this paper over to the other side and draw a wolf. You can draw it anywhere on that side and any way you want. Your server will deliver your wolf personality analysis with your meal. This is for entertainment purposes only. Enjoy!"

They dutifully turned over their sheets and followed the instructions. Their meals arrived and the server smiled, "Oh good! You're doing the wolf personality test. The analysis sheet is right here for when you're done." She placed their meals and the paper in front of them, adding with a grin, "No peeking until you're done drawing!" Before heading back to the service area, she asked, "Can I get you anything else?"

The Morins both half answered her with a distracted response, to which the server replied, "Okay. Well, enjoy yourselves. You can use that table topper if you need anything else, and make sure you check off the room where you're sitting."

This time only Julie acknowledged the young lady with a smile and a nod, as Mike was now rushing to complete his drawing so that he could get on to the business of eating his anxiously awaited meal. His face lit up as he picked up his utensils. "Look at this food! It looks and smells amazing! As Chef Big Wolfe would say, 'Awwwoohoo wonderful!'" He gave himself a chuckle of approval for his own humor.

Julie finally put down her pencil while looking at her husband and this moment with smiling satisfaction. *This is happy. This is good. We need more good.*

The Morins spent the next half hour eating their meals and enjoying every aspect of it as they discussed tastes, textures, and ingredients along with the upcoming events over the next few days. Julie tremendously enjoyed the times when they were in sync. She remembered a piece of advice her mom had offered her a long time ago, at the first few disagreements in her marriage to Mike:

Honey, a bike has two wheels and the only way it's going to work is if both wheels are spinning in the same direction. Otherwise, you're not going to get anywhere, girl! Sometimes you have to pedal more or brake for a bit, or repair the links that hold your chain. Just fix that bike and agree on a direction! A couple, like those wheels, has to work together in the same direction to get past life's hills so they can enjoy the ride.

It was great advice from a wise woman. Julie knew her sons John, Jake, and Brett would take great care of GG on this trip to Wisconsin, and she was thrilled that her mom was going to be able to witness her firstborn grandchild getting married. She picked up the personality-analysis list that was left for them.

"Well, honey, here it is. Are you ready to look at your wolf?" Julie asked.

"As long as I can keep eating, sure. Go ahead," Mike replied. He picked up his drawing of a wolf. "Shoot."

Julie began reading the analysis sheet aloud, seeing her husband was in such a good mood: "'Wolf personality test results—analysis of your inner wolf. Remember that this is for entertainment purposes only! A: If your wolf is drawn near the top of your paper, you are an optimist and like to think positive. Near the middle, you are most likely a realist. Near the bottom, you are a pessimist and you tend to act in a negative way.'"

Mike's wolf was at the center of his paper. He spoke up right away. "Well, they got that one right. Beginner's luck. What's the next one?"

Julie noticed that he was hooked already. She continued, "'B. Size of the wolf: This reflects the size of your ego and how you see yourself or how you think others perceive you.'"

Mike's wolf was not overly large, but it was big enough. "Okay," he remarked, "I'm good with that."

Julie shared the next one. "'C. Details: The more items you put in the background shows how attached you are to things and memories. If the background is crowded with lots of items, you may be a hoarder! You are also very analytical. Fewer items shows that you tend to be a minimalist and like to get straight to the point. You like to keep it simple!'"

"Ha!" Mike interjected. "See? Now that one they only got half right, because I know I am good at analyzing things, but I do like to keep things simple. It's one or the other according to them, and I'm both. So, see? Silly."

Julie deliberately reread the last part of the directions with emphasis to Mike before moving on to the next item on the analysis list: "'This is for entertainment purposes only. Enjoy!' Did you hear that, honey?"

"Yes, dear. I understand that quite clearly."

Julie continued. "'D. Ears: Your listening skills are based upon the size of the ears drawn. The bigger the ears are, the better a listener you are.'"

Both of them noticed that Mike's wolf did have large, pointed ears, and Julie added, "Look at that, hon, you're a great listener!"

"You sound sort of surprised at that," Mike countered.

Julie returned a big grin. "It's not that I'm surprised. I just think sometimes you cut people off a bit too soon when they're talking. That's all."

"I'll have you know that I am a very good listener. I just don't like what I hear."

"Well, maybe your wolf's ears are pointed because you like to get to the point. Let's just move on to the next one, and . . . let's see . . . here it is: 'E. Teeth: The size and amount of teeth show your self-confidence and vitality. Gaps between the teeth show insecurities. Sharp teeth show anger. You are either feeling angry or you know someone is angry with you. If your wolf is lacking teeth, this shows a lack of any self-confidence or sureness.'"

Mike bared his teeth so that his smile matched the wolf's. "Lots of teeth. Natural-born leader. Natural-born, *confident* leader!"

Julie looked at her husband, then at the drawing, then back at her husband with no response except to share the next analysis on the sheet: "'F. Eyes: The eyes are the windows to your soul. The larger the eyes, the more open and trusting you are as a person. Small eyes may show a level of distrust or shyness and a tendency to keep to yourself or protect yourself.'"

Mike and Julie looked down at his drawing as he curled up his face. "There's nothing wrong with protecting yourself."

"Nothing indeed, my love," Julie kept her reply simple so Mike would not feel challenged and the fun could continue.

"'G. Legs: If your wolf has four legs, it means you are a secure person, but you can also be stubborn. If your wolf has fewer than four legs showing, it means that you are insecure or you are going through a major change in your life.'"

Sure enough, Mike's wolf was standing squarely and perfectly on four distinct legs. "Some people call it stubborn. I call it securely determined."

"I know," Julie teased, "No one's arguing with you about that one because it's not like you're going to change your mind about it, being, um, securely determined and all."

"Cute," Mike remarked. "Keep going."

Julie loved the fact that he let her get away with that poke! She read the next part: "'H. Fur: Messy fur means your life is in chaos at the moment due to a lack of organization of thought. Short fur shows submission to others. You tend to be a follower. Longer fur shows that you have or crave freedom or power. You tend to be a leader.'"

The two looked down at Mike's wolf as both simultaneously took another bite of their meals. "Well, see? Now that one's off," he continued as he chewed the small amount left in his mouth. "We both know I'm a leader, and I didn't draw any fur at all in my drawing except in the tail." He chewed a moment longer and added, "Woo!"

"Woo?" Julie questioned his remark, not knowing how that connected with his last statement about the fur analysis.

"What do you mean by woo? The wolf is woo, or is just the fur woo?"

"Mmm. Neither. The jalapeno cheese grits. They have a spicy kick to them, but the cheesy layer keeps it all under control. Boy! This meal is so different, but it's so delicious! I love it! Woo!"

"My coleslaw is really good too. So are the black-eyed peas. They have just the right ingredients that pull it all together, like the pork I ordered. It plays in your mouth for a little bit and then gracefully goes on its way, leaving a delicious memory in its place before the next bite enters."

"Now add kicked-up spicy to that, and you get a woo!" Mike said with a grin. "That's why Chef Wolfe's food is so amazing!"

Julie grinned back this time. "I get it." She paused a moment or two and added, "Woo."

Woo indeed! We both need less tired and more woo!

For the next few moments they ate in silence as they savored their separate morsels of "Southern food done right." Mike broke the silence first. "You know, longer fur means the craving for freedom, it said, and that's what we craved and are having now—a little bit of freedom by ourselves. That's probably why I drew that. I really wanted this freedom, and you probably did too. Don't you think so?"

Julie thought Mike was overthinking this instead of enjoying it for what it was—a fun exercise to keep them busy while they waited for their dinner. "Sure," she replied, going along with his analysis to avoid spoiling yet another fun activity.

"That's what I thought," Mike said. "I pretty much already know both of us darn well, if I say so myself. I told you, by the way, that we didn't need some personality quiz to learn about ourselves, *but* you were right about it being fun—sort of—in a way that confirms what we already know. Okay, so are there any more, or is mine done? I want to see how you did with your wolf. I bet I could probably guess it all up front too."

Julie replied, "There's just a couple more, and the next one says, 'Tail: A tail that is down and between the legs shows fear and a tendency to be easily humiliated. The longer the tail is, the better your sex life and the more satisfied you are with it. The wider or bushier your tail is, the more you like to experiment with new things/people in your sex life.'"

Though it was out of character for them, both Morins broke out in laughter as they looked down on the very long, curled-up tail on Mike's wolf, which also grew bushier at the end. Mike confirmed this analysis with a short nod and a proud grin.

"What can I say?" he joked. "I'm a happy man with a tail like that!"

"I can see that!" Julie joked along with him as he looked back over his drawn wolf, chuckling intermittently. She took in this moment and savored it like the food she was eating. Mike was actually enjoying himself with something fun and trivial. They weren't discussing how to fix some matter that required their attention or some issue about their kids or their parents. They were having fun alone together, enjoying the food, the atmosphere, and their own company.

"Hey," Mike piped up, "you said there were a couple more items. So what's the last one?"

"Oh, that's right," Julie agreed. "It's cute and a really nice touch. It says, 'Most importantly, if you drew a big belly on your wolf, you must be a regular at Big Wolfe's Barbeque—just sayin'!'"

The Morins smiled and Mike remarked, "You're right, it is a nice touch. Fun personality quiz, too. Leave it to ol' Big Wolfe! And now it's *your* turn. I bet I can guess everything on yours."

Julie welcomed the challenge and asked her husband to predict her analysis.

"Okay, you probably have a small wolf at the top of the page, items in the background but not much," Mike began as he scanned the analysis sheet. "You have no teeth, huge eyes and ears . . . let's see . . . probably standing sideways on two legs, short fur, if any at all, no big belly, and if there's no tail, I'm going to draw a long, bushy one and insist that you were the one who put it there!" Mike capped off his guess with a wink and a grin. "So? How close did I get?"

Julie smiled as she flipped over the paper and looked down at it as she tried to conceal the wolf she had drawn. "Wow. Almost all good guesses." She placed the drawing down on the table so they could both view it. "It does have big eyes and ears and it's at the top of the paper, but I did draw some items in the background. See? I gave him a ground to stand on. There's grass, a tree, a moon, a rock, and some flowers."

"What's the analysis say about that again?" Mike scanned the sheet. "Mmm, attached . . . memories, yeah, analytical . . . okay, I can see that. You do put a lot of meaning into all the things you hold onto at home—all your little souvenirs of memories."

"But I'm not a hoarder."

"No, you're not," Mike replied. "*But* you do tend to analyze all of us. 'How did he say it?' 'Did she look upset when she said it?' 'Do you think he meant it?' 'I wonder if she's going to go through with it.' I don't get hung up on that stuff, but you always do. Analyzing things is not going to change whether they happen or not. It's wasted time if you ask me."

"It's called caring about others' feelings, honey," Julie was quick to defend herself, "and I did also draw four legs, so we'll have to chock up a few extra points for confidence on my part. What do you say about that, my dear?"

"Well, I'm looking at what you drew, and I can confidently say that I love your wolf's tail!" Mike stated with a grin and waggling eyebrows.

Julie shook her head and teased, "You're incorrigible!"

They finished the last bites of their meals with light laughter, agreeing that the wolf personality test had indeed been fun. They opened a small, white box that had come with their meals. Its top flap read, *A Happy Ending*. Inside the box were two pig-shaped pink mints and two chocolate kisses. On the inside of the top flap, the message continued: "Hogs and Kisses from Big Wolfe's Barbecue, where every dinner has a happy ending. We're glad you came!"

"Oh, what a great touch! I love it! Don't you, honey?" Julie asked with smiling eyes.

"Cute," Mike agreed.

The Morins enjoyed the mints and chocolates and then got up from their table. Mike placed his hand on his wife's upper back as they left the Little Piggy's Wood House section and headed toward the exit. On a wall in the wide hallway was a large corkboard. The board had several business cards and flyers, some with detachable slips with phone numbers. Big Wolfe's was apparently nice enough to allow local businesses and individuals to advertise to the community that dined here. Under the board was a slender side table that held a large box with a sign that read, "Place your business card in the pig pen and we'll draw one lucky winner each month! Good for a free meal on Big Wolfe!" Next to the pig pen box was a framed sheet announcing, "This month's winner: Carmela Ratchet, Best Deal Movers," and it showed her drawn business card.

The Morins continued past the community board and box and arrived at the two machines that would accept the coin they had received with the receipt for their dinner. One machine had a wolf's head and was entitled "Food for Thought." The other machine was slightly smaller and adorned with three little pigs. It was entitled "Piggle Giggles for Kids!" Julie squeezed Mike's hand and asked with amusement, "Well, honey, do we want some food for thought or a piggle giggle?"

He surprised her with his choice of a piggle giggle and then quickly added, "Just kidding. Of course, I'd prefer some food for thought, but I could be persuaded to choose a piggle giggle if that's what you prefer."

"Food for thought would be nice. Let's do that one," she replied.

Mike inserted the coin into the machine. The wolf came to life and stated that nourishing one's mind and soul was just as important as feeding one's stomach. It thanked the coin recipients for visiting Big Wolfe's, howled, and then fed the Morins a wallet card with a printed message.

Mike took the card and read it aloud for the both of them: "'An old Cherokee was teaching his grandchildren about life and said to them, "A battle is raging inside of me. It is a terrible fight between two wolves. One wolf represents fear, anger, envy, sorrow, regret, greed, arrogance, self-pity, guilt, resentment, inferiority, lies, false pride, superiority, and ego. The other wolf stands for joy, peace, love, hope, sharing, serenity, humility, kindness, benevolence, friendship, empathy, generosity, truth, compassion, and faith." The old man fixed the children with a firm stare. "This same fight is going on inside of you, and inside every other person too." They thought about it for a minute, and then one child asked his grandfather, "Which wolf will win?" The old Cherokee replied, "The one you feed." A Native American tale.'"

Mike and Julie stood quietly for a moment and looked at each other, pondering the wonderful wisdom that had just been bestowed upon them by a mechanical wolf in a simple dispensing machine. Mike spoke first. "Well, that certainly is good food for thought."

Julie agreed. "It's put so well. A really good point. Thanks for suggesting this place, Mike. It was just right and exactly what we needed."

"You are very welcome. I'm really glad too. Great place. We'll have to make a point of visiting here every time we're on a trip, now that we know where it is. By the way, my suggestions are not free, so I will expect payment within the next few hours." Julie shook her head and smiled as Mike added, "Easy payment plan!"

Julie asked, "And what's that plan, I'd like to know."

Her husband quipped, "Simply help me get lucky in Kentucky tonight!" He followed it with a small, whispered wolf howl.

Julie responded, "Oh, you men. I guess I'll see what I can do about paying that bill."

"Yes," Mike said joyfully. "Watch out, Chef Big Wolfe! There's a new wolf in town, and he's a-cookin' himself!"

The two joined hands as they exited the restaurant and returned to their car. As they entered, they were greeted with an incredible sauna full of steamy air.

"Wow! I guess we should have left the windows open a crack!" Mike remarked.

"Well, we didn't know it would heat up so quickly in the evening, although we were parked in direct sunlight in this spot. Gee, who would think that it would heat up this fast after we left it with such cold air," Julie offered.

"True," Mike stated. "We can fix that right away, though!" He turned the AC back on full blast and proceeded to exit the parking lot. The Morins got back onto the main strip and then took the first ramp back onto the interstate. The countryside offered scattered cornfields, farms with tall, slender silos, and working grain elevators. Mike and Julie pleasantly noticed quite a few calves within the slightly silhouetted groups of cattle grazing before the twilight backdrop. Some of them were nursing, while some of the more adventuresome ones were exploring close to the outer ditches and others were playing with each other and romping around.

There was music playing softly on the radio, which Julie had chosen instead of a Thelma Bermback CD, just for a change of pace once they had reentered the car back at Big Wolfe's. She was soaking in the relaxed comfort of being together, happily journeying toward the wedding of their firstborn. Their stomachs and hearts were nourished and refilled. Their senses were basking in the sights of the passing scenery and the soothing sounds from the songs that were serenading them. Julie thought about the Native American legend the mechanical wolf had fed them. She believed that it was truly important for her and Mike to focus on feeding the good wolf in their marriage. There were so many demands placed upon them from the two generations that sandwiched them that it was hard to find the right time or recipe for their own happiness. How does one find time for romance and growth in a relationship while caring for the needs of an elderly parent and children at the same time? These "panini" problems constantly challenged Mike and Julie in twos, threes, and sometimes even fours, each vying for their attention.

Which one will win? The one you feed.

Julie decided that from now on, she and Mike would just have to take those paninis and feed them to the good wolf. How could they be good for the others if they first weren't good for themselves? There was strength in the unity of two, and even more strength in the unity of a happy two. They would choose to be happy, and as long as they knew that they had done the best they could for others while being true to themselves and each other, they would choose not to feed the bad wolf one morsel of regret or disappointment. It felt good to make that statement. Now she just needed to share these thoughts with Mike. Perhaps they could discuss this after he got past his focus on gettin' lucky in Kentucky!

Julie reached down and pulled her cell phone from her purse to check for any texts from her children. Already her worried thoughts of them and GG were challenging her declaration! As she lifted the cell phone from an outer compartment of her purse, a pen came along with it and fell to the car's floor. Julie bent down to retrieve it. As she sat up back into her seat, a car passed theirs in the opposite direction and the reflection of its headlights caught the visible line of the worsening crack in the Morins' windshield. Julie let out a quick gasp as she realized the crack was getting worse!

"What's wrong?"

"It's the crack, honey—it's worse! I could see it in the reflected lights of that car that just passed us! We need to get it fixed before it gets any bigger or longer. It's getting dangerous!"

Mike rolled his eyes. "Oh, for Pete's sake, why do you keep harping on that? It can't be that big because I can't even see it from here! Besides, how could it be cracking more? There's been no pressure on it or anything like that."

"I'm telling you, it's getting much longer," Julie insisted, "and you probably can't see it from where you're sitting because of the angle. Why can't you just pull over for a couple of minutes and check it out from where I am? Then you'll be able to see it for yourself."

Mike let out a sigh of defeat. "Fine. I'll make a deal with you. If I pull over right now to check it out instead of waiting for Wisconsin, will you finally let it go?"

"Deal," Julie said with a short nod. "I just want us to be safe, that's all. Thank you, honey."

"You are welcome," Mike replied with exaggerated patience.

He continued to drive for a minute or so until he found a wider and safer spot to pull over on the side of the roadway. Mike slowed the car until it came to a full stop at an unfinished graveled entrance that led to a dirt path. It looked like some type of ATV or horse trail. He shut off the motor, grabbed the flashlight that he had placed in the lower compartment of his door, and then opened the door, only to be greeted by a heavy stench that stiffly hung itself in the humid air.

"Oh, man!" Mike complained with disgust. "How many cows died out here? It's Barn City!"

"You know, Mike, with all our adventures on this trip, we could write a book together!" Julie tried to make light of their situation at hand, knowing that her partner was getting grumpy again.

"Yeah, well, if we write a book about the cow-patty air out here, we can call it *Cow Crap on Tap!*"

Julie didn't know whether to laugh or stay silent at that moment. Was he joking or getting angrier—or maybe both? It was a funny joke spoken like a cutting comment. As he closed his door, she commented, "Feed our good wolf, honey, feed our good wolf!"

Mike walked around the front of the car until he came to his wife's side of the windshield. He turned the flashlight on and angled it toward the spot where Julie was pointing from the inside. He examined the area of windshield that had caused such great worry for her, and sure enough, there it was. She could tell by his facial expression that he would have to agree that she had a valid concern. He walked back to his side of the car and opened his door again.

"I can tell you agree with me," Julie spoke up. "So we're going to stop somewhere and see what can be done, right?"

Mike replied, "Look, I do agree with you that the crack is becoming a problem, but I still think it can wait for Wisconsin. You are making a mountain out of a molehill."

"But honey," Julie argued her point, "what if the windshield completely cracks or, God forbid, falls in on us while you're driving? I just think it's dangerous and unwise to continue on the way that it is right now."

"Well, dear," Mike spoke as he entered the car, "you may be right, but I'm the one making the call! We're not stopping unless that crack gets a *lot* longer! Otherwise, it can wait until Wisconsin. Period!" Mike sat down in his seat and slammed the car door with great effect.

CRRRRRAAACK! The windshield of the car now presented itself with a long crack that extended from the middle-lower portion of the pane to the upper corner. The two sat in silence for the longest five seconds possible. Julie spoke first and with confidence. "Honey. It's longer." She could tell Mike was now seething while he glared at her as he reached his hand out toward the On Track service button in their car.

Before pressing his finger on it, he stated with an impatient sigh, "Well, I guess we don't have a choice now. I'm contacting On Track to get some help."

Julie thought of making an "I told you so" comment but instead replied, "Feed the good wolf, honey. Feed the good wolf."

Chapter 7

Julie watched as Mike reluctantly pushed the On Track button.

Oh how he hates to ask someone for help.

Julie had offered all the self-help windshield-repair options that she could think of or find while surfing the Internet, proposing everything from the clear nail polish in her purse to the superglue and duct tape in the auto safety kit that was stowed away with the spare tire.

"On Track expert car-care service. How may I direct your call?"

"I need to know where I can get my car's windshield fixed."

"As your live advisor, I first need to verify your account and contact information. What is your account number, sir?"

"Hey, I don't know my account number. Isn't it enough that I pushed that green button and you answered the call?"

"I do see by the logistics on my computer screen that you have not been involved in an accident, and since this is not an emergency, it is a perfect opportunity to update the data of your account."

"How about if I get disconnected from my live advisor and you put this call through to the dead, automated, call-forwarding regimen of push one for unlocking car doors, push two for roadside assistance, and push three to fix my windshield!"

Julie cringed.

"Just following proper procedures, sir. As I said, the automatic crash-response system has not been activated, so this call has been classified as a nonemergency on my computer screen."

"Well, let me clarify some details for you and your computer screen. While this might not be an emergency for you, it is for me. I am out in the middle of nowhere, and my windshield is badly cracked, which I am sure you already know by your logistics. The one thing that you don't know is that some thoughtless farmer decided to clean out his barn this evening and subsequently make the entire atmosphere reek of cow dung. My wife and I can hardly breathe. So I suggest that, unless you want to call an ambulance to bring us oxygen tanks, you tell me how I am going to get this windshield fixed and drive to our son's wedding!"

Julie raised both her hands with palms forward in an attempt to get Mike to calm down.

"My apologies, sir. I will direct your call to my supervisor to assist you."

As the hold music began playing, Mike turned toward Julie. "Want to explain to me one more time why we needed this? We have never needed it up till now, and it certainly doesn't have the level of customer service their advertising promotes."

A softer voice came over the speaker. "Henrietta here, sir. I see your current position and am happy to report your windshield-repair location is a mere ten miles down the road."

"Henrietta, are you telling me no one can come to me and fix it? You expect me to drive ten miles with this damaged windshield?"

"Yes, sir, I am sorry to report that. There is no mobile windshield-repair unit available within a forty-mile radius."

"That's just terrific. What's the address?"

Henrietta cleared her throat. "The name of the business is Diesel's Wreckovery Shop. If you press Local Services on your On Track menu, you should see the business and its address listed there. Simply select it, and you will then see the directions to get there. I'm seeing a notation for this business as well. The contact person is Diesel. I'm sure that he'll take good care of you."

"Terrific. Just terrific," Mike replied.

Julie couldn't decipher if Mike was a volcano waiting to erupt or just so tired of the ordeal he would do almost anything to bring the phone call to a close.

"Thank you, Henrietta. You've been very kind," Julie interjected.

"Why, you are most welcome!" Upon hearing Julie's pleasant voice, there was a noticeable change in Henrietta's tone. "Thank you for calling On Track, where we do just that—keep you on track! Bye-bye."

Julie started to say, "Goodbye, Henrietta," but was interrupted with a loud zapping sound that must have been triggered by the call disconnecting.

"Did you have to be so cheerful?" grumbled Mike.

"Did you have to be so cranky? Those folks were just trying to do their jobs."

Mike started the van, activated the directional, checked the mirrors for any approaching traffic, and pulled out with a slight screeching of tires. Julie prayed that his driving wouldn't be hampered by the lightning-bolt design in the windshield, especially if he was going to drive with lightning speed. She prayed even more earnestly that the stench would vaporize before any feelings of nausea could take hold. It had been a long time since she had smelled that robust barnyard odor, and it was worse than she remembered. She rolled her window partially down. Was it the cooler temperatures of early evening or her imagination that the disgusting odor was dissipating?

"Mike, please roll down your window, even if it's just a tiny bit. I think we're past that barnyard stench."

After following the On Track directions, Mike pulled onto the graveled shoulder and turned in to the repair shop. Julie cringed as she surveyed the premises and hoped the exterior did not reflect the workmanship of the owner. The two-tone, rust-colored posts appeared to barely support the roof's overhang, let alone the partial gutter section that was hanging haphazardly off to the side of the building. The only saving grace for the impending gutter tragedy was the immense number of tires stacked underneath. Mike skillfully maneuvered their van past the accumulated tires and pulled ahead to the garage entrance.

"Coming in?" he uttered.

"No, thanks. I might stretch my legs and walk around a bit, or maybe I'll just sit here. I'm not sure . . . If you need my help I'd be glad—"

"It's just a yes or no question, Julie, I don't need an essay." He swung his door open almost as quickly as it slammed.

"Okay, so that's a no," Julie commented softly to herself. "Well then, you got us into this mess. You can get us out of it." After all, this could have been totally averted if he'd just paid attention to what she was saying four hours ago! Julie watched as Mike entered the shop and approached the silhouette of a figure bent over a wooden bench with an array of tools randomly hanging on the pegboard above it. Try as she might to understand the conversation by watching their body language and facial expressions, it was no use. As usual, her desire to help in any way possible overtook her indecisiveness, and she got out of the car. She was about to enter the garage when Mike shot her the silent communication that every wife has learned over the years. The look that reads, "Leave it alone. I will handle this."

Julie managed to nonchalantly continue walking past the entrance as if she were heading toward the older-model soda machine. She was still way too full from dinner to even consider a drink. If anyone were watching her, though, at least they would not have known her original reason for getting out of the car. Julie surveyed the rocking chair next to the vending machine and decided to sit there. It was a convenient spot to be out of sight for Mike's benefit, but perhaps still close enough to overhear the conversation. Julie sighed. *What a day! Maybe I should—*

The ding-ding of tires rolling over a rubber hose lying across the gas-station lanes interrupted her train of thought. An old, red pickup truck came to a stop by one of the four gas pumps. The elderly, coverall-clad farmer got out of his vehicle and began pumping. Julie wondered if he was the individual responsible for the impudent scent that had permeated the countryside earlier. Was he the man who had been cleaning the barn? How could anyone function in that environment? Julie knew she would never know as he replaced the gas pump's handle, got back into the truck, and tipped his hat toward Julie in a farewell gesture. As he drove past her, she noticed a shotgun suspended in the back window's gun rack. Julie had thought those things had pretty much gone away when all the gun-free school-zone laws were enacted.

"I sure hope this area's safe," she murmured.

"Area's safe, all right," answered Mike. Julie jumped at the sound of his voice. "Sorry. Didn't mean to startle you. Windshield will be fixed by tomorrow morning. Diesel already called and got us a room across the street. He's committed to staying late tonight to get it installed so the adhesive will have plenty of time to cure. Should at least be able to leave first thing in the morning."

"Wow, we sure were lucky to have the blessing of On Track," Julie noted.

Mike rebutted, "Lucky? Blessing? Are you kidding me? Your problem, Julie, is you're always looking at the world through rose-colored glasses. All you can think is how blessed we are tonight when, in reality, we are not having even one ounce of luck!"

"How can you not find such a simple blessing as the one I mentioned?" Julie asked back.

"Because we're not going to be in a great room that I picked out in Paducah tonight! No wolf, no romantic night, no—no gettin' lucky in Kentucky!" he stammered.

Julie was not fazed by his comment. She sighed. "Guess you should have had the beans."

The Morins both rolled their eyes at the other as they headed out of Diesel's Wreckovery Shop toward their lodging for the night. Julie felt Mike grab her hand as they crossed the deserted two-lane highway and approached the Notel Motel. The oversized yellow arrow blinked in a syncopated rhythm with the vacancy sign and was ready to welcome new guests with the promise of color TVs, in-room coffee service, and vibrating beds. For Julie, it was a moment of déjà vu. Her mother had owned a sixteen-unit motel in the small town where she and Mike had gone to high school, and this current establishment bore a striking resemblance to her teenage residence. As she surveyed the door to the office, her mind flashed back to that cold February evening when an extremely nervous fifteen-year-old girl was saying goodnight to a very handsome eighteen-year-old senior, and she was convinced he would never, *ever* ask her out on a real date. The Sadie Hawkins event had turned out to be a bona fide fiasco, and without a goodnight kiss, or even a moment of handholding, she had opened the door and fled upstairs to her bedroom. As she had cried herself to sleep that night, she had been positively convinced she would never spend any more time with him. Boy, had she been wrong about that!

"Are we going inside, or are we going to sleep in our car?" The voice of her less than happy prince charming, who was already holding the door to the office open and waving her to enter, interrupted her melancholy moment. Julie managed a small smile as the silhouette of that fifteen-year-old girl disappeared.

"I'm sorry," she said and brushed past him.

Even though the lighting in the small lobby was not very bright, the inside of the motel seemed to mirror the exterior. It appeared clean but visibly dated, with 1970s-style avocado-green vinyl flooring and a desk made from tongue-and-groove pine paneling. To their right was an arched opening with a small sitting area. An undersized sectional leather sofa, which appeared to have aged with a crackled faux finish, was pushed into the far corner with an array of magazines spread across the coffee table. There was no one behind the desk, and Julie wondered if the owners had already gone to bed for the night. It was then she saw the bubble-lettered note that read, For Service— Ring Me. She lightly touched the bell once and the clapper dinged appropriately, but no one came.

"I don't think anyone's coming, Mike. Maybe we should just leave."

"And go where, Julie? Diesel said this was the only place to stay in town, and he didn't exactly offer to take us home

with him either. Do you want to sleep in the car and romantically gaze at the starry sky through the cracks in our
windshield? That sure would make a passionate evening!"
Mike slapped the desktop bell repeatedly, and Julie started
to secretly hope no one would answer; she was so embarrassed by Mike's persistence!

A voice came from the top of a stairway down the hall.
"I'm coming, I'm coming!"

Julie could hear the stairs announce that someone was
indeed coming to their assistance, and a girl who looked
about twelve, with bright, curly, red hair, came bouncing
around the corner. "Hi! I'm so sorry we kept you waitin'!
My momma sent me down to let all y'all know that she'll
be right down. She's just finishin' talkin' with my sister,
who just had a baby boy! I'm an auntie and she's a grandma
for the first time, and we are so excited and thankful! You
know, she just got married six months ago and she had a
ten-pound baby! I don't know where y'all come from, but
around here that's pretty amazin'! I don't know why, but
that's what everybody's sayin'."

Julie glanced at Mike and could tell instantaneously
that he had absolutely nothing to say to this sweet, young
girl. "Well, congratulations! That is amazing, and we're
very happy for you and your family," Julie offered. "Do
they have a name picked out yet?"

"Yes ma'am. It's South on account of all the other
directions were already taken."

Julie thought Mike was going to choke, but somehow
he kept his reaction mostly to himself.

"Here's my momma now," she said as the stairs began
to creak again. "I told them our good news, Momma, and
apologized for bein' late with gettin' down here. Is Sissy
still on the phone?"

"Yes, and she is waitin' to talk with you. Scurry on up there this instant before her minutes run out!" She motioned her daughter to hurry. "Now, how can I help you kind folks who've been so patient?"

"We need a room," Mike said very matter-of-factly.

"Did Diesel from Wreckovery send you folks over? I saw two cars pull in there right before I got the baby news, and I thought to myself that we are going to be busy tonight! Folks don't pull in over there this late unless they're in a heap of trouble! So what happened to you?"

"Long story," replied Mike, "and we're pretty tired, so if we could just get a room, we'd appreciate it."

"Sure can! Did you read all those wonderful extras listed on our sign that we offer to our customers?"

"Mmhmm," replied Mike. Julie could tell he was barely listening.

"Well, I have to apologize cuz we don't have any special massage beds anymore. The quarters kept gettin' stuck in the coin box, and people would pound on the box to try to get that massagin' bed to vibrate. Plus, we'd get lots of complaints from the adjoinin' room due to the repeatin' wall thumpin' they'd hear. So, to make a long story short, we need to get that old sign outside fixed so that we don't get in trouble for false advertisin'. I am real sorry if you were expectin' to get one of those."

Julie glanced at Mike, and she could tell that he had started to listen. It was probably the vibrating-bed comments that caught his attention. She could also tell he was about to say something inappropriate to this sweet woman, so Julie quickly interjected. "That's perfectly all right. We don't need anything fancy."

"Well, aren't you the sweetest, most understandin' person! For bein' so nice and considerate, I'll tell you what I am goin' to do. You can have our very best room with the brand-spankin'-new mattress! That should put a great big smile on the faces of you two lovebirds!"

Lovebirds? Me and Mike?

Julie tried to smile at hearing the woman's comment and glanced at Mike, who was now busy filling out the registration card in triplicate. It was the first time Julie observed there was no computerized system, just an old-school style of registering. Mike slid the registration card back across the desk, along with his credit card, and Julie noticed he was starting to drum his fingers on the top of the desk; she knew from past experience that signaled impatience with a capital I—not a good sign. It took a moment to run the card before the owner slid the key toward Mike.

"Here's your key to lucky room thirteen. Take these extra towels and a couple extra packets for the in-room coffee service. I know you two are goin' to sleep like babies on that brand-new mattress! And don't worry about checkout time for tomorrow. Y'all are welcome to stay as long as you like! Just place the room key on the dresser, and then flip the little security lock over so the maid-service sign shows when you leave. Have a good night now." Mike quickly grabbed the towels and coffee packets without uttering a word and headed for the door.

"Thank you," said Julie as she followed Mike.

What is wrong with that man? If he can't be friendly, can he just be civil?

She knew the day hadn't gone the way either of them had hoped, but shouldn't they each be able to put the day's disappointments aside and try to make the best of things? After all, they were alone together, and that was worth something, wasn't it?

While Mike was fumbling with the room key and trying to get the door to unlock, Julie thought back to the last time they had a car break down on an interstate highway. That had been an experience they had never forgotten. As Julie stood in the moonlight staring toward Diesel's shop, she certainly hoped this small windshield incident would not balloon to anything of grander proportion.

"Well, are you going to come inside this lucky-number-thirteen room, or are you still considering a romantic view of a starry sky through a cracked windshield?"

"I'm coming in," Julie responded. "I am tired and really looking forward to sleeping on that brand-new mattress."

"Yeah, me too," replied Mike as he set down their overnight suitcase and hung their garment bag. "I'm going to take a shower."

Julie looked around the room and could only imagine what had gone through Mike's mind. As a salesman who traveled about 75 percent of the time, she knew what he liked in a hotel room, and she knew this wasn't it! Julie took a second look. The gold wallpaper flocked with the black-diamond pattern was obviously continuing the '70s theme. The brass table lamps on the matching nightstands were nice, but the gold-foil lampshades were a bit much. Also, she definitely would have traded in the bright-yellow bedspread for something more subdued. As she ran her hand across the top edge of the headboard, she realized it was clean. There was no dust or sticky residue from too much furniture polish. She turned back the covers to check the sheets and was pleasantly surprised with the feel of Egyptian cotton. The décor might be lacking, but the comfort of the new mattress and the soft, cool silkiness of the sheets were far more important. She reached for the remote and clicked through the list of available television stations. There wasn't much to watch, but Julie didn't care and just clicked on the family-sitcom rerun. She didn't even want to shower; all she really wanted to do was just lay her head on her pillow and go to sleep.

The sound of running water coming from the bathroom increased, so Julie turned up the volume on the television.

How could a shower be so loud? No wonder people had complained about noise from adjoining rooms. There must be no insulation in the walls between the units.

It sounded as though they were at a quaint motel next to Niagara Falls. Julie fluffed the pillow and turned onto her side. Losing interest in the sitcom rerun, she began channel-surfing until she came to a weather channel. Julie hoped the rainy pattern that had been plaguing the Midwest would be gone soon. After all, it was only three more days till the wedding.

Suddenly the sound of running water lessened, and Julie heard Mike ask, "Could you come here a minute?"

What else could possibly go wrong? Was the shower drain plugged and had water flooded the bathroom floor? Did I forget to pack something in his shaving kit?

Julie opened the bathroom door, and the questions in her mind disappeared. Mike had done the almost unthinkable— he had transformed this '70s bathroom into a spa-like retreat. There were at least a dozen tea lights placed around the small space, filling the room with a flickering softness and the aroma of gardenias, her favorite scent. The pale-pink bathtub was brimming with bubbles. The towels had been fluffed, and a small bottle of moisturizer had been placed next to the tub. Her husband had even managed to sneak a brand-new bathrobe into the space without her realizing it and had hung it on the hook to the left of the door.

"Surprised?" asked Mike, who was wrapped in a bath towel from the waist down, leaning against the pink tile in a steamy calendar-style pose.

"Well . . . yes. I am."

"Happily surprised, I hope."

"I am."

"Good, that was my goal. So now you can slip into that tub, take your time, and relax."

Julie couldn't help but smile. A nice, relaxing bath would be just the thing to help her sleep. Mike continued. "And then we can . . . you know . . ." He wiggled his eyebrows with great enthusiasm. "See you soon. I'll be waiting for you." Mike closed the door.

Julie stood motionless. She realized at that very moment that Mike hadn't done this for her; he had done this for himself. He had done this because he wanted something, and she knew exactly what it was. Julie knew she had a healthy attitude toward intimacy—after all, they did have five children, and they certainly didn't just show up miraculously! In her mind, there was nothing wrong with make-up sex either; in fact, there were some really special moments in their years of marriage where the closeness they experienced, after being in the trenches of a battle, was beyond compare. The majority of today, however, had been infused with disagreements, and before you can have make-up sex, you need to make up. Right? In Julie's mind they just hadn't made up yet. There was no "I'm sorry" or "I was wrong" or "Please forgive me." Julie undressed and got into the tub. She was thankful that the water temperature was not too hot. She planned to soak in the bubbles for a while and try to think all of this through. Her mind began to fill with thoughts.

If only he'd said something! It didn't have to be an apology, but something at least sweet or kind. He knows that I am a word girl! Why couldn't he just innately know what I wanted?

The bathwater was cooling off quicker than she had anticipated, so she pulled the plug and reached for a towel as she stepped out of the tub. While drying herself off, Julie wondered if it was possible that Mike could already be asleep.

Ha! Not a chance! She turned and reached for the robe, but it was gone from the hook. *That man! I've got half a mind to just get fully dressed!*

She then realized that he had taken every single piece of her clothing with him. She had no choice; it was towel or no towel, and she knew darn well that she was coming out wrapped!

Julie opened the bathroom door to a darkened space with more flickering candlelight and the aroma of more gardenias. The television's volume was much lower, and as she peeked around the corner, she could see that the covers on her side of the bed had been turned down. Then she saw him in the dimly lit room, and he was grinning like a mischievous cat on the prowl. Julie approached the bed, lay down, and pulled the covers up to keep the air conditioner from blowing directly on her. She wondered just how quickly Mike would pull the covers right back down again. He probably wouldn't let anything interfere with his lascivious scheme for the night, including the fatigue she was feeling at this moment. Julie really wanted to sleep, but she did not want to add any fuel to the bickering and discord between them. She decided that Mike would get his way, but like all women from time to time, she would be a silent partner rather than a zealous participant. Mike probably wouldn't even notice that. All he would need her to do is just "show up."

Chapter 8

Julie could not sleep. She lay on her back staring at the ceiling. She looked at the face of the clock on her nightstand. Two thirty a.m. The only consolation to the thought that she might not get any sleep tonight was knowing she could sleep in the car later, and that way, there would be no arguing with Mike. They might actually arrive at Larry's home with no further problems. She gently rolled onto her left side to see if Mike might still be awake; thankfully, he wasn't.

Her mind dwelled upon their issues. To Julie it seemed that every time they had a special event, there was a cloud of irritability that followed them. It routinely happened at Christmas, New Year's, the Fourth of July, and even Veteran's Day (and that day recognized those who fought)! Their problem had reared its ugly head in the French Quarter, Marco Island, Padre Island, NYC, and DC. It even struck during a five-day cruise as they gazed at one of the most romantic starry skies Julie had ever seen. She knew she had found more romance with Mike while playing in their backyard swimming pool, sitting in their parked car in the garage, or just laughing at silly jokes while washing dishes together in their kitchen. Those romantic times led to incredibly wonderful intimacy. Why couldn't they reconnect so it was like that now?

Mike's thoughtfulness in creating a spa to help her relax was a caring gesture, but it came with strings attached. Julie reflected on the comment he had whispered in her ear an hour earlier: "How was it for you? Gold-medal performance or what?" In the pitch black that enveloped their room, she'd murmured her answer out of a sense of obligation and the need to please him more than herself. Julie decided that was the conflict: she didn't want to feel obligated. Julie wanted to be able to make love when she really "wanted to," but that would mean the two of them finding a mutual meeting place, somewhere between fun and romance.

Julie glanced at the clock. It was now three thirty. She hoped she wouldn't be exhausted and yawn excessively during their lunch with Larry and his bride later that day. Even though she was not overly happy about the scheduled meeting, she certainly didn't want to be rude. During their years of double-dating in college, she hadn't appreciated Larry's "love 'em and leave 'em" attitude. However, Larry had been a good friend to Mike, and she was not going to be an embarrassment to her husband. At least, she hoped she wouldn't be an embarrassment. Larry's gorgeous-gorgeous wife must truly be gorgeous-gorgeous if those were the words he chose to use in describing her. After all, for Larry, a girl's appearance had consistently outranked intelligence. Julie's thoughts wandered.

What should I wear? Hmm…

Sleep finally did come, bringing her temporary peace.

※ ※ ※ **✻** ※ ※ ※

Julie rolled over expecting to see Mike still asleep, but instead she found an empty bed with turned-back covers. Where had he gone? Mike couldn't have gone to get the

car; Diesel had said it wouldn't be ready before seven
thirty and it was only a few minutes after five o'clock. Julie
fluffed her pillow and lay back down. Should she try to
get back to sleep, or rely on the morning drive for a nap?
She voted for the nap, pushed back the covers, and made
her way to the bathroom.

In the absence of candlelight, the pink-tiled bathroom
looked entirely different. Julie took a serious look in the
mirror. Her eyes were puffy with pretty serious dark
circles. She knew a steaming shower would not help but
turned the tub's faucets on full force anyway, figuring
there would be enough time to lie down after the shower
and apply something cold to erase the signs of minimal
sleep. The shower felt incredibly wonderful and invigorating, much different from the spa bath the previous night.
With Mike's disappearance came the chance to relax and
genuinely let go.

Who lets go at this crazy hour of the morning?

Julie couldn't answer that question, except to think she
would be the crazy one, and she began to sing a favorite
song of hers that captured the moment. She had not been
blessed with an incredible voice, but she certainly did enjoy
singing without Mike present to critique her. Stepping out
of the shower, Julie quickly dried off and slipped into a
matching lingerie set. For a moment, she wished she were
at home pulling out a bag of frozen peas or a chilled cucumber
slice to apply to her eyes. Then she remembered that the
suitcase had last been used for her mom's trip to the
hospital. She scavenged through the piece of luggage for
the item that just might double as her eye cure, and yes,
there it was—hemorrhoid cream! Julie knew it sounded
gross, but she was desperate! Somewhere she had read that
the main ingredient would help in just such a predicament,

so she dabbed a small amount, being careful not to get it in her eyes. It stunk to high heaven, and where she applied it did look a little oily, but Julie kept hoping it would work its magic. She'd just have to wait to apply her makeup.

Julie walked over to the closet and unzipped the garment bag. What should she wear? Since she hadn't known about the lunch plans and seeing Larry, she really hadn't brought something special for this part of the trip. Julie thought that Thursday she'd just wear shorts and a top that would be comfortable for traveling, but that would no longer work. In fact, nothing seemed the right balance between respectable and sexy. There were only four items to choose from, but Julie finally decided on her favorite sundress for the reunion of the "part-time drunken degenerates," a name Larry and Mike used to describe themselves jokingly. Catching her reflection in the full-length mirror, she was thankful for being diligent in watching what she ate. Mike may not have said anything regarding her changed appearance, but at least she was satisfied with her reflection. She sat down in the overstuffed chair, turned on the television, and located a weather channel.

There had better not be any rain in the forecast for this weekend!

Julie heard a funny sound and then the turning of a doorknob. It was Mike. "Hey, you're awake! I thought you'd still be asleep. Did I wake you when I got up?"

Julie kept her focus on the television's weather report. "I didn't hear you get out of bed at all. When I did wake up, I figured you would want to get an early start, so I rolled out of bed and got ready for the day."

"That's too bad," said Mike.

No surprise to me, Mike. I know what you want.

Mike continued. "I have another surprise for you, but since you're ready for the day, I guess it won't work out."

Yup, that's right Mike. I am dressed and staying dressed. After all, you owe me an apology for yesterday's argument, and I am waiting to collect.

Julie saw a small, brown paper bag that had been hidden behind Mike's back.

"I thought you might like breakfast in bed," said Mike as he placed the bag on the end table. Julie was totally surprised. This was coming from the man who would never, *ever* eat while in bed. Even on their honeymoon, they had to sit at a table when room service had been delivered. Mike had said at that time, "I'm not sleeping on the likes of sand or gravel. I'm not sleeping with the roaches who are looking for the crumbs. I am sleeping with you and you alone. End of story." Then he had looked at her with those blue eyes that made her melt. She remembered how he had reached across the table to hold her hand, had kissed the back of her hand and then her wrist, had worked up to her elbow, and then her neck, and then—

"Have you already had coffee?" Mike asked. His question snapped her back to reality.

"No," sighed Julie as she got up from her chair, "but it won't take long."

"Sit down, Julie, I'll get it." Mike headed off to the bathroom sink to get the water.

Julie opened the brown paper bag and a sugary scent of apples, mixed with the very slightest hint of butter, filled the room. The aroma reminded Julie of the way her mother-in-law's kitchen smelled on a Sunday evening before heading back to college. It seemed every time they stopped, she had fried chicken and a homemade apple pie waiting for them.

"Where did you find fresh pastry in the middle of nowhere, Mike? The only possible place I saw last night was one called The Country Store, and it had an old, wooden sign propped up against it. Do you remember? It was just before Diesel's shop. That place didn't look occupied to me."

"It wasn't. I got the fritters from Aunt Patty's food truck. When I got up this morning, the lights were on at Diesel's, so I went over to check on the car. There was this constant stream of cars cutting through to get around the back of his shop, and I asked Diesel what was happening. Seems his Aunt Patty makes these great apple fritters and sells them at his place a couple days during the week on her way to deliver pies to restaurants in Cadiz or Hopkinsville. She's got a nice little business going, calls it Pie a la Road. Clever, huh?"

"Mmhmm," Julie said as Mike handed her the steaming Styrofoam cup.

"Ladies first," he said and winked at her as he tilted the open bag toward her. Julie could feel her heart melting once again as she reached in and pulled out a fritter.

"This thing is huge! Want to split it with me?"

"Nope. I am going to deviate from my healthy food regimen, and if it's as good as I've been told, I'm going to eat a whole one all by myself. Just nibble what you want and throw away the rest. After all, your mom isn't here right now, and you don't have to belong to the Clean Your Plate Club!"

"Right," said Julie. "Speaking of my mom, I sure hope everything is going all right at home. Do you think we should give the guys a call? They should be on their way to MARTA right now. What if they oversleep and miss their flight?" That had been a genuine concern for Julie right from the start, even before their flights had been booked. For some strange reason, she intrinsically carried the concern that, if she wasn't there, something was going to go wrong. She didn't consider herself a helicopter parent, but then again, she wasn't a free-range believer either. Was there such a thing as a happy medium? Mike's voice interrupted her internal debate.

"If everything wasn't all right we would have gotten a call. I'm sure no one has overslept. After all, your mother is always up before the crack of dawn!" Julie almost laughed but then considered the reality of the matter.

"But what if they did oversleep, Mike?"

"There are lots of flights leaving Hartsfield today, Julie. If they miss it, they'll catch a later one either today or tomorrow. They'll certainly get there by Saturday and the wedding!" Mike said with a grin. Julie could tell he was trying to be funny, but it wasn't funny to Julie.

"But what if—"

Mike interrupted before she could finish her sentence. "Look, no more what-ifs. I don't want to talk about your mother, and I don't want to talk about the boys. Take a bite of your fritter and try to be in the moment, okay?"

Julie glanced at Mike as he took another bite and brushed the crumbs off his pants leg and onto the floor. She knew he would never have done that at home. Julie looked back down at the floor and nibbled at the apple fritter. His reply had been curt, and her mind reverted to the two thirty–a.m. thoughts that had swirled around her.

Why do short tempers and snide comments have to happen?

Mike's voice broke the silence. "Hey, remember that early morning wedding when your hippie friend Tina got married?" Julie nodded as she continued to look at the floor and nibble. "Remember their wedding cake?" Julie shook her head no. "I know why you don't remember it," continued Mike. "There was no cake. They had blueberry-fritter donuts instead of a cake."

"Now I remember," Julie replied. "Tina's mother thought she and Patch were insane, but it actually was a pretty cool idea."

"Yeah," replied Mike. "Remember when Larry took the box that had the table number on it and stuffed it with fritters? You were so afraid that we'd all get caught doing something so terrible!" Mike laughed. "It's going to be so terrific to see him today. I can hardly wait! Be sure to remind me to jog his memory about that day!" Mike laughed and as he stood up, he said, "I'm going to shower and then we can hit the road."

Julie heard Mike laugh again as he shut the bathroom door behind him. Julie was not laughing though. She may not have remembered the doughnuts, but she did remember how Larry had broken the heart of his date by flirting with the maid of honor. The arguing that ensued had spoiled the day's affair as far as she was concerned.

Julie turned her focus back to the television's weather map. The entire country was sprinkled with smiling-sun notations, so there was no need to worry about the weather, at least for the moment. The boys and their precious, ninety-year-old cargo should arrive safe and sound today in the Badger State, giving her mom time to rest before the weekend's festivities. Julie grasped her steamy Styrofoam cup and was ready to take a sip when the blaring ringtone Jake had programmed into her phone startled her. The coffee showered her floral sundress with an array of bronzed polka-dots. "Damn!" she exclaimed. Now she would have to find another outfit for today and somehow get this cleaned before the weekend. How could she have been so clumsy? Why had Jake thought it was so clever to download that crazy, earsplitting tune onto her phone just so she would know when he was calling? Julie decided to ignore the call and take care of the newly created mess.

She knew there was no appropriate outfit for the lunch date in their suitcase or garment bag. Her formal mother-of-the-groom dress was certainly out of the question. Behind that were a simple black sheath dress, her classic boot-cut jeans with tunic top, and a brightly tie-dyed V-neck dress that was a cross between a kaftan and a muumuu. She had packed the sheath for the rehearsal dinner, just in case the sundress was too informal for the evening. At the last moment, she had thrown in the kaftan for the car trip home, just in case she ate way too many goodies over the weekend and didn't want to battle with a tight waistband.

Wonderful. I can meet Larry's gorgeous wife looking like I am ready to attend a funeral, or be a hippie going to a luau!

Neither seemed to be an appropriate alternative, but she had to make her choice. She had heard Mike's infamous farmer's blow and knew that signaled his time in the shower stall was soon ending. She definitely wanted to be fully clothed when he reappeared.

After slipping into the clean garment, Julie took a serious look at the coffee-stained fabric. The outfit was one of her favorites, the hard-to-find kind that, when you first put it on and look in the mirror, makes you look good and feel great. Since Julie really didn't enjoy shopping, she wanted to somehow salvage it, but would cold water and some hand soap be enough? Or was it just not worth trying to save it? Should she just toss it?

"Hey, you changed clothes. How come?" Mike asked as he walked through the steamy doorway.

"Spilled my coffee," Julie muttered as she turned on the cold-water faucet. "I hope I can get the stains out, or I'll have to throw it away."

"Well, we can always get another one. It's not irreplace-able," said Mike with complete indifference. He obviously didn't understand the way Julie felt about that dress, and of course, she instinctively knew that this had better not make them late for their lunch date. "Here," Mike continued, "just put it in this plastic bag with our other dirty clothes, and you can deal with it later." Julie turned the water off and did as she was told, stuffing the bag back into their luggage where she figured it would be forgotten. The sundress wouldn't get the attention it needed and would remain stained, not to be worn or enjoyed anymore.

Why even hang on to it? Probably should throw it away now. What a shame.

"Could you speed it up? Let's go!" Mike snapped as he grabbed their luggage.

The tone of his voice made her jump. "I'm sorry, Mike. I guess I was still thinking about the sundress. What did you say?"

"I said I thought we were ready to leave. Let's go!"

Julie grabbed her pillow and purse before following him out the door. How could she have been so deep in thought not to have heard him? Maybe it was a consequence of not getting a good night's sleep or being too sentimental about her dress. Whatever the cause, it hadn't made for a very smooth start for the car ride. Julie plopped onto the passenger seat and shut the door.

"Don't slam the door! Do you want to damage the new windshield too?"

"I didn't want to damage the first one, Mike. I just happened to see something was wrong with it. Maybe if we would have stopped at that point and checked it out, we could have saved ourselves some money and time!" She hoped that dig would hit home. He hadn't listened to her yesterday, and it seemed to Julie that this day was beginning just like yesterday ended.

Well, it takes two to argue, and I refuse to participate. I'm just going to nap. Good luck, Mike. Enjoy the drive!

She rested her elbow on the door's armrest, cupping her chin in her hand, and closed her eyes. The decelerating of the car and the faint, repeating sound of the blinker woke Julie from her nap. "Where are we?" she asked, rubbing her eyes before remembering she was wearing makeup.

"We're in Illinois, Julie. I just want to make a stop at the rest area."

"All right," Julie replied. After all, she was in no hurry to arrive at Larry's in Effingham. Getting out of the car, Julie stretched and surveyed the area. It was a park-like spot with plenty of trees that provided welcome shade from the summer heat. There was a wooden playground dotted with preteen boys roughhousing on the slide and using the monkey bars like a balance beam.

Where are their parents?

Julie looked around for any adults. The scene brought to mind how her boys had wanted to behave once released from the confines of a car during a long road trip, but neither she nor Mike had allowed it. As Julie walked toward the restroom facilities, she noticed the blue emergency boxes with red push buttons to call 911 for help. She momentarily stopped to look at them, having never seen a device like that.

Good to know that if one of those boys falls and breaks his leg, his parents are able to get in touch with medical personnel immediately!

She walked toward Mike, who was surveying the oversized map in the glass case.

"Where are we again?" Julie asked.

"Right here," Mike replied, pointing to marker seventy-three. "More importantly, which restroom is the men's and which is the women's? The signs on the doors are gone and no one is exiting. I don't want to walk in on someone."

How ridiculous. All he'd have to do is open one of the doors and peek. It's far less risky for him to view the women's stalls than for me to glance at a wall of men standing at urinals.

"Well, Mike, the men's restroom is most likely to the left because women are usually right," Julie offered, barely able to finish her statement without laughing.

"Ha. Ha," Mike countered as he headed to the left. Julie pulled the door open and let it close behind her. She burst into laughter instantly as she came face to face with women's stalls. She was right. Of course she was right! It was just like she had said.

Despite the obvious vandalism of the signs, she could tell the interior of the restroom had been recently updated. The stainless-steel partitions were void of any type of graffiti, and the tile reflected its newness. Julie washed and dried her hands. As she was taking a serious look in the mirror to evaluate the smudged makeup, a young woman entered. She was carrying a crying newborn, swaddled in what appeared to be an ugly, mustard-colored receiving blanket. She hurried into the handicap stall and exited just as quickly, surveying every wall in the room. To Julie the young mother's expression was a mixture of confusion and disgust, so of course, she just had to ask.

"Excuse me, miss, is something wrong?" Julie inquired.

"It sure is. I'm out of diapers and there's no vending machine, let alone a changing table."

Julie gave a reassuring smile to the new mom. "Well, you're in luck. I just happen to have a whole box of newborn diapers in my car. Come on, let's get that baby cleaned up. By the way, I'm Julie."

"Deidre," the woman replied, looking baffled.

Julie understood the young mom's surprise—why would a woman Julie's age have newborn diapers in her car? It didn't take long for Deidre to find out. Julie moved suitcases and baby paraphernalia out of the car in search of wherever Mike had positioned the diapers. While doing this, she shared the details of their trip and the upcoming wedding with the young mother. Deidre told Julie how she was headed to Lambert–St. Louis Airport to welcome home her husband, who was in the army and had done a short tour overseas. In all the anticipation surrounding his return, she had forgotten to check the quantity of diapers in the diaper bag before leaving this morning. Her darling little Henry seemed to be reacting to all the excitement with a fine case of diarrhea. Once the baby was clean, dressed in a soft, blue onesie, and comfortably placed back in his car seat, the two women hugged goodbye. Deidre was back on the interstate and Julie turned to face a not-so-smiling Mike standing next to a towering stack of items.

"What the hell happened? And who's the new friend?"

Julie could tell Mike was agitated. "There is no short explanation for this, Mike. Spare me trying to explain. You won't understand anyway."

"Really? Well, try me. I'm sure it's another story in the Julie to the Rescue series."

"Yup. That's exactly it. Deidre ran out of diapers and her baby was in desperate need of one. I was happy we could be of help. End of story."

"Not quite," replied Mike with a huff. "The story doesn't end till the car is repacked. Unless, of course, you think there might be someone else coming soon who may be in need of a diaper, or perhaps our ice, or anything else you want to give away. It's not enough that you're the mother of five? You need to be the mother of the world as well?"

"Yeah, well that's enough out of you, father of two!"

"Only in my dreams, Julie, only in my dreams."

Julie watched as Mike seemed to heave the items back into the car. "You know, Mr. Cheery, we had the opportunity to help someone, and your only reaction was to be grumpy and cantankerous!"

"No, Julie, we didn't have the opportunity to be helpful. You did, and once again, you did it without any thought to us and how this could make us late meeting up with Larry. You unpacked half the car and then had to 'ooh and ah' over somebody else's kid that you will never see again. Couldn't you just have handed her a couple of diapers and said, '*Have a nice day*'?"

"That would have worked if I'd known where the diapers were in the car, Mike. Mr. Organization Man, of course, packed them where they wouldn't be easily found because we have to pack everything in order according to importance. Excuse me! Whatever happened to the golden rule and helping others?"

Mike pushed the last piece of baby paraphernalia into the car and slammed the door.

"Hope the windshield survives," Julie murmured sarcastically as she opened her door.

"Okay. That's enough with the wisecracks. My back is really hurting right now. You want to drive to Effingham? It's only about an hour away, and I'd rather not with this annoying pain."

Julie really didn't want to do the driving. Looking at Mike, though, she felt a small amount of empathy. "Sure," she replied as she let go of the door handle. Her eyes were downcast as she approached the front of the car. When Mike grabbed her arm and turned her to face him, it caught her by surprise when he spoke with a much calmer tone.

"Look, Julie, I'm sorry for the way I spoke to you. I really don't know why I sometimes say what I say."

"That's okay. I understand," she answered just to make peace. She tried to continue on her way to the driver's side door but was stopped by Mike's continued grasp. Once again he spun her around to face him so they were now standing toe to toe.

"No, Julie. Really," Mike uttered with emphasis. "I am sorry. I want this road trip and upcoming wedding to be a fun time for us."

"I do too, Mike," Julie replied matter-of-factly, and she tried to continue on toward the driver's door, but his grasp was firm.

"Don't brush it off, Jules. I meant what I said. I want this time alone together to be wonderful for us," and he pulled her closer. Julie could feel her heart start to race. Was this her husband, one of the most publicly unaffectionate men on the face of the planet? He drew her to him with his other arm and wrapped it tightly around her waist. Letting go of her forearm, he placed his fingertips under her chin and ever so gently lifted her face so his lips would meet hers. The tenderness of the moment made Julie's defensiveness melt, and for a fleeting moment she felt as though her knees were going to buckle. When their lips parted, Julie laid her head against Mike's shoulder and sighed. Was everything right in their world now with one passionate kiss? Julie opened her eyes to see Mike smile. Maybe parts of the world were okay again.

"Still willing to drive?" Mike whispered in her ear.

"Mmhmm," she softly replied, thinking that this small, affectionate gesture had triggered an inner feeling she hadn't experienced in a very long time. The warmth of his embrace intermingled with the fragrance of his cologne, and Julie felt as though a magnetic force was pulling her closer to him. Closer . . . ever so closer . . . but suddenly she felt herself standing alone, somewhat dazed. Mike had released her from his loving embrace. As she stood there suppressing a sigh, Julie knew it had ended all too soon for her.

"Well, let's hit the road then, shall we?" Mike said as he clapped his hands together in anticipation. "Sure don't want to be late for Larry and Mrs. Gorgeous-Gorgeous Wife!"

Julie felt as though her emotional stick shift had been forced into reverse from arousing revitalization to an exhaustive timetable. Despite her disappointment, she managed a small, if not somewhat fake, smile and walked to the driver's door. "So we'll be there in about an hour?" Julie asked as she fastened her seat belt.

"More or less."

"So what do you think Mrs. Gorgeous-Gorgeous is going to look like, Mike?"

Julie glanced at him. She could tell he was giving her question serious consideration and was half anticipating him to be noticeably salivating at the thought. *Men! What is this with the preoccupation with a female's appearance?*

"Well, it's no secret that Larry was definitely a selective shopper, and my guess is that her body rivals any runway model. You know he always found redheads extremely attractive, so my guess is she has long, auburn hair and an hourglass figure that defies gravity and the ability to stand up straight," Mike concluded with a chuckle.

"That is so not appropriate, Mike!" Julie countered without a second thought as she merged onto the interstate. "Guys that make those comments remind me of those construction workers who ogle, whistle at, and make rude comments to a young woman as she passes by a work site. That comment you made, Mike, is so degrading to a woman."

"Julie, come on. I was just joking. Anyway, what do you think the new missus is going to be like?"

"Be like or look like, Mike? There's a difference!"

"Just for fun, let's start with looks, then," Mike replied.

Julie furrowed her brow for just a moment. She had given a lot of thought that morning to what she would wear and how she would look, but hadn't really considered what the woman she was about to meet would look like. It really didn't matter to Julie; she herself just wanted to make a good first impression.

"You shouldn't have to think that hard. You know as well as I do what he's like," Mike interjected.

"I remember what he was like, Mike. People change. Even Larry has probably changed, and I bet his wife looks nothing like the girls he used to date." In her mind, Julie could picture the exact opposite of Larry's former conquests. Her appearance would be simple. Her figure would be minimally curved, or perhaps she'd even be chubby. She probably didn't wear any makeup, and although she wouldn't be homely, she would not be exactly attractive. She'd be more of a plain-Jane type. When Julie shared her thoughts with Mike, he couldn't have laughed harder!

"You've got to be kidding! I'll bet you she is queen of the bimbos, half his age, with an hourglass figure beyond compare. She'll have the face of an angel, a perfect smile with teeth white as pearls, and gorgeous Lady Godiva hair that's either naturally red or full of peroxide."

"You're wrong about the hair, Mike. There won't be any peroxide. I don't think any holistic, organic-loving folks choose anything with chemicals."

"Who said anything about holistic or organic?"

Julie shook her head. "Have you forgotten about the card that was sent announcing they had one of those 'quickie' weddings in Las Vegas? It was held at that fancy organic resort. Don't you remember the photo featuring their vegan chocogasm cake? I mean, how could you forget that?"

"Easily forgotten," replied Mike. "That card you're talking about was just a publicity piece sent promoting destination weddings for health nuts. I'm sure that request came straight from Mrs. Gorgeous Wife. What happened to beer, brats, and cheese? Larry's from Wisconsin, and I'm sure he hasn't given up those three staples. I just don't see him having changed into a lover of tofu and alfalfa sprouts. Can you honestly picture Larry dumping a bunch of vegetables into one of those blenders with a one hundred–hp motor and liquefying it into a concoction that resembles horse diarrhea? Nope, won't ever happen, Julie."

Julie swallowed hard, as if trying to force the sludge she was picturing down her throat. "Thanks a bunch for describing horse-diarrhea drink right before we join them at their home for lunch. I'd say maybe we should eat before we get to Effingham, but right now I don't have any appetite at all."

"Well, hungry or not, Julie, it won't be long until we get to Larry and Honey's. What kind of a first name is that, anyway?"

"An unusual one, that's for sure, but it must be for real. Larry wouldn't have put a pet name for his wife on that fancy announcement."

"It just adds to the bimbo personification. I'm telling you, Julie, be prepared to be wrong."

Julie chose to refrain from commenting on that allegation. *How can one of the characteristics I love most in Mike be one that often irritates me?*

The combination of his methodical, rational thinking and aura of self-confidence was helpful in business situations, but a little less self-assurance in personal discussions would be more than sufficient for Julie. She turned the radio on and pushed the search button.

Sports channel, farm report, talk radio, hard rock, golden oldies . . . golden oldies it is.

As one of their old dance favorites filled the car, Julie let her mind wander back to that unexpected affectionate moment at the rest area. She could picture him placing his fingertips under her chin and gently lifting her face so his lips would meet hers. She could still feel the warmth of his hand as it moved downward from her chin and tenderly pressed against her neck. Long ago she had asked Mike to kiss her just like that after watching a movie where the leading man had done the very same gesture. Mike had not forgotten. Julie's defensiveness softened a bit at that thought.

"The crossroads of opportunity," stated Mike.

"What?"

"Effingham is the crossroads of opportunity," said Mike. "It's on the water tower. Did you see it?"

"No. I missed it," Julie replied as she exited off the freeway. Seeing a billboard advertising a flower shop's monthly bouquet special, Julie exclaimed, "Oh my gosh, Mike, we have got to stop and pick up something to take with us. We can't arrive empty handed!"

"Why not? We already sent them a wedding gift. What did you send them, anyway? Was it a gift card, or did you decide on something else?"

"I told you, Mike. We sent them a beautiful, fully stocked, wicker picnic basket."

"Oh yeah, I remember. That's nice, Julie. We don't need to get them another gift."

"I'm not suggesting shopping for another wedding gift. I just think we should take flowers or wine to give them when they receive us."

"Well, I vote for beer."

"Not going to happen, Mike. We can stop at that boutique shop that was on the billboard we just passed, or I'm sure there's a grocery store where we can get flowers or wine or maybe both."

"Just make it quick, if you really think that it's necessary, Julie. I don't want to be late. Hey, there's a gas station up ahead on the right. Just pull in there."

"We aren't buying flowers and wine at a convenience store, Mike."

"Sure we can, Julie. I bet we could get wine, flowers, *and* beer there," Mike replied with a chuckle. "Besides, the GPS is saying we turn off the main street in less than two miles. What if this is the last possible place? We don't have time to search everywhere for some unnecessary, last-minute gift."

Julie held her tongue. This was not some "unnecessary, last-minute gift." Well, on second thought, maybe it was last minute. However, she felt it was necessary, and she sure didn't want to arrive empty handed. "Oh, all right. We'll give the gas station a try," Julie said as she signaled her intention to turn in to the service station.

"Wonderful. I'll top off the gas tank while you run inside," Mike offered.

Julie pulled up to the pump and turned the ignition off. She surveyed the multitude of window signs advertising everything from lottery tickets to liquor to cigarettes and beer prices.

I hope it wasn't a mistake to do what Mike asked.

She walked toward the automatic doors. Although the inside of the store was small, it was clean and neatly organized. Julie immediately saw to her left the flower display, strategically placed for impulse buying, but upon closer inspection, none of the last-minute romantic bouquets would do. A well-meaning man who hardly ever brings flowers to someone might purchase a bunch of petals showing their age with brown edges, but not Julie.

So, a nice bottle of wine it is.

Julie walked past the refrigerated wall section. There certainly was plenty of beer to pick from, but Julie did not consider that option for one fleeting moment as she continued toward the back of the store where the wine display was located. She scanned the shelving for a nice label she could recognize. There was only one bottle that looked familiar, and when she picked it up, she realized why—it was the brand with the red-white-and-blue twist cap. As newlyweds while Mike was in the military, it had been their low-cost liquor of choice. There had been an assortment of nauseating sugary flavors with strong alcoholic aromas, all of which delivered the same results. Julie rolled her eyes as she thought back to those times.

I can't believe we actually used to drink this, but at least it didn't turn our lips and mouth black like the wine some of our other friends chose!

Mike had tried that other stuff once, and the weird reaction made Mike look like he had been eating charcoal! Julie laughed out loud; she could still picture that moment in her mind! There weren't any flowers or wine suitable here to give to Larry and Honey. Julie shook her head, and because she hurried to set the bottle back on the shelf, the worst possible incident occurred. The base of the red-white-and-blue screw-top bottle nicked the edge of the metal shelving and the bottle cracked, creating a cascading waterfall of alcohol that just missed the hem of her kaftan and shoes. Almost immediately the cashier was at her side, apparently scolding her in a language Julie didn't recognize. He was wildly waving his hands as if calling for someone to come clean up the newly created mess. Julie quickly dug in her purse, retrieved a twenty-dollar bill, handed it to the cashier, and made her way to the front doorway. She could not get out of that place fast enough! Mike had finished fueling the car and was sitting behind the wheel, ready to depart.

Thank God he's ready to leave!

"In a hurry?" Mike asked as Julie jumped into the car. "Did you just rob this place?"

"No. I just want to get out of here. Let's go!"

"But where are the flowers or the wine or the beer?" Mike asked.

"I didn't get any. They didn't have what I like."

"What do you mean, they didn't have what you like? Why can't you just like what they have? It doesn't have to be perfect! And what's that smell? Did I get gas on my hands? Kind of not what gas smells like, though," Mike wondered as he stretched his right arm toward Julie.

Without taking the whiff that Mike was looking for, Julie said, "No. It's not you. You smell the wine that spilled on me from the bottle I broke. Please, just go!"

Mike continued with questions as he started the car and pulled away from the pump. "You broke a bottle of wine and that's why we didn't buy any? Did they only have one bottle?"

"No. It's just too much to explain right now," Julie responded. "Let's just stop one more time and try to get something." Mike pulled out into traffic and continued down the road.

"We are not stopping again, Julie. We're going to run out of time, and I am not going to be late."

"Well, I am not going to be empty handed, Mike. Okay, it looks like there's a strip mall coming up on the right. Just pull into the parking lot. There's gotta be a store I can run into there."

"The GPS is directing us to make a left turn at that intersection, though, so I'm following the GPS."

"Mike, I literally can see a sign for a grocery store in that plaza and can run in there."

"No."

Julie let out a gasp of annoyance. "Stop being such a stubborn man, Mike! This is not out of the way. I never wanted to stop at that gas station for wine and flowers in the first place, but I did it for you. Why can't you do this for me? It's what we should have looked for in the first place!"

"All right, but you'd better hurry. In fifteen minutes, we'll be late!" Mike muttered something else under his breath that Julie couldn't hear, but she didn't care; he was turning into the parking lot.

"Well, will you look at that," Julie said. "The grocery store's named Mighty Mike's and it's located right next door to the Flying Mule. How appropriate!"

"Well, while you're in there, why don't you buy a shovel for all those digs you're making."

"Sure will, and I'll see if I can buy a map, too, so you can find your way back into my heart." They silently mouthed ha-ha-ha at each other as Julie grabbed her purse. She made a quick exit and cringed ever so slightly when she heard the thud of her closing car door. As she strode toward the store's entrance, she was confident that Mike would once again be reminding her how to properly close a car door after a windshield installation. She gave a raspberry to the whole idea of it, and then chided herself that she had better hurry indeed. Taking too long would offer one more opportunity for a critical remark.

As Julie entered Mighty Mike's Market, she decided to concentrate more on making the perfect selection of wine and flowers for Larry and Honey and less about her own "flying mule" back in the car. After all, she was the one who was going to be judged for the hostess gifts they presented the Dymawiczskis. It seemed to her that it was the first rule on the secret list of the understood but unspoken unofficial rules for visiting couples. If it's nice, they're a great couple; if it's terrible, then it's "Did you see what she brought?"

Think, Julie!

She arrived at the floral section of the supermarket and decided upon a beautifully vibrant, full bouquet of yellow daisies.

Perfect! Yellow for Honey. Yellow for blonde bimbo or sunshiny plain Jane. Also, yellow for somebody-color-me-a-happy-housewife face!

Julie next walked almost the whole length of the store before locating the aisle offering alcoholic beverages. She found the perfect wine to give as a hostess gift. It was a pricey ice wine produced in the Niagara area, simply called Bliss.

Perfect again! Ignorance is bliss — good motto for newlyweds, good motto for blonde bimbos, good motto for Honey and Larry, "bliss" their hearts!

Julie purchased the two items in the express lane and headed back out to the car. As she got back into her seat, Mike put away his smartphone and started the car's engine. "Wow, Julie, great job! That *was* fast, so we're still pretty much on schedule — and the flowers look great!"

"But not as great as the love of your life, right?" Julie prodded, half joking and half hunting for a compliment from her husband.

"Is that really the name of the wine?" Mike asked, not realizing what his wife wanted to hear.

Disappointed, Julie replied with a sigh, "No. The wine is called Bliss."

"Oh. Okay," Mike uttered with a mild confusion that dissipated almost as soon as it had appeared. "Well, great then. Next stop, Larry's!"

Julie looked out the passenger side window as her mind complained to itself: *God bless Mike's bliss and my feeble attempts at romantic banter. Our blind, deaf, broken-winged cupid is shooting with crooked arrows at a reversible, swiftly falling target! Time to get a new cupid, one that doesn't say, "I'm tired and busy. Can I aim and shoot you tomorrow in a more comfortable set of orthotic wings? Maybe get some lighter arrows too? My back's killing me!" We need to get our oomph back!*

"... WKRV, 107.1 FM. You're listening to classic hits on the Kurv. Local news coming up on the hour." The voice of the radio station's announcer brought Julie's attention back to the car.

She looked at the brochure she had spotted and picked up while exiting the supermarket and remarked, "Wow. They have a winery right here in town. We could have purchased a gift bottle there if we had known. Oooh—they have plays and shows and lots of things going on at a place called the Effingham Performance Center as well."

Mike shot out an idea. "Well, maybe we can come back for a long weekend or a week and enjoy a longer visit with Larry and Honey sometime. Besides, it's probably a good idea for us to start having some time away again, just the two of us. Right?"

Julie put down the brochure. "Time away to relax sounds great, but let's see how lunch goes first. Maybe you won't want to return if Honey is not such a, you know, sweet honey."

"Well, we're going to find out soon enough," Mike proclaimed as he turned the car onto Brittany Lane, where their GPS indicated they would find Larry's house in two-tenths of a mile.

As the car headed down the lane, Julie quickly opened a compact mirror from her purse.

Okay, ol' girl, this is as presentable as you can be right now. I'm sure Honey's assets are a lot younger, firmer, and perkier than anything I have to offer! My assets are probably more like bypass-its now. Okay, Julie. Whatever you do, stop comparing! Comparing leads to swearing, and you don't want to put yourself on the cuss bus! You deserve better than that! Enough with the Honey this and Honey that already. If they don't like me the way I am, hey, it's just lunch!

Julie finished her inner pep talk, snapped her compact mirror closed, and deposited it in her purse as Mike pulled into the driveway of Mr. and Mrs. Larry Dymawiczski. It felt strange to think of Mike's old friend as a married man now. He had always been the big catch that no woman could reel in, though so many had tried. His playboy aura allowed him to nibble at a lot of lines without ever getting snagged. Julie personally never cared for his style of handling women, but he was always a good friend to Mike. That she would give him. Mike never needed to be asked twice to share stories of their college escapades, and today would be a quick parade down memory lane. It made her chuckle to think that the aging memories of those two men always seemed to create new and improved "facts" to each story they told. Everything seemed to get bigger or longer or faster with each repetition of the tales they shared. At the rate they were going, their biographies would become great works of fiction for Alzheimer's book clubs across America. They were legends in their own minds!

Mike put the car in park and silenced the engine. In front of one of the garage stalls sat a compact, shiny red Prius. "Someone went environmental," Mike said. "Hmm. Really nice place." Julie replied with a muffled "mmm" as she was busy paying more attention to the items she was fumbling around with in her purse than to what Mike was saying. The Morins found themselves sitting outside a brick-and-stone English Tudor home that was well dressed with tall peaks and neatly tucked bay windows. The house itself had clean, modern lines that gave a slightly new twist to an older, classic style. The front lawn had been cut to perfection and offered a landscape containing colorful flower beds and well-manicured bushes. It begged to be on the front cover of some home-improvement magazine. Julie zipped her purse closed as her eyes swept the scenery that greeted them.

Great—perky, young, gorgeous-gorgeous, and *has a beautiful house.* Julie let out a big sigh.

"All set, honey? There they are now. They're coming out," Mike announced as he opened his door. Julie pulled the strap of her purse up onto her shoulder as she put on her happy-housewife face.

She mumbled through her smile like a ventriloquist, "Don't call me that 'honey' name anymore." Mike's door unknowingly closed abruptly on her last remark. He was already raising his right hand in a wave as he turned to see if Julie was exiting the car yet.

She grabbed the bouquet of daisies and the bottle of wine and then followed Mike's lead toward the Dymawiczskis. The couples greeted each other by the shrubs at the end of the front walkway, which curved effortlessly up to the grand entrance of the house and was filled in with beautifully fitted fieldstone. Julie and Honey gave each other a quick, smiling glance as they waited to be introduced, while the two college buddies gave each other a bear hug accompanied by testosterone-fueled pats on the back. Honey giggled and silently mouthed the word "men" to Julie. Julie politely returned a knowing smile, which masked her thought that the whole exchange was just an indication of how long the afternoon torture of silly masculine antics would be for her.

After exchanging a few words and a laugh or two, Larry turned, walked over to his wife, and proudly introduced her to both Mike and Julie. "This is my wonderful, beautiful, sexy, eco-caring, perfectly made-for-me Honey!" His thirty-six-year-old wife sported a shoulder-length, blonde shag haircut that complemented a knock-out, fat-free figure, one that probably would bring any plastic surgeon to tears of artistic appreciation. She was wearing a white, cutesy-cute sundress with a light-golden trim and a matching short-sleeve jacket. Julie's eyes travelled downward to Honey's Birkenstock sandals, which presented golden-yellow daisies at the center of their top straps. Mike and Julie exchanged quick hellos and hugs with Larry's wife as they offered her their gift of flowers and wine. Honey blushed at Larry's comment and accepted the gifts appreciatively as she commented on how perfect they were for the occasion. Julie couldn't help taking inventory and making a comparison.

Just lovely. Perky, younger, gorgeous-gorgeous, beautiful house, perfect body, adoring husband, cutesy-cute hair and clothes . . . and no kaftans! Just lovely. Please, Lord, there has to be something wrong with her! Bimbo? Bad tempered? Maybe? Anything?

Honey gave a blushing smile as she returned back to hold Larry's hand. "You just don't know how happy I am to meet you! Larry goes on and on about all the fun you have had together. I've heard so many stories, and it's just great to meet the people that go with those stories!"

Mike's face lit up. "The pleasure is all ours, right, Julie? We couldn't wait to meet the lady who could bag this guy here and get him to commit, right, Julie?"

"Oh, yes," Julie answered. "Congratulations on your wedding. I've always said he should be committed."

The group laughed and Larry replied, "Ah, Jules, witty and pretty, you haven't changed a bit! Mike's a lucky man, but I'm the luckiest one because I landed my Honey here!" He stepped over to his newlywed wife and gave her a big squeeze.

Honey giggled again. "I think we're both lucky." They kissed, and then Mike put his arm around Julie in a defensive move that said, "We're in love too . . . right?"

Honey broke up the moment as she scolded, "Well, where are our manners now? Why don't we all go inside and have a drink before lunch? I have years of catching up to do with the three of you musketeers! And Julie, I hope I can learn a secret or two about marriage from you! From all the stories Larry shares with me, you and Mike were just about cut out of the same cloth for each other!" If only she had known that they were so busy lately trying to tie some of the loose ends that were beginning to unravel from that cloth of their life together.

"More like two musketeers and a damsel in distress," Julie kidded as she became more comfortable with the lunch date. "At least I'm not outnumbered anymore! By the way, your yard is beautiful!"

"When did you become talented in yard work?" Mike asked Larry.

"I didn't! I hired a company, and they have all the talent!"

"Well, it looks great! Boy! Nice house, new promotion at work, gorgeous new wife . . . good thing I came to rescue you from all this bad luck!"

"Yeah, right," Larry laughed.

"I love this walkway! It's pieced together perfectly! What did they use to build it?" interrupted Julie.

Larry replied, "I was just going to let the contractor put down whatever he thought was best, but my Honey here, my pride and joy, was really smart by doing a lot of research, and she found this material that is environmentally friendly."

"He's always flattering me," Honey gushed. "Anyone could have gone on the Internet and researched it. These are called permeable pavers, and they actually are very eco friendly. I just feel that we all really need to be responsible and take good care of the earth. I'm just trying to do my part."

Larry added, "See that outline decoration of the words 'I DO' next to the front steps? Honey carved that from reclaimed wood, and then she filled it with desert sand from Eternal Springs Preserve, where we got married. Who knew all the things you can create from recycled goods? It does make you feel great that you're doing your part and all, know what I mean? Honey's great at that. She's better than anyone I know when it comes to being creative with recyclables! Even her dress she's wearing is oregano cotton!"

"Organic cotton," Honey corrected. "Good for the planet and absolutely comfortable to wear."

"That's really neat!" Mike replied. "So I bet Honey is the owner of that nice red Prius parked in the driveway, then. Am I right?"

"Correct!" answered Larry. "I might get one too. Honey is inspiring me to see the world in a whole new light."

"Which is ironic because most of your fun used to take place in the dark!" Mike teased as he elbowed Larry. "Isn't that great that they're environmentally conscious, Julie?" Mike continued. "What do you think?"

Maybe she can help me consciously recycle my marriage and get more mileage out of it! "Wow. That is wonderful indeed!" Julie exclaimed with her happy-housewife face.

Honey thanked them for their compliments and reminded them that drinks and lunch were awaiting them. The four walked up the stairs and through the door of the grand entrance to the home so they could enjoy the refreshments that Honey had offered.

The four chatted as they entered the wide-open foyer of the Dymawiczski home. They were welcomed with a spacious area boasting a cathedral ceiling, hanging crystal chandelier, beautiful arched windows, and a sweeping grand staircase. There was a large bouquet of fresh white daisies with yellow centers sitting in a crystal vase in the center of a long entry table. Julie made a mental note to herself that the flowers in the vase matched Honey's outfit, and that they now made her gift flowers look redundant. Her eyes moved on and surveyed the rest of the room, looking for an error, a problem, some imperfection. Anything!

Mike let out a low whistle. "Nice! Very nice. And I still can't believe that someone tamed the beast in you, Larry, and that you've finally settled down." The boys and Honey laughed.

"Well, it was actually easy putting the whole bachelor life behind me once I found Honey. She's the best. She really gets me," Larry explained in a way that exposed how his lovebug–bitten heart was suffering with newlywed ramblings.

"You have a lovely home," Julie offered. *Something, Lord, anything, just one fault. No one is* this *perfect!*

"It's just perfect!"

Was that God answering me? No, it was just Mike.

Chapter 9

The two couples were standing in the middle of the entry room of the Dymawiczski home. Julie could not stop dwelling upon the duplicate set of daisies.

"Sorry about the repeat in flowers," she explained. "I didn't know."

"Oh, please! Don't apologize!" Honey replied with reassurance. She held up the bouquet of yellow daisies next to the white ones in the vase. "See? The flowers will actually complement each other, and they'll add such a natural beauty to the entryway. I love your taste!" Julie was beginning to understand that Honey was a genuinely sweet and gracious person and that Larry had just happened to strike it lucky again. At least he seemed very appreciative of his good fortune this time around.

As if on cue, Larry piped up, "Well, Mike, it sounds like you and I need to toast our luck in finding amazing wives! C'mon, everybody, let's have a drink in the solarium before lunch."

The four walked through the entry room, down a short hallway, and into a bright room encased in windows on three sides. It was painted in a soothing, rose-tinted orange hue, which Honey explained to them was called Northwest Sunset. A ficus tree, a hanging spider plant, a large corner fern, and natural wood pieces made the room look warm, cozy, and very inviting. An overstuffed, cream-colored sofa was placed at the opposite end of the room from them, and three cushioned chairs were positioned to fill the room while all facing each other. The sofa had beautifully carved wooden arms and was adorned with various-sized throw pillows bathed in sunset shades and tones. The variety of colors seen in the decor fit perfectly with the columns of various drapes tied together between the window casings. A coffee table sat in front of the sofa, offering a filled pitcher that was accompanied by a set of four glasses resting upon a wicker tray.

Honey picked up the pitcher as the Morins sat themselves down on the cream sofa. "I made a pitcher of strawberry-basil lemonade for us and I used a vegan vodka. Anyone here a vegan besides me?"

"No. Sorry, but Julie and I aren't vegans. We pretty much like to chew the moo, so to speak."

Larry chimed in, "Yeah, I tried to go vegan with Honey, but I guess I'm just too set in my ways. At least my beer is vegan, which is what I think I'm going to have. Want one, Mike?"

"Sure. That sounds good, thanks," Mike replied.

Julie decided to try the lemonade cocktail, so Honey poured two glasses for the ladies. "Oh, that looks so good," Julie said as Honey handed her the drink. "And the sliced strawberries floating in it look delicious!" Honey agreed with Julie's assessment and added that it was her favorite summertime drink. She also added that the basil gave it a wonderful little kick. After her first sip, Julie was hooked. "Oh my goodness! No wonder it's your favorite! I love it! Could I get the recipe for it from you?"

Honey smiled. "Of course! I'll e-mail it to you. I know Larry has an e-mail for Mike. We'll just have to check before you leave to make sure I have a direct e-mail address for you. It'll be nice to communicate with each other. I'd like that a lot!"

Julie replaced her happy-housewife smile option with a genuine smile. "Yes, I'd really like that too." *You're okay, Honey, and I should've known that right away. It takes an angel to convert the devilish habits of a man like Larry Dymawiczski.*

Once again, as if on cue, Larry returned to the room with the beers and some frosted steins for the men. The four drank and updated each other with details of the elopement, the upcoming Wisconsin wedding, and other family events. Honey showed the Morins her wedding ring, which she and Larry pointed out was a fair-trade ring.

"What? You traded rings with someone?" Mike asked. "That's not like you, Larry! What happened to 'go big' or 'go with the best'?"

Larry chuckled. "No! That's not it! Honey taught me all about the fair-trade market practices and its issues around the world. She asked if we could switch the first ring I chose for another one that could be certified as fair-trade marketed. That means that the people who mined the original materials or made the ring were fairly paid for their work. They weren't duped by some slick businessperson who pays them cheaply and then pockets a huge profit for him- or herself."

"Got it. Well, what if the person who made the certificate paper that says the ring was fairly traded wasn't fairly paid, meaning that the paper wasn't fairly traded, but the ring was? What do you do then?"

"Hmm. That would be an issue, wouldn't it?" Honey contemplated.

"Teasing, Honey, he's teasing. Right, Mike?" Larry reassured his wife.

"Guilty as charged," Mike replied. "I actually think it's pretty neat how you care about the world and others so much."

"I do too," Julie added. "Caring about others and thoughtfulness go a long way no matter who or where you are. It doesn't matter if it's home, local, or worldwide."

"Exactly!" Honey chimed in with her agreement. "And it's easy to make it part of your everyday life. I could show you lots of ways, just like I did with Larry."

"Perhaps we can take you up on that offer the next time we get together, because unfortunately, today we have to continue on our way in a just a few hours," Julie replied.

"Oh, yes, of course. That's what I meant," Honey explained. "Speaking of time—Larry? Shall we serve lunch on the backyard patio now?"

"Sounds like a great plan, my love," Larry answered, "but first, I just want to point out the photos we have hanging on the walls of this room. Mike and Jules will probably recognize some of the ones on my side." He explained how, on one side of the room, the theme of the pictures was his family and his hometown, which did indeed offer many settings that the Morins recognized and enjoyed. On the other side, the theme was Honey's family and her native home of Portland, Oregon.

Well, that explains our eco-friendly, vegan, Birkenstock-wearing, fair-trading Honey, thought Julie. *She's so sweet, though. I'm going to force myself to find something in common with her besides our two UW husbands! I may have to become a modern-day, high-class, happy hippie myself!*

After enjoying the photos together, the Dymawiczskis led the Morins out through another door of their beautiful solarium. This brought them to the outdoor patio. Larry and Honey continued to talk about the house and backyard while the Morins finished sipping their drinks, looking around and making occasional comments. Julie saw that the patio offered a glass, rectangular table that could seat eight and held a large, wheat-colored umbrella at its center. The woven, webbed chairs were cushioned and matched the umbrella. Near the table was a long, cement island that seemed to serve as a sidebar. This was confirmed by the four stools that were lined up on the other side of it. A grill was nearby, offering them little wisps of telltale smoke that let them know something was simmering for their palates to enjoy. Its size and accessories, as well as the barbecue tool rack next to it, showed them that Larry was a pretty serious grilling man. Past the patio was a wonderful little area nestled in between shrubs and small trees, where some wicker furniture was arranged around a beautifully layered, stone fire pit.

As the group arrived at the table, Julie said to Honey, "You decorated everything so beautifully, and it all fits together so well." Honey thanked her once again for all the compliments.

Mike laughingly commented on the nearby outdoor heater. "Nice heater! And it's close enough for everyone to stay warm, but far away enough so the umbrella doesn't catch on fire and give you a whole different show, right, Lare?"

"You've got that right!" Larry chuckled with him.

Sitting at the center of the patio table was some sort of wide, flat, crafted ring that sat around the umbrella's pole and matched the top of the sidebar. Both displayed a colorful variety of ceramic tiles that were broken yet filled in together in a neat, glossy, patterned arrangement. There were four plates that sat upon what looked like jute placemats with matching napkins, rolled up and tied with natural raffia. Julie grinned when she saw the mason jars that were converted into drinking glasses. Though they had only met a little more than an hour ago, Julie already knew how fitting this setting was for Honey.

I'm sure it's all either recycled, homemade, or fair trade! It's so natural that it looks like it practically sprang up out of the ground and improved itself. Julie's eyes roamed and reviewed her surroundings once again. *Maybe I should plant and recycle Mike here.*

"Have a seat! Make yourselves at home while we get this all rolled out," Larry said as he headed toward the grill, its accessories, and their meal.

"Can I help with anything?" asked Julie with her perfect manners.

Honey replied before exiting the patio, "Thanks, that's sweet of you, but I'm just getting a few things here and there out of our basement fridge. Be right back in a dash and a flash!" Honey ducked into another door that most likely headed into the basement of their house.

"Did someone say flash?" Mike and Larry exclaimed in unison and then broke out in laughter.

"It's not that kind of flash! You silly UW Badger boys never miss a chance for some guy fun, do you?" Julie scolded them jokingly.

Larry shot back, "Foiled again by Jules' rules!"

Mike smiled along with Julie as she replied, "I haven't heard that phrase in years!"

"I'm so glad you guys decided to stop here on your way up to William's wedding. I told poor Mike that I wasn't going to take no for an answer. I'm also glad he didn't challenge me on that!"

Julie looked at Mike as he grinned as if to say, "See? I'm innocent! I told you so." He returned her gaze as he replied, "Can't deny a Badger bro, Larry!"

The next hour flew by as the Dymawiczskis served up a summer feast filled with grilled squash quesadillas, marinated veggie kabobs, fruit and potato salads, a mushroom and risotto medley, and an amazing barbecue sauce–soaked chicken, the latter being served for the enjoyment of Larry and the Morins. The delectable lunch was followed by ten to twenty minutes of rest for the happily satiated stomachs gathered at the patio table as old stories intermingled with lighthearted repartee. Honey stood up with a look on her face that showed her thorough enjoyment of this time spent together. She announced to the group that it was time for a little dessert.

"Now folks," Larry announced, "we must be prepared to surrender ourselves to the incredible baking talents of my sweet, lovely Honey! I also want to point out that it was the absolute wisest decision of my life to give the key to my kingdom to this queen of my heart. This way I may forever enjoy all that she has to offer this world, including her ability to please my taste buds while sneaking healthy food into my body. We are about to enjoy one of my favorites that Honey makes from scratch."

"Oh, Larry, thank you for saying such sweet things. Isn't he just the best? Well, my happy hubby asked me to make a certain dessert. I'll go get it so we can all have some."

Honey left the table to enter the basement of the house once again and returned with a two-layered tower of deluxe, thickly slathered, twirled chocolate cake that sat at attention on its serving plate. There were small murmurs of "wow" as she approached the table with her offering. "This is my Larry's favorite dessert that I can eat as well."

"Eat as well? So it's vegan. Is that what you're saying?" Julie asked.

"Uh-huh," answered Honey to the Morins, who no longer showed quite as much excitement as Larry. "And I'll tell you, I would've never guessed that you could make good ol' chocolate cake from garbanzo beans until I found this recipe!"

"Here's the kicker, guys. Honey, tell them what it's called."

"Chocogasm Cake! Cute, huh? It's like you know exactly what they're implying!"

"Well, you know what they say," Julie chimed in, thinking that the cake certainly wouldn't hurt her goal of fitting into her dress this weekend. "I'll have what she's having!"

"Ha! Good one, Jules! How about you, Mike? You in for having a Chocogasm?" Larry asked his buddy.

"Sounds R-rated to me, but I'm up for trying it at least," Mike spoke. "It's good to try new things, especially if it fixes old things!"

"Yeah, old things like us old farts!" Larry answered.

Julie gave a quick glance at the men from the side of her eyes. *If it fixes old farts, then eat up, men, eat up!*

Julie's quick-witted retorts remained for her sole enjoyment, and that was probably a good thing. The next several minutes were filled with a palatable pleasure for the group, the kind that allowed one's soul and body to melt together into gastronomical nirvana. It wasn't real chocolate cake, but it was pretty close—and it was gluten-free to boot!

After enjoying the combined blessing of great food and conversation between gathered friends, the ladies cleared the table together with the men. Julie could tell Honey was immensely enjoying the tales of youthful college escapades, as told by two old Badger buddies, while Julie corrected a few male-bravado exaggerations here and there. She found herself enjoying this get-together a lot more than she thought she would. Honey surprisingly ended up being someone very likeable and someone she could connect with very easily, even though they were different in so many ways. It also amazed Julie just how much marriage had changed Larry from a restless, extreme bachelor into a very happily married and more balanced man. So it was probably very fitting that they get to know more about the lady who accomplished this "taming of the beast"!

She decided that she would talk with Mike about setting another date with the Dymawiczskis, at a later time when they could stay perhaps for a few days. It was long overdue for the Morin children to step into larger helping roles with GG and for Julie to have more faith in their capabilities in this area. It truly was time for her to gradually release some of her self-imposed guilt and daily worries. She had to stop "should-ing" on herself! That was a great new phrase she had picked up from one of the Bermback discs.

When everything had been cleared from the table and brought back to the kitchen, the group gradually split up, with the women heading outside to check out Honey's garden and the men heading downstairs to a basement media room.

The women walked around the outside edges of Honey's garden as they discussed the lush plants the garden offered in return for Honey's diligent care of them. While there, the younger wife mentioned that she was enjoying the challenge of bringing her herbal container gardening from Oregon to Illinois as well. She had to learn different planting times and where to position the containers to gain the most benefit for her plants from the sun's rays. The ladies walked over to the deck so that Honey could show Julie the various herbs that looked so robust and reflected their owner's green thumb. Honey shared her beliefs about using organic foods and fresh ingredients as much as possible. Julie complimented Honey's obvious gardening skills and talent, to which she replied that it was a necessity for her to become good at this. They helped her tremendously with overcoming her health issues. After sharing this, Honey explained to Julie that she suffered from SAD, or Seasonal Affective Disorder, but that it was managed well because she was able to treat it using the knowledge she had gained through long hours of research and various visits to the doctor.

Julie joked, "So what would you grow to help treat Defective Husband Disorder?"

The ladies shared a short giggle. Then Honey pondered the question for a moment and finally answered, "I don't know. I guess I would just grow, well, us! Larry does that too, believe it or not. We are our most important resource, so we make sure we take care of that. We are both crazy about each other, and I don't want us to lose that feeling, so we grow us!"

"Wow," Julie responded. "Such a simple answer, but a really wise one. That's good, Honey. I'm going to like having you to balance out our foursome! We are going to have to get together sometime in the near future, for sure."

"Oh, I would like that!" Honey said with a genuine smile, happy to be accepted by her husband's friends. She offered Julie another glass of the strawberry-basil lemonade, which Julie accepted. They sat down at the patio table, sipping the last round of the summer cocktail, and chatted, getting to know each other more and enjoying the wonderful weather for a while longer before their partners returned.

It was then Mike announced that Team Morin had to sadly continue on their way toward Madison.

Once again the couples agreed that another visit in the near future was definitely needed so they could all enjoy more time together. It was also agreed that it would be in Illinois again, as Julie and Mike currently had too many distractions and not enough room for visitors at their home in Cumming.

Larry and Honey walked the Morins back to the driveway where the Traverse was parked. The four exchanged hand-shakes and hugs and made promises to call each other soon to solidify their plans. Mike and Julie thanked them again for such a wonderful lunch and shared with Honey what a pleasure it was to finally meet her. After e-mail addresses were updated and Honey's number was added to cell phones, Mike and Julie got back in their car and buckled up before Mike backed out of the Dymawiczskis' driveway. With final smiles and waves, they were back on the road as Larry and Honey faded away in the growing distance. Mike and Julie were now on their way to a hotel for the night, only a couple of hours away.

The Morins were making great time while still enjoying each other, meaning something bad was probably going to happen soon—why hadn't it already? Julie could feel this like an old, arthritic woman sensing that rain was coming. Her bones forecasted to her that a Morin storm was overdue, and it would probably be accompanied by floodwaters, most likely created from her own tears.

Probably happen without warning. One of those tropical storms that comes up fast and catches you in a downpour. Well, let's hope someone throws us a vine if it happens so we can quickly find a safe haven from ourselves!

Chapter 10

The drive into Champagne had been uneventful, and the Morins had spent this time enjoying the passing views and commenting on their visit with Larry and Honey. Both agreed that it amazed them how love had transformed their UW Badger buddy into such a different person. The day had finally arrived when Cupid shot and bagged the great player Larry Dymawiczski. Julie shared how she could see herself and Honey becoming good friends despite all their different qualities. She believed this was because of Honey's down-to-earth likeability, the thoughtfulness that she put into everything, and the basic fact that she truly cared about people and helping them. These were obviously strong qualities in Honey, and that was probably why Julie had picked up on them so easily during their short visit.

"Good thing the next visit is at their place again," Mike stated. "I'm thinking that we could adapt more easily there than they could at our place."

"Well, first of all, there's no place at our home. We'd have no room to offer them, so they would have to stay at a hotel," explained Julie. She looked out her side window and saw a sign announcing their entrance to the city of Champagne.

"Right," Mike agreed, "and the last thing you need is more stress added to your plate by figuring out what Mrs. Larry can eat or drink, not to mention making sure everything in our house means something or honors someone in some way. Can you imagine her with a husband, five kids, and a parent to take care of as well? I think her pretty little head would implode!"

"Oh, Mike." Julie shook her head at his naughty comment, biting her lip to hide a smile. "She would probably rise to the occasion and surprise us all," Julie contended as her mind was distracted once again by the city-entrance sign she had just seen. It was not their usual route, and Mike was generally a "life and business as usual" kind of guy. *Why did Mike choose this way?*

"You're actually probably right about Honey. Larry got lucky once again but so did I, not to mention how lucky *you* got in choosing a husband! I can say at this point that you should be prepared to be *wowed*!" Mike replied, making it evident that he was quite proud of himself.

"You mean like 'wow'-ing your lungs off out the window?" Julie asked.

"Forget that. It wasn't one of my best moments, but this may very well be!" he stated with great bravado.

"What are you talking about, Mike, and, by the way, why are we going this way? This is not our usual route," Julie wondered aloud.

"An old dog *can* learn new tricks, and this old dog still has some up his sleeve! With my good buddy Larry's help, I have made reservations at a new place for us to stay! What do you say to that, Mrs. Michael Morin?"

Julie stammered, "I—I guess—wow."

"Ha-ha! I did it! See? I have officially 'wowed' you! This is exactly what we need, and I think we are going to love this place."

"Well, Mr. Michael Morin, I have to say that I love how thoughtful you've been about us this afternoon, even trying to surprise me. It beats arguing. It's also nice to have some alone time for just us. So here's to new places and new things, I guess! What's the name of the hotel?"

Mike smirked. "You'll have to wait to find out, but not for long. GPS is showing that it's straight ahead in . . ."

"On your left in point five miles."

The GPS and Mike ended their sentence in unison. Mike and Julie laughed together at the serendipity of the announcement and its moment.

This is actually exciting. Please, God, let this place be okay and not some crazy Larry the Player idea.

Julie pictured a strange version of Mike the Player, complete with an oversized gold chain and dollar sign hanging from Mike's neck along with a pimp hat, saying, "C'mon, Jules, a threesome never hurt anyone!" She shuddered to clean the "gross" off of her.

"Here we are—our happy home for the night!" Mike proclaimed as he pulled their car into the parking lot of Fantasy Dream Suites. Julie's eyes quickly scanned her surroundings so she could decide whether to nay or yea this idea right away.

"Are you sure this place is okay? I mean, it looks okay on the outside, but are you sure?"

"Absolutely sure of it. I booked it at Larry's after he strongly recommended it for us. I wanted to surprise you and maybe have some fun while trying something new. We have to stop somewhere, so it might as well be here," Mike explained as he pulled the keys out of the ignition.

"True. Okay, I guess. You know I trust you, so Fantasy Dream Suites it is!" Julie accepted the plans.

Mike continued lightheartedly. "You know, Larry's words were, 'This place gives you horizontal dancing and romancing, and neither one of those ever hurt a couple.'"

Julie shook her head. "Well, that sounds like something Larry would say. I get it, honey. Do you want me to check in with you or stay here?"

"You can stay here. I'll be right back, my dear, and then we can head up to our theme room. It's going to be great," Mike said happily as he exited the car.

"Theme room? What do you mean by theme room?" Julie called out to him. Mike simply turned toward her direction, gave her an extra cheesy smile, and held his finger up to his mouth, as if telling her to keep a secret. Then he continued on his way before she could protest, not knowing what to expect about any of this.

Julie watched Mike walk toward the entrance of the hotel. He had a higher spring in his step, and she could swear that he was even whistling. She knew the inevitable expectation of some "horizontal dancing" was always the way to renew his spirit. After about ten minutes, he returned to the car so the Morins could grab their overnight bags and accessories. They crossed the parking lot, entered the hotel lobby, and then took the elevator up to the second floor.

"Okay, so now is a good time to tell you. There are rooms here made up to be different themes, and I took the jungle room for us," Mike announced. "Don't you think this will be fun? I can't wait to see what it's like!"

"I guess so. I just don't know what to expect, so keep in mind that I'm playing catch-up. Jungle, huh?"

The door opened and the Morins exited the elevator. After reading a sign, they headed toward the jungle suite. Julie started to imagine something tropical with exotic flowers. She pictured cuddling with her man in a lush bed with clean, white, linen sheets and thickly stuffed down-feather pillows, while large, tropical leaves fanned them. This whole fantasy-suite idea was actually growing on her very quickly. It did sound enticing and fun, and putting some of that fun in their time together certainly couldn't hurt at all. So why not? Life always seemed to have a way of throwing curves at them, but what could possibly happen in a harmless hotel room decorated to fit a fantasy? It's not like a monkey would come out from under the bed and throw coconuts at them. She decided to invest herself in the fun and really enjoy it with Mike.

Julie continued to envision her sketch of the events for the night ahead as the couple arrived at their fantasy suite's door. She wondered with intrigued excitement what surprises were awaiting them on the other side of it. The door's construction invited her curiosity as it gave telltale clues about what this room would hold for them. It had deep, rounded grooves carved into it with long, slender, wooden vines attached to its face, and the twisted, round doorknob sat in the middle of a recessed tree knot. An awning of fabricated leaves sprang outward above the door, creating a partial replica of a jungle canopy. Julie's eyes scanned the door from bottom to top and then upward again, stopping at the leaves above, which were painted in deep, lush hues of green. "Wow," she barely said aloud.

"Wow is right," said Mike with a smile of anticipation growing on his face. "If this is the door, can you imagine the inside? Well, here goes nothing." He put their two overnight bags down and was about to swipe the key card but stopped short in hesitation.

"Uh, hold on. I want this to be perfect for you," Mike hesitated. "You think I should carry you over the threshold? You know, just for fun? I don't know. What do you think?"

"Well, I think that would be wonderful and awful at the same time," Julie replied. "You and I both know that it would be magical for about five seconds until our old age and your bad back kick in. Then what would we do for the rest of the trip and the wedding? We just can't risk it for some quirky moment of honeymoonitis."

"Okay, what if I carry you, but you sort of . . . help me?" offered Mike.

Julie wasn't sure what he meant. "Huh? I don't get it."

"Sure. I could carry most of you, and you could just keep one leg down and sort of walk in with it."

"What a fantastic idea!" Julie faked a smiling face.

"Yeah?" Mike looked hopeful.

"No! Of course not!" exclaimed Julie. "We're not risking your back to lug me in some hop-along pretense of youth!"

"All right, all right! I was just trying to make it fun and, uh, you know, romantic!" Mike explained.

"I know, honey," said Julie, "and that's really sweet of you. Just open the door, though, and you can deliver inside our room, Mr. Rooster!"

"Yes, ma'am! Right away. And I'd like to just say that I don't mind being cooped up with you one bit!" Mike remarked, proud of his witty reply. He finally passed the card through the security slot, and the door's lock released itself. Mike picked up the overnight bags and opened the door far enough to allow Julie in. He closed the door and placed the bags down while she flipped up the synthetic wooden twig that served as a light switch. Their fantasy room came to life.

"Oh, wow. You Tarzan. Me Jane," Julie said while visually surveying the room that was decorated in lush greens and earthy browns. Her ears detected water trickling leisurely somewhere in the suite. "Do you hear water running?"

Mike replied, "Yes, I hear it too. I wonder what's causing that?" He walked off to inspect their surroundings and to discover the source of the watery noise. Julie joined him in exploring their temporary "habitat" but headed off in a different direction. The walls had 3-D trees cropping out from them with bunches of leaves scattered at the top here and there, while the floor was covered in exotic animal skins from a jaguar and a couple of smaller ocelots. There was an amazing chair that was carved into an oversized howler monkey with arms curved inward, so one could sit on it and feel embraced in its lap. The room's masterpiece, a king-sized bed, was wrapped with bamboo around both ends and was topped off with a thatched, grassy canopy that looked like it jumped out of some South American–travel magazine featuring rainforests.

Imagine the dust that must collect in all that grass . . . and those leaves! Glad I don't have to dust here! Boy! And that jaguar skin must get eaten up by the vacuum cleaner at least once a week. Looks so soft, though. Ooh, nuts!

Julie stopped her roaming for a moment, reached down, and picked up some nuts from a bowl on a table next to her. She began to eat the nuts. *Mmm. Macadamias and cashews with a bit of Brazil nuts—yummy combination. I could get into this!*

"Pretty neat, huh, Mike? There's a bowl of delicious mixed nuts here. Want some?" Julie asked once she swallowed more of the tropical mix.

"Not right now, thanks," Mike called. "I found the water noise. It's a cool, small waterfall next to a hot tub that's been carved into a wall. It's made to look like some sort of recessed cave. You know, this place is really neat. They went all out. And they could, too, judging by what they charge."

"Probably," Julie replied. She was still standing by the table and grazing on the nuts. Her head turned upward toward the ceiling and her eyes came to rest upon a very realistic, colorful, and feathery toucan perched on a swing inside a cage. Intertwined between some of the bars were a few vines with one that hung lazily from the cage all the way down toward Julie. "Oh, wow," she said to herself. "They even have a cute tropical bird. It looks fake, but the vines look real." She tugged on the longer-hanging vine to check its authenticity and was caught off guard when the toucan started up with a recording.

"*Scraaaawk!* Toucan! Who can do it? Toucan do it. You two can do it too! *Scraaaawk!*" Julie half chuckled as the recorded jungle noise in the background came to an end.

Cute. A tiny bit tacky, but still cute and clever.

She then glanced down toward the table again and saw two sets of thick, plush, white towels, as well as baskets that held lots of miniature bottles, things with handles, and other assorted items.

Why are the towels out here and not in the bathroom? That's weird. Towels in every room. Glad I don't do the laundry here! Gosh, these nuts are good!

Julie's eyes continued to browse through the curious treasures set before her. She picked up and inspected a few sealed bottles from one basket. *Hmm. Peppermint foot lotion, coconut massage oil, shea butter massage lotion . . . well, that explains the towels.*

She closed her eyes and felt a surrendering release within her body while imagining the wonders of Mike's hands massaging her. *Oh, we are most definitely using these lotions!*

After enjoying the moment and then letting it go with a sigh, Julie switched the bottles in her hands with thin, red packages from the same basket. *Strawberry, passion fruit, cherry . . . well, they're fruity, whatever they are—OH! They're edible panties! Hmm, one size fits all. Well, now there's a claim to challenge!*

She returned the edible panties to the basket and continued. Next she picked up a black stick with long, colorful plumes of ostrich feathers attached at the tip and a slender, satin-covered handle on the opposite end. A sticker on the handle stated that this teaser was a complimentary souvenir of this evening from the hotel. Julie also noticed a small tag protruding from the handle, which read, "Teasers by Tess, Inspected and approved by #27."

Could there really be twenty-six teaser testers before number twenty-seven?

Julie humored herself with a mental vision of a teaser-tester factory line. She twirled the stick back and forth in her hand and watched the feathers dance in a colorful circle before her. *Well, we'll see if the Morins approve of it tonight! I think I am just going to have to dust off the cobwebs that have built up between my husband and me. Yes, I am!*

Julie grinned as she thought fun but slightly naughty thoughts. She was actually enjoying this little fantasy adventure of theirs. She put the feather teaser down and saw some battery-operated candles, in case guests wanted to enjoy their evening by candlelight. She also noticed there was a basket just for packaged eye masks and blindfolds. There were gel, satin, herbal, and masquerade masks accompanied by long, satin blindfolds of various colors and animal patterns for purchase. Then there was yet another basket with items that seemed a bit too weird for Julie's taste, like fuzzy handcuffs, a paddle, and some kind of strange-looking leash with studs. There was a ribbon attached to the basket's handle that read, "For Freaks, Shrieks, and Tweaks."

Now there's a basket that scares me! Thank you, but no thank you!

Julie left the long table and wandered over to a corner not far from the bed. Her curiosity was called upon when she saw before her a shiny pole that went all the way from the ceiling to the floor. It too had vines of different lengths hanging near it from the ceiling. *Now why on God's green earth would someone put a firefighter's pole here? Maybe it's for hanging up clothes and things? No. No hooks.*

"Hey, Julie, honey," Mike called out in a provocative tone as he headed down the short hallway back toward their bed. "Want to get undressed and relax in the hot tub with me? We have our own little rainforest cavern to explore together!"

"Uh, sure," Julie replied, not really paying attention to his words. "Sweetheart, would you happen to know why there is a firefighter's pole sitting in our fantasy suite? It's supposed to be a jungle, not a firehouse." Mike looked at his wife and then looked at the pole.

"Well, people might slide down it, but that's no firefighter's pole," Mike replied with a grin. "It's actually a stripper's pole."

"Oh. I've never seen one this close before now," Julie answered while her eyes traveled up and down the pole. "Are you expecting me to get undressed using that thing?"

"Well, I'll understand if you don't, but I certainly won't complain if you do," Mike answered in a playful tone. "So. Are you going to try it? I'll be the adoring fan!"

"Oh my . . . honey . . . I'm not sure I can do that. I don't even know what to do or how to do it or anything." Julie put her hands around the pole. "Do you have to spray it or polish it first or something?"

"No, I think you just swirl around it and dance, you know, kind of sexy-like. Go ahead and try it. It's just us here," Mike suggested.

Julie gradually turned around so she could face Mike while she leaned her back against the pole. He sat down on the edge of the bed, and she could tell he was ready to visually consume whatever entertainment she was about to offer him. It felt fantastic to have his full and undivided attention for a change, and it made her feel like somehow she had a renewed worth to him. She began to sway slowly in a somewhat awkward attempt at being provocative. Then it happened. "Oh!" she exclaimed as her moves picked up the pace. She pumped her body up and down the pole in short, precise rhythms that turned into a frenzied vacillation, more like a mini seizure than a dance. "Oh my gosh! I didn't realize my back was so itchy and this feels good. Who knew this pole could scratch a back so well? Ah, wonderful . . . Okay. Oh! I'm sorry, honey, I'm so sorry. I got so carried away with the scratching that I forgot about the stripping dance thing! Want me to start over?"

Mike sighed, smiled at her, and stood up from the bed. "Tell you what. How about we get undressed right now and use that hot tub together after all? We'll be more refreshed and comfortable. Then we can have some wine and see where the night takes us. How about that, honey?" He walked over to her and they embraced.

"Good idea," Julie agreed. He lifted her chin with his finger, and then held her face with both hands as he reclaimed her lips. Julie responded with a kiss that said she was his all along. They began to move in sync as their kisses took on a new urgency. Their bodies moved as one toward the wall and he pressed her up against it. They both froze in fear as her back pressed a console button on the wall. The room jumped to life with high-pitched jungle cries, squawks, and a nearby growl that seemed to be hunting them down! After their brief paralysis, Mike and Julie broke out in laughter together as they realized that the room came complete with sound effects.

"Boy, these interruptions are one after another, just like at home—only without your mother!" he added light-heartedly.

"Or the kids," Julie concurred. "Oh, look! There's another wall button just like it on the other side of the bed."

"You're right, I see it now. They're low so you can reach them while you're in bed, I guess." He continued. "Well, honey, tonight belongs to us, and I'm not giving up on catching you yet! I'm going to trap you with my legendary jungle charm!" Julie gave him a wink and a quick sexy growl. "Ooh, she's on the prowl!" he replied. "C'mon, Jules, let's get undressed for the hot tub and hunt each other down!" They got undressed quickly before anything else could intervene and ruin the moment.

Julie piped up, "By the way, don't forget to try the nut mix, honey. It's delicious!"

There was no reply.

Men! You offer them the slightest possibility of a little horizontal hula and everything else gets zoned out, even food! One-track mind! Oh well. What was that saying all the girls said in high school? "Since the beginning of time, only sex is on his mind, so remember, no milk, no how, unless he buys the cow! Choose bad and be sad, choose wise and get the prize!'

Julie smiled to herself. *Time to dust off my prize!*

Mike headed into the water-cavern room first. Julie gave her hair a quick brush so she could look her most enticing self for her husband. Then she quickly placed her purse and cell phone on the nightstand next to the bed, in case there were any emergency calls from their family during the night. There was no use mentioning this to Mike. It would just upset him, and that was the last thing Julie wanted to do at this time. She finally followed him into the room as the tub was filling with water. Mike was busy fumbling with some knobs and levers next to the tub. The room itself looked so tranquil and lush with rainforest colors, vines, and a bamboo wall. The hot tub and sink, however, had cave-like backsplashes behind them. The toilet was a fabricated replica of a gigantic coconut sliced in half with the top lid opened up in a standing position and the cushioned seat resting in the down position. The edges of the seat and lid looked like the white, meaty part inside the fruit.

Never went to the bathroom in a coconut before. This will definitely be a first! Julie thought.

Her eyes continued their journey throughout the room, and she noted that not far from the spa were plastic bamboo buckets hanging on dark-green wall hooks. Julie walked over to peek in them and saw that the buckets held an assortment of packaged aromatherapy items.

I bet there are some great scents here we could use. This is so lovely! What a wonderful night this is going to be for both of us, finally! Ooh, I love musk. That's sexy. Rainfall would be good too. Smells clean. The scent burner is on this short, little, cute wooden wall shelf and plugs in to that outlet just above it. It must have been built just for this little aromatherapy station. She sighed. *Ahhh! Enjoyable peace at last!*

"Darn it all! Why do things always have to go wrong for us at the worst times possible?" Mike called out in frustration.

Julie's aromatherapy-shopping spree came to an abrupt halt. "What's wrong, dear?" she asked.

"I can't get the flippin' jets on this darn whirlpool to start!" he exclaimed.

"What are flippin' jets?" Julie inquired.

"They're what you call whirlpool jets that won't start when you are trying hard not to swear and ruin the mood!"

"Oh," she answered. "Well, did you see if there were any instructions?"

"Already did that, blasted things that won't work when you want them to! Now I'm going to have to call the front desk to get someone up here to fix this. We paid too much for this fantasy suite not to enjoy all of it! Sorry, Jules, we'll have to get dressed again so they can send someone."

"Hey! Wait a minute! What about this button here?" Julie asked as she walked over to a wall button on the opposite side of the room. She pressed it and the sound of birds filled the air, along with other tropical noises.

Mike said with disappointment, "Must be wired into the same audio system as the bedroom. Good try, my love, but it doesn't solve our problem with the jets, and it's just not the same without the bubbling water, I'm afraid."

"Well, let's get dressed and wait for them to fix our flippin' jets, then," replied Julie, trying to make the best of yet another ruined attempt at romance. The Morins returned to their bedroom area to get dressed once again. Mike dressed quickly and then placed a call to the front desk. Julie continued to dress herself in a nighty and covered it up in a robe with matching slippers.

He got off the phone and told Julie that the management was sending someone up as soon as possible, but that it might not be until tomorrow morning. "Either way, they're going to give us a discount for our inconvenience," he added, "because they don't have any other fantasy rooms to offer us as a replacement. Hotel is full." She nodded in acknowledgment as she took out her facial cream and other cleansers. Mike walked over to the bottles of wine and the ice bucket. "Hey, Julie, I'm going to go find the ice machine so that I can fill our ice bucket. They have a bottle of white wine here that I know you'll like better if it's chilled." He walked over and gave Julie a quick peck before leaving.

Julie lay herself down on their spacious and comfortable thatched bed. While waiting for Mike to return, she thought it would be best to become better acquainted with the details of all the things their suite had to offer. She kicked off her slippers, grabbed the welcome manual from the bedside table.

"Aaagh!" Julie let out a shriek as she caught the first glimpse of herself in a full-body mirror attached to the inside of the thatched canopy. It happened to be, much to her horror, placed directly above her! She kept her eyes squeezed shut until she felt brave enough to have another look at herself lying in bed.

Well, at least I'm wearing something! What were they thinking, putting a mirror in a place like that! Who wants to see themselves at this age? I think I'll read the manual in the monkey chair.

Julie started to get up from the bed and let out another shrill yell as she came face to face with a replica of a boa constrictor that was left to hang at the pole next to her pillow. "Oh my heart! I don't know if I'm going to enjoy this room or die from it!" she complained out loud in spite of being alone. Leaving her slippers behind, Julie headed over to the howler-monkey chair with the welcome manual in her hand. She made a detour to get another handful of the tropical-nut mix. As she turned to head back toward the chair, she stubbed her big toe on the leg of the table offering the nuts. The pain seared through her toe and shot straight up the neural pathway to her brain, registering a direct hit. Dropping the manual on the floor, Julie tried flexing her toe and shaking her foot vigorously, hoping it would make the pain subside quickly. Fate refused to allow such a quick solution, so she hobbled over to the chair and sat herself down, elevating her leg and resting it upon one of the chair's curved arms. Now she would be able to get a good look at the toe and assess the degree of damage done to it. After a few pokes and squeezes, Julie decided the toe would be okay but sore. She rose from the howler-monkey chair and retrieved the basket containing all the various lotions she had perused earlier and brought it back with her to the chair. Bending down, she picked up a tube of peppermint lotion from the basket, opened it, and applied it to her sensitive toe. Hopefully the lotion would refresh her foot enough to bring it back to its previous state.

Julie placed the tube back in the basket with the other lotions, edible panties, and feather teaser. She decided to bring the basket to the bamboo nightstand next to their bed. This way she and Mike wouldn't have to go very far to use these treasures during their stay. Once she placed the basket on the nightstand, Julie began to walk around to make sure she would be perfectly fine by the time Mike returned. It was then that she spotted it, some sort of strange, black object hanging a short distance from the corner ceiling, between the nightstand and the windows of their room. She had not noticed it when they first arrived. It was placed close to the imitation banana leaves that were woven to create window shades for the double rolling windows. This way, when the shades were parted, one could look onto the walkway outside the suite.

Julie approached the object to inspect it more closely. It had a large, smooth horizontal bar with a wide, black, rectangular, cushioned strap hanging from it. There were also two more separate pairs of black straps, with some sort of padded loops attached at the end of them. One pair of the looped straps, a bit larger in size, hung much lower than the other. There were slender, green vines attached to the bar, and the straps met them at various connecting points that formed a network of unified support. Julie talked herself through her inspection of this item that had now grabbed hold of her curiosity.

Trapeze swing? No. That wouldn't fit the jungle theme of this suite. Ah. Yes, of course. Some sort of exercise piece! Workout equipment would be something a hotel would offer its guests. Hang there to do lifts or chin-ups, probably. Make it look like some swinging jungle vine. Wow! They thought of everything!

Julie took hold of the large bar with both hands and let her body hang. It had been decades since she had been on a set of monkey bars, and she was amusingly curious enough to test her endurance. She learned just then that her spectacularly mighty, steadfast endurance could last approximately three seconds. So much for performing a feat of amazing strength! She knew the straps were obviously there to help, but she wasn't sure what part of her to put where or how on this contraption. Julie surmised that she could sit on the long bar if she could just figure out a way to get up there. She placed her feet in the lower strapped handles and reached up to grab hold of the higher looped handles. This left her with the puzzling obstacle of getting herself seated on the bar, especially with her long, flowing bathrobe in the way.

Well, first things first, ol' girl!

After letting herself down from her position and removing her bathrobe, Julie took a step and tossed her robe at the foot of the bed. She usually wasn't this easily willing to prance around in her nighty, but they were not at home with the usual interruptions. Tonight was her and Mike's special fantasy night alone, and it was going to be an unforgettable night; she could just feel it in her bones. Julie stared at the hanging black apparatus. Right now, she just had to figure out how to get her bones sitting up on that bar so she could surprise Mike when he returned. She didn't realize until now just how much she was enjoying their attempt to bring romance back to their marriage. As a matter of fact, he would probably be returning any moment now, so she had better hurry.

Deciding to double up on her support, Julie slid her left arm straight through the top left cushioned handle and then the bottom one. She executed the same clever maneuver with her right arm. Now she could grab the nearby hanging vines with her free hands and still give her arms the extra help they needed. She planned to just jump up at the same time, and with just a tiny bit of extra push from her elbows off the handles, her bottom would easily lift up and land on the bar. Then all she would have to do is find the pose she wanted to strike for her seductively captivating moment. She couldn't wait to see the very surprised—but pleased—look on Mike's face!

Julie grabbed the vines on each side of her and tugged as she simultaneously leaped up and forward to her desired destination. The swing convulsed with Julie as the straps constricted immediately around her wrists and arms. Landing back on her feet, Julie was very confused as to what had just happened. Her arms were now fully confined by the straps that were apparently controlled by the vines, and those vines were now tangled with the banana leaves that formed the window shades, thanks to the dancing commotion caused by the contraption and her body. With her arms trapped, there was no way she could reach the vines to reverse her predicament!

What kind of exercise equipment would leave a person trapped like this, anyway? I need to loosen all these straps . . . hmm . . . but how? Think, Julie, think!

She spotted her solution. In the basket she had placed on the nightstand was the ostrich-plumed teaser with its wonderful thin handle. If she moved forward as much as she could and stretched her leg and foot, she could probably grab the stick with her toes. Then she could use the stick to loosen the straps. Julie congratulated herself, then stretched her leg and foot as far as they could go toward the object that would hopefully free her from her entrapment. On her second try, with the addition of some pain, Julie was able to use her stubbed toe to drag the basket a bit closer to the edge of the nightstand. She was promptly able to grab the stick of the feathery teaser between her toes and retrieve it. All Julie had to do now was place the stick in each of the loops, push outward, and she would be released! She hopped up and down trying to transfer the stick from her foot to her entrapped hands. At one point the stick dropped, and Julie had to repeat the process of picking it up with her toes before she could attempt the transfer again . . . and again . . . and again. She was growing more and more frustrated with each failed attempt.

It dawned on Julie that perhaps her hands were confined much too close to the long bar. She most likely would be more successful if she tried to get the teaser from her foot to her mouth instead. Julie was indeed able to accomplish this but with little relief. What a ridiculous situation and night this was turning out to be—and where the heck was Mike? Her toe was stubbed, her wrists were getting pretty sore, she was being held captive, the hot tub wasn't working right, and her husband was missing in action! Really!

There was a knock at the door. Julie called out, thanking God that Mike was finally back and praying he would hurry in and help her. Unfortunately, with the feathered stick in her mouth, all that came up was garbled talk. Another knock came to the door. *Are you kidding me, Mike? Now is not the time to play games!* she thought angrily.

Julie clenched her teeth down hard on the stick so she could articulate better and he could hear her seriousness loudly and clearly. "WELL, DON'T JUST STAND THERE! PLEASE GET IN HERE! I'VE BEEN WAITING FOR YOU!" The door slowly opened and a wide-eyed Hispanic lady hesitantly entered the room, taking only a few steps.

"Hello, I am Juanita and I am here to give the hour of massage that was ordered for your room tonight," she began. She spoke cautiously while her gaze took in every detail of Julie and her surroundings. "But, uh, perhaps now is not a good time. Yes, I see you are busy, so I will return later. Okay?" Julie quickly responded, but without clenching her teeth down on the stick, her words came out garbled once again. The masseuse politely spoke, "Look, I'm not sure what you are trying to say. I must tell you though that I do not prefer women and I am not into sex swings or anything like that. We are not even allowed to mix socially with the guests. I was just here to give the massages, but I will give you some time and come back later." Julie's face froze with speechless embarrassment as her mind processed what she was hearing while dangling in such a vulnerable position. Her mind was racing, but her mouth was stuck in the horror of what this masseuse was implying!

Sex swing! Sex swing? Oh my gosh! A SEX SWING! Talk, Julie, talk! Explain to her that she's mistaken! Speak up for yourself now and get her to help you!

Julie pushed her head forward first so she could spit out the stick from her mouth. As the top of her pushed forward, her legs flew out behind her and one of her feet hit the button on the wall. Jungle screams burst forth as the audio effects returned to life in the room. The masseuse panicked as she began to rush out of the room with her equipment, exclaiming, "Okay, I actually have another appointment right now! I'll send a replacement to take care of you! Good night!" Julie tried to protest, but the door was already swinging closed.

I cannot believe this is happening to me! Where are *you, Mike?*

Julie was tired, frustrated, and sore. She retrieved the tickler from the floor once more, held onto it with her mouth, and reached to place her feet on the nearby, narrow window ledge. At least the straps would not feel as taut if she could stand on the ledge instead of hanging where she was. This way the feathered stick would probably fit better inside the loops, increasing her chances of loosening them and freeing her hands! Her feet made it to the windows' ledge, but the tilted angle of her body parted the banana-leaf shades, leaving her exposed to anyone walking by outside. Julie tried to bring the shades back to their original position while keeping her feet on the ledge, but she only tangled them more.

At this moment, a man walked by with a bottle and a serving towel and flashed Julie a surprised but approving smile as he walked by the double windows. Then he came to a stop at the suite's door, gave her a look again, and then returned his eyes to the door. He knocked on it. Julie spat out the stick once again and shouted in resignation, "Yes, you know I'm here! Come in or go, but please don't just stand there and stare at me. This isn't a show!"

The young man opened the door and walked into the suite. "Room service, ma'am. I was told to deliver a complimentary bottle of our finest wine to apologize for some sort of maintenance issue you're having in your room, but I'd say that you don't need any more wine!" The man chuckled. "You might have had a little bit too much already, huh?"

Julie was insulted. "I am just fine, thank you."

The man replied as he placed the bottle of wine on a table, "I bet you are!"

Julie, even more embarrassed now, started to explain what she really needed. "Could you please just help release me before my husband gets back?"

The employee shook his head. "Hey, thanks, lady, but no way! I don't want trouble, you know? I don't want no one's husband coming in and finding me like that and beating me up. Sorry! But hey, have a good one, lady. Or I don't know, have fun or something. Anyway, forget the tip! So just thank you and goodnight!"

"Wait! I—" Julie shouted, but the room-service man, her next hope for assistance, was already gone. Julie felt totally and ridiculously disgraced. She hung her head as she hovered in mounted degradation, resigned to her predicament. Suddenly there was a knock and the door to their fantasy suite opened. Mike walked in with a bucket full of ice and headed straight toward the table at the other end of the room, his back facing Julie.

She listened as he called out, thinking that she was in the bathroom. "Hey, Jules, I'm back! You should have locked the door. Sorry I took so long, but the ice machine closest to us was broken. I had to go all the way to the front desk to find out where another one was located. So while I was there, the manager said they were going to send up a free bottle of their best wine and discount our room. Maintenance isn't coming until tomorrow for sure. Less interruptions for us, right Jules? Great news, huh? Oh, the bottle's here already; great! By the way, I also ran into the masseuse I hired for us, and get this! She told me that some crazy lesbian lady in a sex swing was trying to come on to her! I told her it takes all kinds in this crazy world, you know?" Mike made room for the bucket of ice and put it down on the table. He placed the hotel's complimentary bottle in it and then continued talking. "I told her that I hired a masseuse too and wondered if it was her. She took my name and said she'd go back to the front desk to look for the order card for our room. Then she's going to come up to take care of us right away, seeing she refused her appointment with that lesbian sex-swing lady. Isn't that great, Jules? . . . Julie?"

Mike turned toward the whirlpool cavern to see why Julie wasn't responding. As he turned, he saw her body half hanging, half standing in the corner between the bed and the rolling windows. When she saw that he finally noticed her, she closed her eyes for a moment, shook her head, and let out a big sigh.

"Julie, what are you doing? Why are you—oh my gosh, you're the lesbian sex-swing lady, aren't you?"

"Is that what's going around the hotel? I probably am, then," Julie said with resignation. "I'm stuck and on display, and it took forever for you to return."

Mike remembered himself and finally rushed over to help her. "What happened for you to be stuck like this?"

She replied, "More like what didn't happen! It was just one ridiculous thing after another, really, mixed in with one misunderstanding after another." Mike reached up to help release Julie from the strapped loops around her wrists. "Wait! Can you please close the shades first, so I can save the tiniest little bit of dignity I have left?" Mike fixed the imitation banana leaves, which had become more mixed than woven. The shades returned to their proper places and the Morins' privacy was restored.

Mike then rescued Julie from her uncomfortable imprisonment, and they checked all of her sore points. He swept her into his arms and allowed her to linger in the security of his embrace. "C'mon, sweetheart. Let's have a glass of wine, and you can tell me all about how these ghastly twists of misfortune happened to you."

Julie replied, "I do hope the rest of this evening goes a lot better for us, though. It certainly can't get any worse! Oh, Mike, I'm so glad you're here now. I'm not letting you go anywhere else now that you've rescued me!"

"Yes," Mike said. "About that rescue, you need to fill me in with the details on how you became a sex-swing lesbian. That's a whole new sexy side of you I've never known!"

Julie shook her head. "Well, please pour the wine and I'll share those details!"

Julie and Mike spent the next hour learning about what happened where and to whom as they finally relaxed and enjoyed their complimentary bottle of Beaujolais. They chuckled and sipped their time away, lost in their own little world together. Julie let go of her inner critic and learned to laugh at herself just a little bit more. It was so much better than chiding herself for any shortcomings or self-professed failures she possessed only in her own eyes. They finally stopped when there was another knock at the door.

"You can get it this time," Julie said as they both grinned at each other.

"No problem, my lady," said Mike. "I'm sure it's our masseuse—a different one, as the one I saw told me that she was sending a different one to the sex-swing lesbian's room. I'm proud to say that lady belongs to me!"

Julie replied, "Well, after the events of this evening, I'm ready for a relaxing, normal massage!" They winked at each other as Mike got up to answer the door. They were back in love, more than ever. It was a love so strong that they could survive anything that the jungle of life could swing their way. Now it was just a matter of rearranging the vines that held them back from each other's hopes and expectations.

Chapter 11

Mike parallel parked with ease. Julie turned toward him. "I thought we were heading out to the interstate. Aren't you in a hurry to get back on schedule?"

"Not this morning, especially after last night," Mike replied with a smile. "In fact, I know William and Elizabeth could get married tomorrow just fine, even if we didn't make it to the rehearsal and dinner tonight. Want to test that theory?"

Julie detected a twinkle in his eye and furrowed her brow for a moment in actual contemplation. "Are you serious?"

Mike chuckled. "I'm halfway serious. Those two lovebirds would get married tomorrow even if it were just the two of them standing in front of the judge, but I also know there would be an extensive list of 'shoulda, woulda, couldas' in years to come. You, my sweet one, would probably own a list longer than mine, and despite wanting to pursue my own selfish desires of keeping you all to myself, we are going to be at that rehearsal. I just want to share some breakfast with you before we get on the highway." Mike turned off the engine and exited the car.

Julie watched him as he passed in front of the car and began feeding the parking meter. She, too, had similar selfish desires. *Is that such a terrible thing? No, it isn't terrible; it's normal. It is normal!*

After all, who wouldn't want some time away from an aging parent plus several high-spirited teenage boys learning to navigate their ever-expanding world? Everyone values having some truly free time to do what they want when they want.

Mike beckoned her to hurry up, and she opened her car door. "Let's go, Julie. At checkout the front-desk clerk told me about this new café. He was here last weekend and said it was marvelous."

I hope that is all that he told you.

It had been challenging enough for her to rush through the lobby and hurry to the safety of their car, after dodging the hot-tub repairman walking down the hallway. She didn't want to risk anyone recognizing her as "that sex-swing lesbian lady" from last night. She was so very thankful that Mike had not suggested the establishment's continental-breakfast option; she would have felt humiliated even if no other guests were there. Julie joined Mike at the parking meter.

"Need any more nickels?"

"Nickels, Julie? Try quarters. You forget we are in the twenty-first century. Nickels are practically obsolete, at least in regard to parking meters. Besides, I've already secured two hours of uninterrupted parking security, and if we don't use all of it for dining, we may want to try reenacting parking with backseat pleasures."

"Except right now there is no backseat space, Mike," Julie reminded him. The thought of parking from their dating days brought a small blush to her cheeks. Those times had seemed so romantic. As if on cue, Mike took Julie's hand and together they strolled toward the newly launched bistro. It might have been open for only several weeks, but its outward appearance suggested it had been open for much longer. Mike pushed the oversized iron gates inward, and they walked the cobblestone pathway through the café's courtyard.

"Bonjour, madame. Bonjour, monsieur. Bienvenue à La Table Bleue!!"

Mike leaned toward Julie and whispered, "That desk clerk didn't tell me all they spoke is French!"

"No, monsieur, I speak English. I just wish for you to feel as though you are in Montreal or Paris, or another romantic city like Champaign, Illinois! Welcome to my restaurant, The Blue Table, named in honor of my *grand-mère*. She was the proud owner of the first blue table that I ever saw, and she did all of her cooking preparation there in her kitchen." He closed his eyes for a brief moment and seemed to travel back in time to that magical era. Coming back to the present, he asked, "Would you like to sit inside or on the terrace?"

"Terrace, please."

"Bien sur, monsieur. Par ici."

Again Mike grasped Julie's hand as the owner led them through a short, extremely narrow maze of dining tables to the back terrace. He seated them in a quiet corner surrounded by old-world brick walls covered in honeysuckle with only tiny patches of brick and mortar peeking through.

"Your server's name is Andre," the owner stated as he handed each of them a menu, "and he will be right with you."

To Julie the breakfast menu seemed quite extensive. There were all different types of French pastries and coffee cakes, fruit plates, crepes, and egg entrees. How would she ever decide? Immediately she remembered her wardrobe selection and realized she should forgo the higher-calorie items; after all, she knew she had splurged at Big Wolfe's. Ugh! She was so tired of having to be logical in choosing what to eat. It was so very tempting to choose pain d'oré, which was described as French toast that had been soaked in an orange batter and sprinkled with lavender honey, or gingerbread crepes that would be served with poached pears. She had never had either and they both sounded so adventurous, but somehow she would find the strength to resist. After all, there would be photos to reflect on, and she did not want to look even the slightest bit overfed! She would order the blueberry creamy oatmeal dressed with a variety of other berries. That did sound yummy to her, and it did not come with a giant serving of guilt!

"What's with the home fries?" Mike asked. "You know how I love potatoes, but I didn't know that home fries had a French origin."

"Neither did I," said Julie, "but I can tell you this background music is French." She smiled. Although Julie didn't know the title of the song, the melody playing was her absolute favorite. It was a composition that radiated an enticing blend of passion and romance.

"Well, I am definitely having some of those home fries!" Mike's enthusiasm for potatoes rivaled Julie's romantic fervor. "I'm ordering the orange-marmalade omelet and home fries. I know it doesn't sound like something I'd choose, but I am ready to try some new things, especially after last night. How about you, Julie?"

Julie hesitated slightly in answering, as a menagerie of last night's sights and sounds flashed through her mind. *Is sex all he ever thinks about?*

She was ready, but only if he equated sex with romance and thoughtfulness. After all, she had survived the awkward moments of the previous evening and now found herself to be a somewhat more liberated woman. Julie smiled. "Yes, Mike. I'm ready." Mike closed his menu and reached across the table to hold Julie's hand, bringing her fingers to meet his lips, kissing her hand tenderly.

"Bonjour, mes amis. Are you ready to order?" Julie wished Andre's arrival at their table had been a bit delayed. After all, how often did Mike do something like this? Public displays of affection were rare and whenever they happened, Julie treasured the moment.

"Oui," Mike replied, pretending to know French. "Please bring us two coffees. I'm going to have the orange-marmalade omelet with home fries, and my bride would like the blueberry creamy oatmeal."

Andre grinned ear to ear. "Very good, sir. And I apologize for interrupting your romantic interlude. You must be jeunes mariés. Que magnifique!"

Mike and Julie traded awkward glances, since neither was quite sure what their server was saying. "Well, I know that we are magnificent, or perhaps you mean that the food we chose will be magnificent, but I am not sure about the rest of whatever it was that you just said."

"My apologies, sir. I thought you spoke French. You are newly married, no?"

Julie was the first to reply. "Oh, no, we've been married almost thirty years."

"Amazing!" replied Andre. "You must have been an extremely young bride, and you sir, how is it said, must have robbed zee cradle?"

Julie could feel the smallest tinge of redness appearing on her cheeks. It was a somewhat awkward compliment, but she did hope it was more accurate than she personally believed.

"Well, I almost committed the offense," offered Mike. "Let's just agree that she is beautiful, that I am a very lucky man, and that you are done taking our order. We are on our way to a wedding celebration and don't want to be late."

"Absolutely, monsieur. Efficiency is my middle name," said Andre as he picked up the menus, pivoted, and headed straight toward the kitchen.

Efficiency was not only Andre's middle name, it was the flawless description of how their time at La Table Bleue elapsed. It seemed to Julie as if the breakfast came from a well-choreographed, starry-eyed novel that encompassed every aspect of a picture-perfect date. The French music combined with the old-world setting had established the ideal atmosphere for romance. The scent of the honeysuckle vine in full bloom, winding its way across the old brick walls, was perfume to Julie. She was captivated by the fragrance and by how the blue, linen tablecloth mirrored the color of Mike's eyes. It was the perfect setting for a perfect moment.

Julie broke the silence. "I just love this café, Mike, don't you? It's like we've been transported back to a simpler time."

"Totally agree with you. Why don't we do this more often?"

Julie answered matter-of-factly, "It's because we both work full time and have a small army to feed, Mike, but let's not talk about that. Let's talk about the fun we are going to have this weekend. Does it seem possible that William is getting married? Wasn't it just yesterday we were bringing him home from the hospital?"

"Now that was an experience—and not a pleasant one! That first night was almost a deal breaker for me. I thought he would never stop his wailing!"

"Oh, I remember. I was in tears and felt so inadequate. Thank goodness that behavior didn't become the standard routine!"

"Well, I can guarantee if it had, we wouldn't have had four more," Mike replied.

Julie wasn't sure how to respond to that remark. She loved having a big family and couldn't picture her life without any of them. As she continued to ponder Mike's comment, Andre arrived carrying an antique silver tray with matching creamer, sugar bowl, and two steaming cups of coffee.

"Enjoy," he said as he placed the tray alongside the floral arrangement. "Your breakfast will be out shortly." He then disappeared.

Mike spooned two rounded teaspoons of sugar into a cup along with a touch of cream and stirred it gently before handing it to his wife. Preparing the coffee was one of those little customs that they had always shared, and it meant a lot to Julie. It had become one of their most pleasurable moments of the day. She savored the invigorating aroma of the steaming cup.

"So fill me in on the final details Elizabeth has been sharing with you about the wedding," Mike said. "You've been pretty tight lipped since your last rant about the ceremony."

Julie cast her eyes downward and hoped he wasn't bringing up the phone conversation he'd overheard two weeks ago! She had to admit she probably overreacted to having a judge perform the wedding ceremony instead of a pastor. She thought a preacher should always be the one to unite a couple in marriage, but then again, this was not her wedding; it was William and Elizabeth's.

"There's really not much to tell," she replied as she sipped her coffee. "After the rehearsal tonight, there's a fish fry. Then the girls are going to have a little party at the spa where Elizabeth works, and I think you guys are going to a sports bar. The wedding is tomorrow at two with the reception immediately following, but you already know that."

"Yeah, I was just wondering if they'd changed their minds regarding the officiating."

Julie grimaced as it became clear he was referring to her error in judgment. "If you are asking if I apologized regarding my judge versus pastor comments, yes, I apologized."

"I knew I married a wise woman, one who is never too proud to admit making a mistake!"

Julie forced a smile in response as she took another sip of her coffee, hoping it conveyed the message to drop this particular discussion. She really didn't want to bring up who was too proud to acknowledge an oversight, such as a windshield. In her opinion the answer was sitting right in front of her.

Andre's arrival with their order could not have been more appropriately timed, obviously diverting their attention from a potential difference of opinion to yet another beautiful presentation. The delicate white-china pieces, hand-painted with cobalt-blue scrolled edges, were a perfect canvas for the chef's masterpieces. As Andre set the bowl of oatmeal in front of Julie, she was happy to see it had been perfectly prepared, neither too soupy nor too dry. The array of additional blueberries, blackberries, and strawberries was flawless, the fruit being served at the peak of maturity. Mike's orange-marmalade omelet was both beautiful and aromatic; the crème fraiche and minute wisps of candied orange peel adorning the omelet made it look almost too good to eat. The home fries balanced the delicate look of the omelet with a very robust, masculine presence. "Would you care for me to warm up your coffee?" Andre asked.

"Oh, yes," Julie replied. "Thank you."

"None for me, Andre. Please let the chef know this looks absolutely delicious."

"Merci! Enjoy."

Their breakfast was scrumptious, and Andre's service was observant but not attentive to the point of being intrusive. The meal was truly enjoyable as they chatted back and forth between bites, talking more about the celebration tomorrow and reflecting on their own wedding day.

Once they had finished their food, Andre approached their table, set down the check, and said, "I am so very happy that you enjoyed your breakfast here at La Table Bleue. It has been my pleasure to serve you! And, if I might add, may the couple whose wedding you are going to be continuously happy as the two of you are! Bonjour, mes amis!"

Continuously happy as the two of you are . . . continuously happy?

Now that struck Julie as being a very thought-provoking comment. How long had it been since she had been that? Or Mike, for that matter. Yet here was a man they barely knew who perceived a sense of cheerfulness between them. Julie smiled to herself; it was as if she and Mike were waltzing through the same rhythm of life. That had not happened in a very long while. Perhaps the fault finding, the nit-picking, the disagreeing, and fighting were now behind them. They had been on their road trip less than forty-eight hours. Could the elimination of demands created by their family members be the prescription for change they had been seeking? Could it be that simple? Maybe, but totally disregarding all their family's needs certainly wasn't feasible. After all, by midafternoon they would once again be with their family . . . with her mother, who would require assistance, a daughter who would never ask for but welcome an extra pair of hands in caring for her children, and a trio of sons, aware that an invisible pair of eyes and ears were ever watchful.

Mike finished signing the credit-card slip. "Let's hit the road, Jules. Time to get back on schedule to make Madison before four." After standing up, he walked over to Julie's chair and held it out for her in a gentlemanlike fashion. As she stood, once again Mike took her hand in his. She hadn't held hands this frequently since she had had a toddler by her side. They walked back through the dining room and the courtyard to their car, where the parking meter displayed thirty-five minutes remaining.

"Any second thoughts on parking with backseat pleasures? You would be surprised how quickly I could unload all the baggage!" Julie giggled and Mike smirked as he opened the door for her, and she slipped into the front passenger seat.

"I knew that would be a no!" Mike replied. Julie smiled as he closed her door. It appeared to Julie that they were back on the road to having fun and looking forward to an enjoyable time celebrating William and Elizabeth's wedding. That was all they chatted about while they drove through the farming country of Illinois. It was a wonderfully entertaining three-hour drive as they passed cornfield after cornfield.

"Hey, remember when we stayed at the Clock Tower Inn?" Mike asked as they passed the Rockford landmark.

Julie nodded affirmatively. "I don't remember a whole lot of the details except that the corporate Christmas party was there. I do remember having a great time, though!"

"Mmhmm," Mike replied. "We did have fun. Do you remember playing truth or dare? You were pretty risqué back in the days before kids. Want to give it another whirl?"

The previous night's antics were still fresh in Julie's mind as she questioned the sensibility of Mike's suggestion. "In the car? While you're driving?" Julie thought the idea was a bit over the top. After all, they weren't in their twenties anymore.

"Sure, why not, Julie? It will help this last hour and a half fly by quickly. It can't get out of hand, Julie. I'm driving!"

After a moment of doubtful introspection, Julie yielded to the request. "Oh, all right." *After all, how bad can this game be if it's played in a car traveling seventy miles per hour down the interstate?*

"We need some ground rules, though, Mike."

"Well, what do you request?"

"I think I have only two. One is that everything has to take place in the car, and the other is that there is no stopping the car for dares. I'm sure you will agree with both of those, right? I really do want to get to the rehearsal on time."

"Absolutely," Mike declared. To Julie he sounded almost too agreeable, as though he had an alternative plan that would really surprise her, not to mention get the better of her. "You can go first if you want," Mike offered.

"Thanks, but I'm going to need a minute or two. Hope that's okay."

"Understood. Just let me know when you're ready."

Julie knew she had to act fast. "Ready, Mike. Truth or dare?"

Without skipping a beat, Mike replied, "Dare."

Seeing that they were approaching a tollbooth, Julie blurted out, "I dare you to convince the person in the tollbooth that we don't have any money to pay and to let us just pass."

"That's the best you can offer? Piece of cake, Julie."

"Spare me the sarcasm, Mike. Good luck!" Julie replied with a giggle.

Their car slowed to a complete stop and Mike rolled down the window. The attendant looked to be about sixteen years old and was totally focused on her cell phone. "One dollar, please," she robotically stated, never lifting her eyes from her phone's screen.

When Mike didn't reply, the young girl repeated the request and held out her hand, expecting the money to be placed into her palm. Mike never answered the teenager's request but turned to Julie, silently mouthing, "Third time's the charm. Watch this!"

"Sir, you're going to have to pay the toll so you can proceed." She had finally set her cell phone on the booth's ledge and was meeting Mike's gaze.

"Mandy, that is what's on your nametag, isn't it?" Mike squinted as he leaned partway out the window and waited for her to reply.

"Yes, sir, but that really doesn't matter. It's a dollar, please."

"Mandy, I am so sorry, but the wife here and I are out of money. Do you Illinois folks happen to have a layaway plan? We can make payments." Mike was continuing to plead his case, but his words were drowned out with brutal horn-honking by the car behind him.

"Sir, are you trying to prank me? Is there a hidden camera?" Mandy asked as she fluffed her hair and scanned the immediate vicinity. It was as if a lightbulb appeared over her head as she uttered, "Am I going to be on TV?"

"No, Mandy. The wife here and I just don't have a dollar to our name. Won't you please just let us pass?"

Horn honking resumed as an aura of hostility emerged. "Just take this mini envelope, sir, and mail the stupid dollar. Have a good day," she mumbled as the barricade rose, clearing the way for Mike and Julie.

"Mandy, I just feel so guilty not being able to pay. It's just that—"

"Will you just leave? Have you not noticed how upset you are making everyone? Have you not heard of road rage? Just go!"

Mike then put the pedal to the metal and screeched his way to what he thought was a victorious dare. Raising both arms in a V symbol, he proudly stated, "I win! One to zero. Uh-huh, uh-huh!"

"You call that a win? Not only do you have an envelope to pay the one-dollar fee, you've probably got our license plate recorded as well. Now every Illinois State patrolman might be on the lookout for the weirdo who managed to block other drivers at that tollbooth. And what about road rage? What if that guy behind us has a temper that fires up quicker than a TNT fuse?"

"You worry too much, Julie. The dare was to advance without having to pay, and I accomplished that. Score one to zero, end of debate. Now on to you. Truth or dare?"

Julie didn't think she could handle a dare; she would cave too quickly. Then again, choosing truth could be a huge problem since she had never been able to get away with a lie. She surprised herself when she uttered, "Truth."

Mike smiled. "Here it is. Do you have any irrational fear that you never shared with anyone?"

Julie returned Mike's smile. She already knew her very clever answer. "Yes."

Mike waited for the explanation behind her yes, but it never came. "Okay. So what is it?"

"Wrong question to ask, Mike. I already gave you my answer. It was yes. You didn't ask me what it was, just if I had one." Julie saw a look of disappointment spread across her husband's face. "Guess the score is tied, huh? One to one!" Her husband did not respond. Julie could tell he was deep in thought, strategically considering his next move. "Okay, Mike. Truth or dare?"

"Hold on. Need a minute to consider my options. That all right with you?"

"Not a whole lot of options, honey. It's truth or dare. Pick one." Julie noticed the sign that stated South Beloit's tollbooth was two miles away. *He's stalling!*

"No stalling, pick one. Truth or dare."

"Dare," Mike reluctantly stated.

Seeing his frustrated expression, Julie decided to go easy on him. "I dare you to sing The Hokey Pokey to the tollbooth attendant."

"Oh, come on, Julie, you know I hate that song! And what if they do have our license plate and are tracking us and now I'm acting goofy? We won't make it to Madison."

"Are you starting to think like a conspiracy theorist?"

"No. I just don't want to sing that song. You know how I hate that song and those silly actions!"

As they approached the tollbooth, Julie replied, "You chose the dare. Not my fault!"

Mike rolled down the window, fixated his gaze onto the floor mat, and began singing in his most annoying voice while doing the appropriate accompanying actions:

> You put your left arm in; you pull your left arm out;
> You put your left arm in, and you shake it all about!

You do the hokey pokey and you turn yourself
around;
That's what it's all about!

Julie began laughing midway through the song, but as
Mike raised his head from the floor mat to look at the
tollbooth attendant, he understood why. She was holding
a preprinted sign that read, "I am deaf; please deposit
$1.00 in the coin collector. If you don't have change, I will
be happy to give you change from your $5, $10, or $20
bill." Then at the bottom of the sign, in very small print, it
stated that the tollway authority was an equal-opportunity
employer. Mike quickly deposited four quarters and barreled
his way through the embarrassment. Julie could hardly
stop laughing.

"That song will forever make me smile, and to think
with all your singing ability, your audience was deaf.
What a waste!"

"Knock it off, Julie, you know I can't carry a tune!"

"That's what makes it so perfect—she couldn't hear
you!" They continued to banter back and forth as they drove
past Beloit and on past Janesville. It appeared to Julie that
Mike was delaying the truth-or-dare challenge in the
hopes of running out of time, retaining the winning score.

By the time they were passing Edgerton, Julie figured
if there was going to be an opportunity to tie, she would
have to initiate it. "Mike, are you never going to ask me
truth or dare?"

"Sure. Go ahead. Pick one."

"Truth." Julie felt confident. After having no challenge
with the last question, certainly she would be able to handle
this one.

"What was the last lie you told?"

That challenge caught Julie off guard. She was caught in a dilemma. She knew the lie she had told and when it happened, but she certainly didn't want to share it. However, if she wasn't honest in her answer, Mike would know by the look on her face that she was lying.

"No stalling!" Mike said with a grin. "Out with it!"

"Well, you remember when we were at Notel Motel the other night and you whispered a question in my ear?"

"Yes."

"Well, my answer was not a total truth. It was okay, but it wasn't a full ten for me."

"You lied about that?" The shocked tone of Mike's voice surprised Julie.

"Well, not a total lie, but sort of a partial lie."

"I don't know how you tell a partial lie, Julie. That certainly puts a whole new light on what I thought had been a couple of great evenings."

"Don't go off the deep end, Mike. So what's the big deal if it's a ten for you but not for me? So what? It happens to women all the time."

"All the time? Really? You're saying it happens to you all the time?"

"Not me. I'm speaking about women in general."

"I don't care about women in general. I care about you and pleasing you, and now it's obvious to me that I am failing in that department."

"Don't get so defensive. I'm not upset."

"Well, I am!"

"C'mon," said Julie. "Truth or dare is supposed to be fun!"

"Not anymore. Not now," Mike fumed. The conversation stopped dead in its tracks.

Chapter 12

Silence permeated their car as they drove onward toward Madison. Road signs forced the Morins to detour via US 151, which would postpone their hotel arrival. Julie reached for her phone to check the time and breathed a voiceless sigh of relief; even if Mike chose to shower before the rehearsal dinner, they still wouldn't be late. To Julie the silence seemed to be expanding like water when it freezes. She also knew that she'd need to be the one to initiate any resolution regarding her partial lie. She just couldn't bring herself to begin the discussion. The absence of chatter felt awkward. After all, they had been having such a great time laughing and joking. Why did it always have to be a roller coaster?

Exiting the interstate and anticipating the view of the capitol building reigning over East Washington Avenue, Julie wondered if Three Dolls' Diner was still in business. They had served the best ice cream, and the old-fashioned carousel in that restaurant was loved by young and old patrons alike. The painted ponies, mirrors, and bright lights rotating to the calliope music were probably more of a draw than the addictive ice cream served in homemade waffle cones. It had been a great spot to stop after a movie date. Julie had loved to sit on the pink pony adjacent to the lion that Mike always chose. He had humored her by saying that if he had to sit through a simple ride that just went round and round without really going anywhere, he at least was going to ride a wild animal!

One particular night's discussion had developed into a debate regarding Mike's love of roller coasters versus Julie's preference for merry-go-rounds. Julie could still picture Mike saying, "On a roller coaster, I can be laughing but feel sick at the same time. I can be anxious and upset but still be really happy. To me it's a lot more fun! Merry-go-rounds are just plain boring!" Julie had countered his opinion that evening but did not win the exchange. As she reflected on the past few weeks of pre-trip stress and conflict, Julie was positive that they had both viewed their married life as more of a gloomy-go-round with an abundant amount of "anti-merry-isms."

Mike bore to the right onto East Johnson Street, heading toward State Street and their old stomping grounds from college. Julie rolled down her window and let the light breeze refresh her. As she surveyed the city's landscape, block after block, it seemed as though time had stood still; the street looked the same. Front porches were cluttered with student bikes waiting for their riders, team flags were hung from second-story windows, and the faint aroma of charcoal smoldering for a cookout floated through the air. School calendars might have changed since she was a student, having classes begin in August instead of September, but college life and the atmosphere surrounding it remained the same.

As they approached the intersection with State Street, Julie was disappointed that turning onto that route was no longer an option. The thoroughfare was now a mall area with quite a few cyclists weaving their way amongst food-truck concessions. Groups of soon-to-be college freshmen, who were obviously trying to disassociate themselves from the parents that were following them, occupied almost every other available concrete space. She had hoped to catch a glimpse of Bascom Hall, but there was just too much other activity that caught her attention.

As Mike continued driving, Julie realized that one of their favorite spots no longer existed. The Great Pooh-Bah Lounge, which had been a popular dance club when they were students, was now a four-story parking ramp.

How disappointing to have "moving and grooving" replaced with concrete!

As they made their way toward the West Beltline, Julie noticed there were a lot more changes but hesitated to share any of her observances. Confident that Mike would not appreciate her attempt at small talk, she kept her comments to herself. The silence might be deafening, but a verbal cold shoulder would be worse!

The standoff continued much longer than Julie anticipated. She was sure there would be some attempt at conversation by the time they arrived at the hotel and were getting checked in, or perhaps when they got to their room. Certainly they would be communicating by the time they had unpacked, freshened up, and gotten back into their vehicle to go to the rehearsal and dinner, but the silence remained. She hadn't even called to check on the family for fear they would be able to tell by her voice that something wasn't right. As they pulled into the parking lot of the resort where the wedding would be held, their lack of interaction was becoming more than awkward. She knew if she didn't try to resolve the conflict, what should be a joyous and exciting evening would be ruined for Mike and her at the very least.

Mike brought the car to a stop, and as he pulled the key from the ignition, Julie blurted out, "Hey, wait a minute!

Don't you think we need to clear the air? Shouldn't we talk about the last hour and a half of silence?"

"So talk. I have nothing to contribute, just the same as not contributing to your pleasure the other night. Obviously you have something to say, so speak!"

"I'm sorry if I upset you, Mike! I didn't mean any harm. I was just answering that silly truth request. Can't we just call a truce? I want this to be a wonderful evening for our family." Julie tried to read Mike's mind, but his face was stonewalled. As he reached for the door handle, Julie knew she had to make one last effort and softly said, "Mike, you're a wonderful lover. I have no complaints. Please be reasonable. There are people waiting for us."

"Oh, that's right. It is back to being about everybody else but us." Mike exited the car so quickly that Julie had to hurry to catch up to him. "Don't worry, Julie. You can go pay attention to our family and take care of everyone else. I'm used to it." Then without skipping a beat, he added, "I'll see you inside," as he took the sidewalk up to the building.

Julie looked at the venue before her. At first glance, it suggested everything its Native American name intended. William and Elizabeth had explained to Mike and Julie that the venue's name, Hopa Akigle Place, was pronounced *Gho-pah Ah-kee-glay* in the Lakota Sioux language and it meant "beautiful times." It was built with round, wide, dark-brown logs that met grand blocks of cemented flagstone at each corner. The spacious front porch that greeted patrons was dotted with hanging flowers and dreamcatchers along with Native American wall art. There were benches, rocking chairs, and two porch swings at opposite ends, and they tempted visitors with relaxation right from the start. One could see from the graveled parking lot the vast, rich-blue lake behind the building. The view was simply gorgeous. Julie turned to take the pathway leading to the grassy area where the ceremony would be held and was almost immediately surrounded by Elizabeth, Erin, Grace, and the additional bridesmaids. Excitement was running high as Julie listened to their conversation about the rehearsal and the plans for the evening. A deep voice interrupted. "Okay, ladies. Let's move on down the path and walk through tomorrow's ceremony. How about it, Elizabeth? Ready to get married?"

"I am!" she exclaimed as she led the way.

"Who's the mystery man, Erin?" asked Julie as she fell in step with her daughter.

"He's the judge who's going to officiate. Elizabeth introduced us earlier. Seems to be a really nice man, Mom. Maybe the ceremony won't be as bad as you think."

Julie managed a weak smile. In her mind it wasn't that the ceremony would be "bad"; Julie just preferred a "religious" person joining the couple in the sacrament of marriage. *Just another one of my old-fashioned ways.*

As they continued toward the lakeside area set with neatly spaced white chairs, Julie spotted Stan and Micheline, Elizabeth's parents, and waved to them. She remembered meeting Micheline at the bridal shower and had enjoyed chatting with her there. The girls continued to escort Julie down the path where Brett, Jake, and John were gathered around William. The groom's six-foot-four frame towered over everyone there and exuded confidence as he joked with his brothers.

Where has the time gone? Wasn't it just yesterday I held him in my arms? He's getting married. My baby is getting married!

Julie felt an upwelling of tears ready to flow and was determined to find a distraction that would wipe out any sentimental emotion. Almost immediately she saw the so-bering diversion: Mike. He and their niece were standing slightly behind the brotherhood, providing steadying hands to the cane-wielding grandmothers and Mike's beloved Aunt Dee. Julie felt no need for tears anymore.

"Gather round, folks," said the judge. "This rehearsal is very important, and everyone needs to be attentive and follow directions." Julie could tell by the tone of his voice he meant business, but in a nice way. "While I am not known to be a judgezilla, I do know how to herd sheep if needed, and believe me, my shepherd's hook can be almost as painful as a tap of my gavel." Julie found his comment somewhat humorous since he was looking in the direction of her offspring.

I guess he knows how mischievous teenage boys can be!

The judge continued. "We are gathered here to prepare for a great celebration, the marriage of William and Elizabeth. I've attended numerous weddings as a guest where the couple has taken months and months to plan for one day of their lives, thinking only about formal wear, flowers, and cake. It's been very refreshing getting to know William and Elizabeth. I have observed them invest months and months to plan for not only this special day, but more importantly their future together as husband and wife. It's a privilege for me to be officiating at their wedding ceremony tomorrow." Julie could sense her apprehensions regarding the choice of officiant begin to fade. "William and Elizabeth have devoted valuable time in planning tomorrow's ceremony, so this evening we are going to simply walk through the events of tomorrow to ensure that everyone knows who goes where and when. Then we'll all go inside and share a wonderful meal with a couple surprises. So let's get started."

With the precision of a military policeman, directions were clearly given to the ushers, and Julie watched as the cane-wielding grandmothers were slowly escorted down the aisle. The judge said, "Next are the groom's parents." Julie placed her arm through her husband's and offered him a conciliatory smile; Mike's facial demeanor remained impersonal as they began walking down the aisle. Julie took the aisle seat as her mind raced amid a flurry of emotions. She felt disappointment, frustration, regret, even a small amount of confusion regarding why the afternoon had turned out this way. This was a real setback. Julie felt a tap on her shoulder and noticed people were standing as Elizabeth walked down the aisle with her dad. Springing to her feet, Julie realized she'd missed her sons taking their places in front as well as the girls walking down the aisle. She'd even missed Grace practicing her flower-girl duties! *Well, I am not going to let the rest of the evening be dampened because of Mike's attitude. I will not!*

Julie's focus returned to the present and listened as the judge continued with hushed instructions to the bride and groom regarding "repeat after me" and saying the "I dos." She kept waiting for her favorite part of any wedding—the pastor's sermon about marriage, imparting valuable knowledge to the couple—but nothing was said. *Is this what happens when a judge marries a couple? No pastor means no sermon? Not sure I like this!*

When the judge finished instructing the bride and groom, his voice increased in volume as he said, "After I introduce Mr. and Mrs. William Morin to everyone, they will start down the aisle. Once they are totally past the chairs, the bridal party will follow. Next will be the bride's parents and then the groom's. Ushers, you will need to be ready to assist the grandmothers. Any questions?"

"Do I have to pick up the flowers I dropped?" Grace was not bashful when it came to asking questions. "It's not good to litter."

"No, my dear, you don't have to pick up those pretty flowers, but thank you for asking," the judge replied. "You did a wonderful job." Sensing there would be no other questions, the judge continued. "If there are no other questions, let's go have dinner."

As the group made their way toward the restaurant that overlooked the site of the ceremony, Julie continued to admire the resort. The multicolored pansies that lined the path leading to the main entrance were vibrant in the pleasant, seventy-degree weather; she made a mental note to try this color combination when she purchased hers for planting in November. Feeling a hand on her shoulder, she turned to see William walking stride for stride next to her.

"So what do you think of the judge?" William asked.

"I haven't really had a chance to speak with him, but he seems to be a very nice man."

"I'll make sure both you and Dad get a chance to chat with him tonight, Mom. Where is Dad anyway?" Julie had thought Mike was right beside her. As she looked around, he was nowhere to be seen.

"I think he's already inside, honey. I'll pass it along about meeting the judge."

"Thanks, Mom. It's going to be a great wedding. We'll have fun tonight. See you in a bit." He rushed ahead to catch up to Elizabeth, who was chatting with her dad. A Friday-night fish fry was a tradition in their home state, one both she and Mike missed. Her mouth watered at the thought of family-style platters of fish, along with potato salad, baked beans, coleslaw, and bread baskets. She scanned the interior for Mike, but he was still not in sight, so she followed the sign directing the Leary-Morin group to the banquet room for the rehearsal dinner. As she entered the banquet hall, she was surprised to see Mike sitting at a high-top table, talking with his sister and brother-in-law.

"I didn't know you were going to be here!" Julie whispered with a gush of emotion as she gave her sister-in-law a hug. "It is so good to see you! How did you manage to get away? I don't see all your children in tow!"

Rachel laughed, as only a mother of six children would. "Once in a while Mitch and I do still have a life, unless of course we are chauffeuring my mother and Aunt Dee, the sprightly cane-sporting sisters over there." Rachel leaned toward Julie and spoke in a hushed tone so their husbands wouldn't hear. "You know firsthand how it is, Julie. We are in the servant stage of life. Our current life's assignment is to serve the young, the old, and the men we married." Rachel laughed. "That sounds a bit negative considering this weekend's celebration. Even if Mitch and I weren't needed as unpaid chauffeurs, I couldn't pass up a chance to see you. I sure do miss you!"

"I miss you, too, even though it's been only a few weeks since the bridal shower."

"Did someone say bridal shower?" It was Elizabeth's mom, Micheline. "That was a lovely afternoon. We all had such a fun time, didn't we?"

"Sure did. Those surprises you planned for the party were hilarious!"

"Well, there's going to be more surprises tonight, or so I was told," disclosed Micheline. "However, I myself have one more surprise to share with you. Why don't you two follow me and see something unexpected?"

"That sounds very interesting," replied Rachel. "Excuse us, guys, we'll be back soon." Rachel slid down off the high-top stool. "I bet they won't even miss us," Rachel whispered as they followed Elizabeth's mom toward the back of the restaurant.

Julie warned, "The sign on the door says Employees Only. I don't think we're supposed to be back here."

Rachel snickered. "Don't listen to my goody-two-shoes sister-in-law, Micheline. She might be afraid to bend rules, but I'm not. What do you have up your sleeves now?"

"It's not up my sleeve, Rachel—it's what was in the dessert sleeve." Micheline boldly entered the kitchen and made a quick right turn into another hallway.

"We shouldn't be back here," said Julie.

"Stop your fussing," replied Rachel. "Elizabeth's mom is not going to get us into trouble."

They stood in front of a huge, metallic door. "Remember at the shower how each of us included in our gifts something that symbolized a great memory we had of Elizabeth?"

"Sure," responded Julie. "Rachel gave her family recipes because Elizabeth loved to go up to their home and bake with her kids. I gave her a collection of Christmas ornaments because she has spent every Christmas with us since she and William began dating. You gave her the book about the ugly duckling becoming a swan because that was her favorite story when she was little and she was so concerned about growing up. But Micheline, what does that have to do with a surprise for tonight?"

"Did either of you know that swans mate for life?" Both shook their heads no. "Well, I always added at the end of the ugly duckling story that swans mate for life, and when she met her prince charming, the two of them would be together forever like swans."

"How very sweet," replied Rachel.

"You're not about to tell us that there are live swans in this refrigerator, are you?" asked Julie. Rachel rolled her eyes as it was obvious to her that Julie was still convinced that they were all going to get into trouble.

"No, Julie, there's dessert inside. Let me show you." Micheline flipped the light switch, opened the door, and walked to the far end of the refrigerator. There on a multi-tiered rolling cart were trays of beautiful meringue swans.

"Wow! That is gorgeous!" the sisters-in-law spoke in unison.

"But it's cold in here," Julie said. "Let's finish the story outside the fridge."

Julie and Micheline turned and began walking toward the door, but Rachel couldn't resist swiping her pinkie finger in the chocolate cream that rested on the swan's back. "Chocolate mousse. My favorite!" she whispered and picked up the plate to take with her.

"What did you do?" asked Julie in a scolding manner. "Now what if they're short one dessert?"

Before Rachel could reply, Micheline said, "They won't be short. I made extras."

"You made these? They're amazing!"

"I saw it on the Internet. A chef makes these for her restaurant. She fills them with French-vanilla ice cream and has them swimming in a strawberry sauce with crème-anglaise hearts. It looked so elegant that I had to try it."

"There aren't any hearts or ice cream. What made you change it?"

"It just didn't seem practical to expect the staff to scoop so much ice cream at the last minute to finish the desserts. Then I just figured chocolate mousse and Chantilly whipped cream would be delicious."

"You are so right, Micheline. Absolutely delicious!" added Julie as she took a second bite of the swan's wing with a generous portion of chocolate mousse on it. "I sure am glad you confiscated this swan, Rachel."

"My pleasure," she replied.

The group was startled when a young man came around the corner. "What are you ladies doing here?" The women fell silent. At that quiet moment, the pop of Julie's mousse-coated finger exiting her mouth could be heard. "You ladies stay right here. I am going to get the manager." The kitchen staff member hurried away, and only seconds after he left, the ladies made their daring escape amid muffled giggles tossed between warnings from Julie. The group of women made their way back to the rehearsal dinner and slipped back into the event unnoticed. The meal was about to be served and people were starting to take their seats.

"See? What did I tell you?" Rachel quipped. "We weren't missed at all."

"You know, we better have a plan if the kitchen manager comes walking in here," cautioned Julie.

"I have a three-word plan already," explained Rachel.

"What three words would that be?" asked Micheline.

Rachel replied with a devilish grin, "Deny. Deny. Deny."

Chapter 13

The fish fry was filled with small speeches, lots of love, shared laughter, and very touching moments for the group gathered there. After handshakes, hugs, and kisses were exchanged between family and friends, everyone exited the restaurant.

Julie left with Elizabeth, her mom, Micheline, and her sister, Caroline, to join Elizabeth's coworkers and friends for a fun bachelorette party. They had the bride and were the last group to leave. Julie wished her niece, Kelly, along with Erin could join them, but they had to head back to the hotel with GG and the kids. Kelly had been kind enough to take on this duty so that Julie could attend the evening's celebration with her daughter-in-law-to-be. This way GG could also rest for the big day ahead. The bachelorette party would be too much for her, especially after attending the rehearsal and the dinner. Of course, Erin's children were so young and obviously needed her.

All the women seemed so excited and were looking forward to a great time together in celebrating Elizabeth's last night as a single lady. It would be the "fling before the ring," as they had called it at the rehearsal dinner! Caroline had volunteered to take everyone in her car to Elizabeth's workplace, Inn-SPA-ration. Its owners, the bride's bosses, offered the use of the spa and their services for all the gathered hens to enjoy. It was not far from where they were, and so it only took a short time before they were getting out of Caroline's car and walking over to the entrance of the establishment. Julie was looking forward to seeing the people in Elizabeth's life once again and getting to know them more. It had been a quick two months since they had gathered for Elizabeth's wonderful bridal shower given by Micheline and the bridal attendants.

A large, elaborate Victorian house presented itself to the group of ladies. Its carefully painted façade and detailed trim romantically enhanced the building, as the wide but short staircase led visitors to an oversized front porch and Inn-SPA-ration's main entrance. Near the double-door entryway was a large bay window separated into three sections with the middle pane being larger than the two abutting side ones. All three were comprised of frosted glass so that one could only imagine the services offered within the spa. The tops and bottoms of the bay windowpanes were adorned by short, simple, stained-glass squares that complemented the Victorian style of the building.

The Inn-SPA-ration name was showcased with oversized ornate script in the center window, with an etched velvet ribbon that twirled itself behind and around the name. Julie could already feel the seductively soothing relaxation that the spa's front entrance implied. She commented on the beautiful rosebushes the ladies had just passed on the group's way up the steps. Micheline and Caroline quickly agreed with her while Elizabeth shared that she didn't get to enjoy them too often. She normally parked out back and used the employee's rear entrance.

Elizabeth opened one of the front double doors, and the group entered the world of Inn-SPA-ration. They were greeted by Elizabeth's friend and William's cousin, Bonnie, the two owners, Isabella Bella and Scarlett Allbad, the bookkeeper and receptionist, Penny, and Elizabeth's fun but wild coworker, Sophie, who certainly knew how to live loud and large, judging by some of the stories Elizabeth had shared with Julie's family.

The ladies complimented Isabella and Scarlett on their beautiful Victorian building and its bordello chic–styled décor. Isabella was a blonde and buxom woman who spoke with a heavy Southern drawl. "Why, I thank you ever so much for your kind words, ladies."

To this Julie replied, "Ah. I can tell you're a true Southern belle by the way you speak."

"Yes, I am! I'm as Southern as a fine bowl of grits and a couple of fresh biscuits! I will tell you, though, that my mother named me Isabella instead of a good Southern girl's name because she just couldn't stop eating Italian food! My married name is Bella, and that's probably a good thing because my maiden name was Skunkmier! Can you just imagine a girl named Isabella Skunkmier growing up in the South back then? So becoming Isabella Bella was probably a blessing for me!"

Julie smiled as she enjoyed the co-owner's Southern charm. "So then how did you and Scarlett come to know each other and become partners here in Madison?"

Scarlett, with her glossy dark hair, pale-blue eyes, and perfectly bowed lips, replied first. "Well, it's a little bit of a story, and before someone asks the same question I always get, I am indeed named after the main character in *Gone with the Wind*, although my mama had hoped that I would be more like Melanie. Anyway, my husband is a police officer who worked in this city. He said he was going to arrest me for stopping traffic with my good looks.

He got me hook, line, and sinker with that line! So I eventually married that smooth talker, and I figured it was a good way to get out of all the tickets I had accumulated! I opened a small shop, and when Isabella moved to town, she wanted to rent space from me."

"That's true," agreed Isabella. "Now I actually met my husband at his bakery down in Macon. He made great cannoli, and his last name went together so well with my first name! It was a great replacement for Skunkmier, for sure, and I just loved my little round baker to bits! Then our youngest son grew up and became a plastic surgeon. He moved to Madison and we followed him. Now I can get serviced in very good hands at a very reduced price!"

"After several years of working together while Isabella rented from me," Scarlett picked up the story, "we became partners and decided to open a decadent salon as a team! So here we are! We're each other's closest friends and confidantes. Besides, I know way too many secrets about Mr. Bella!"

After a shared laugh, Isabella added, "She's right! Now c'mon in! Scarlett and I will give you a tour so all y'all will know where everything is this evening."

The front parlor of the spa easily impressed the visitors with its open space, tasseled table lamps, and soft, velvet-cushioned wingback chairs with cabriole legs. The area rugs that covered the floor held intricate floral and border designs bathed in deep reds and a plush gold. The centerpiece of this area was the sweeping grand staircase and the main-hall chandelier that crowned its glory. The staircase itself was a showpiece of fine craftsmanship with its round, shapely spindles collectively holding a detailed balustrade and a scroll motif at its base.

Purses, light jackets, and sweaters were hung on the hooks of a large hall tree before everyone headed out to enjoy the tour. Room after room showed the thoughtful care that went into the function, purpose, and décor of each one. Julie especially liked the floral sconces and soft lighting. They adorned the striped red-and-gold wallpaper hanging in the upstairs hallway, matching the patterned floor runners there. It lent itself to a soothing, sensual feeling of being luxuriously pampered while visiting another time and place. The group returned to the bottom floor and was led to a large room off to the side of the entry area. It showcased a tin-stamped ceiling, a small ornate chandelier, and lush furniture saturated in deep, rich colors. Portable massage tables had been set up there, along with two carts that held towels, various jars, and bottles of massage oils and creams, along with hand rollers and other massage tools. The room was also decorated for the evening's bachelorette party.

"C'mon, girls, let's get this party started! Woo! Who wants to join me in a cocktail at our fling before the ring?" Sophie asked, holding up a glass.

"Looks like you had a head start," commented Elizabeth's sister, Caroline.

"Well, I have the duty of keeping us on track with all of our activities tonight. I want Elizabeth to have the best bachelorette party ever, and so-o-o I am Sophie. I come from Eastern Europe, but I just love America! Tonight we'll have Sophie's choices that are all for Elizabeth's naughty fun! Now we begin with cocktails for everyone! Who's going to have a Pink Panty Pulldown with Elizabeth and me?"

Julie and Micheline almost simultaneously asked, "A pink what?"

Bonnie joined them. "Did you say Pink Panty Pulldown?"

Sophie laughed and replied, "Yes, a *Pink Panty Pulldown*! I want you all to try it. It's yummilicious and you will love it! I made plenty for tonight." The women stepped forward as Sophie poured the pink cocktail for each person.

"Mmm. You're right! It *is* yummilicious!" Elizabeth exclaimed after tasting the beverage. Others joined in agreement.

"This is goo-o-o-d! I could have quite of few of these!" Caroline said to no one in particular. "What's in it, Sophie?"

"It's pink lemonade, clear soda, and vodka. That's a little bit of girl, a little bit of fun, and a little bit of naughty! To Elizabeth, everybody!"

The group toasted the bride-to-be and then Sophie added, "Okay now. You must drink up to catch up to Sophie! Woo!" She walked around the room with a large bellied pitcher, topping off the beverages of those who offered their glasses.

"How many, um, Pulldowns have you had already?" asked Julie.

"You have to taste test often to perfect a drink for an occasion such as this one, and on a perfection scale of one to ten, this batch is a twelve! You are welcome, ladies! Woo!" There were scattered giggles and echoed woos.

"I'm all for taste testing. This is good!" Bonnie interjected.

"Okay," Sophie continued. "We all have a good start in our hands, so now let's all have a seat and share our best memories of single Elizabeth before she becomes married Elizabeth!"

The future Mrs. Morin was guided to sit on a vintage, maroon, hooded chair that was specifically decorated for her. Everyone else found their places on elegant chaise lounges, cushioned loveseats, and other pieces of heavily fabricated furniture that were scattered intimately throughout the large room. Julie took in her surroundings and enjoyed it immensely. The lush room was dreamy and nostalgic with hints of seductive undertones that insisted its visitors surrender themselves to indulgent relaxation and chatter.

Julie listened as Micheline started off with her beautiful memories of Elizabeth's birth, her first exciting steps, and the day Elizabeth first spoke of William. She knew this was the man who was going to capture and keep her daughter's heart. Caroline followed with her childhood memories of two sisters staying up late talking and giggling, squabbling at other times about who started what and why, but especially about how they both knew that they would always have each other's back. They were sisters connected through birth and friends connected through the heart. The group uttered a collective "aw" and Sophie added, "That was so beautiful, Caroline, and we must all have another Pink Panty Pulldown to toast it." Sophie refreshed everyone's cocktails.

"Okay, Isabella and Scarlett!" Sophie announced after sitting back down. "It's your turn to speak about our wonderful Elizabeth. Woo!"

Isabella and Scarlett rose from their chaise lounges and spoke about meeting Elizabeth for the first time. It was an interview set up through a mutual acquaintance. They were wondering if it was the right time to build their staff to meet their business goals. Isabella shared that it was one of their best decisions and that Elizabeth meant the world to them. Scarlett added that Elizabeth brought such happiness to the spa through her gifted talents and her personality. They both shared their mutual hope that married Elizabeth would continue working at Inn-SPA-ration as she was such a blessing to them. The two owners led the group in another toast to Elizabeth.

Julie was impressed with all the wonderful compliments being paid to the woman who would marry her firstborn, her William. She believed he had chosen well, and all these comments confirmed it. Julie listened as Sophie took her turn. Sophie's birth name was Zophia, and her family had come from Poland for the great dream of America. She had changed her name to Sophie in order to blend in better in her new homeland. They moved to this city because they knew friends who lived in the area, and she was hired at the spa after formal massage-therapy and aesthetics training. Sophie shared how Isabella and Scarlett had informed her one day about their hiring of Elizabeth and wondered if they would get along. Not everyone understood how Sophie liked to live large and grab the bull by the horns, so to speak. She went on to say that, though Elizabeth and she were almost opposites, it somehow worked so well that one could not imagine her day at the spa without the other. They worked great together like salt and pepper. Elizabeth was the sweet to her spicy.

Sophie explained that the moment she knew the two women would click was when she got a tattoo one weekend and came into work the following Monday. Elizabeth was already at her backroom desk and she greeted Sophie as she entered through the door. Sophie was so excited about her tattoo that she just had to put her things down right away and show off the new artwork. She joyfully announced it and had grinned when Elizabeth looked at both arms and lower legs in a confused search for the tattoo. Elizabeth had asked where it was, and Sophie shared that it was between her breasts. She had showed it to Elizabeth, and even though Sophie could tell that Elizabeth would never do something like that herself, she was genuinely happy for her coworker.

"That's when I knew we were going to be like sisters for life!" Sophie shared.

"You put a tattoo between your breasts?" Julie asked.

The ladies laughed in between sips of their drinks as Sophie confirmed this.

"That's interesting," commented Julie. "Now why did you choose that particular spot?"

"Conversation piece during a date," Sophie replied with a playful pout after a moment or two. More laughter filled the room, followed by a random "Living large, Sophie!"

"Conversation piece?" Julie tried to understand. "What is the tattoo?"

Sophie explained, "Two mountain hikers. Do you want to see them?"

"They're actually really cute," Elizabeth added.

"No, thanks," Julie replied, "but why two mountain hikers?"

"I didn't get it at first myself," offered Micheline.

Elizabeth explained, "Mountain hikers like to climb mountains, and they are in between her breasts."

She waited while Julie filtered this information, and this time the mother of the groom joined in the lighthearted laughter that once again filled the room. Sophie added, "See? Fun! Life is easier when you grab the fun! I am from Poland and my country lost many families in the past, and it knew great sadness at one time. Then we had to rebuild our country and our families. Now we help each other with great love simply because we are happy even to have the blessing of a family. We reach for fun because it is important to enjoy life while it is here. Okay, so live and enjoy already! I have pink refills for everyone! Woo!"

When everyone settled back down, Penny stood up from an overstuffed chair. She spoke of her belief that some of the best memories someone can have are the little everyday moments they share with others. She then shared her favorite memories of Elizabeth's thoughtfulness, speaking of how she would bring in little surprises, always remembering someone's likes and dislikes, or how she would say the perfect thing to brighten the day.

Penny raised her glass and said, "Let's toast to the young lady who lifts our spirits every day. Elizabeth, we're all so happy for both you and William, and we just know you're going to have a great life together. Being the bookkeeper here, I can tell you that I've checked the numbers, and they all add up in your favor!"

Glasses were clinked and the ladies complimented Penny on her words. Bonnie stood next and shared how she met Elizabeth through her friend Lisa, who was the bride-to-be's roommate. The three of them had gone to an event and under a beer tent it came to her that Elizabeth would probably be impressed with her workaholic cousin William. Bonnie initiated the exchange of phone numbers between the potential couple and then, after their initial meeting at a pontoon party and several magical months of dating, Cupid hit its target and became responsible for this bachelorette party. Elizabeth thanked Bonnie for playing Cupid and having such a good aim! The two gave each other a quick hug and Bonnie returned to her seat. Heads then turned toward Julie as the group waited for her to speak.

Julie smiled as she looked around the room and began talking about mothers and their hopes for their children's happiness. She explained that parents put so much of themselves into their children, always hoping that they got it right and that the little ones they raised would grow to have the best and happiest lives possible. She then spoke of her wonderful feeling of satisfaction when learning that William and Elizabeth were engaged. Her firstborn was going to have an amazing partner, and Julie was thrilled that they would experience the fullness of a happy life together. Her maternal soul had held its breath and could now release it and enjoy the growth of her family with the addition of a sweet daughter-in-law. The group laughed when she added,

"Two married kids down and three to go!" The ladies all rose to hug each other after one last toast to Elizabeth.

"Let's get this party shaking!" Sophie shouted as she changed the background music to some pulsing party beats. She danced in celebration and infectiously inspired others to join her. Julie realized that the last time she had danced was at Erin's wedding reception. It felt good to release herself to something festive—something that was long overdue.

"Okay, everybody! Sophie's choice for Elizabeth's fun now is to shake the junk from our trunks!" Julie was surprised as Sophie approached her and tied a belt around her waist while Penny did the same to Micheline. The belt looped through a tissue box that held ping-pong balls and rested at the top of her behind. "Now we will cheer for the mamas of the bride and groom while they shake the junk from their trunks! No using hands, mamas!"

The group shouted and laughed as the bridal mothers first took a drink from their cocktails and then tried their hardest to dance the ping-pong balls out of their boxes. The two ladies twisted, jittered, and cavorted until the last of the junk was emptied from their improvised trunks! The onlookers cheered for them when they achieved their goal, though they took well over four minutes to complete the task. The others all took their turns and were able to reach their objectives in one and a half minutes or less. Penny passed on trying this activity due to a fresh injury from horseback riding, and everyone agreed that she shouldn't put her leg at further risk. Sophie and Caroline tied for the best time at fifty-three seconds, and Bonnie came in a very close third place with fifty-five seconds.

"Now that we have all shaken the trunk from our junks, Isabella and Scarlett are going to give us all very extremely nice massages," slurred Sophie. "That's gonna help your trunks feel better. Shake it but don't break it, baby! Woo! C'mon, ladies, help up and drink yourselves to refills. I'm going to put out some very extremely delicious appetizers for us to snack on while we all very indulge ourselves on our indulgences here. Woo!"

Scarlett helped Sophie to sit down on one of the chaise lounges while everyone else helped to set the appetizers out on a large table. The ladies worked quickly to prevent Sophie from doing any of it—if they left her in charge, the floor would probably see more of the food than them. Isabella and Scarlett encouraged the group to help themselves and to just ask if they needed something.

"We all need Pinky Panty Pullydowns, please," Sophie exclaimed to the room.

After making plates for themselves, Micheline and Julie put together a plate of snacks for Sophie as well and hoped that it would help to absorb some of the alcohol in her bloodstream. Sophie thanked them both after tasting a few pieces and added, "These are really very extremely good, and they look just like some of the food I got for this party. Great minds think alike!"

The two moms smiled at each other and agreed with the semi-sauced party hostess while getting her to eat a little bit more in between bites of the enjoyable appetizers on their own plates.

Isabella and Scarlett took Elizabeth over to a cushioned table and started the bride off with a warm, deep-soothing facial mask. Isabella prepared and applied the mask while Elizabeth enjoyed an oiled hand massage from Scarlett. The two left Elizabeth on the table to bask in the warmth of her pampered coverings. They then walked over and offered the two portable massage chairs to the mothers of the bride and groom.

Julie couldn't wait to enjoy the refreshed feeling of a skilled massage that would melt away any built-up tensions. She was sure that Isabella would find them hiding within the fibers of her muscles and that her professional hands would send them on their way. Massages, facials, herbal blends, and infused elixirs were always such a rare and precious treat for a middle-aged wife, mother of five, and primary caretaker of an elderly parent. Julie knew that even just five minutes of a small neck massage involving some deep, rejuvenating serum would be enough to achieve nirvana.

Isabella gave Julie a smock to wear, and after mixing some herbs with a sweetly aromatic lotion, she lathered the mixture onto her own hands. The co-owner began to slowly but deliberately rub her guest's lower neck as if she knew exactly what Julie had just been thinking! A warm, damp cloth was then placed over her neck, and Julie basked in its deep, tranquilizing sensation. Isabella left her there temporarily while she offered a small deep-tissue massage to Penny for her recovering leg. She then went on to give Bonnie a general back massage.

Scarlett worked her way between Micheline and Caroline while everyone intermittently added to the conversation in the room. Sophie dotted the exchanges with casual comments, causing laughter to erupt here and there.

Once Isabella left Penny and Bonnie to enjoy the effects of her muscle manipulations, she returned to Julie and gave her a very satisfying back massage as well, relieving any tensions she had harbored there. "Can I bring you home with me?" Julie asked the skilled masseuse.

Isabella laughed. "I get asked that all the time! Too bad you don't live nearby. Then I could take care of you on a regular basis."

"I would need it too," Julie replied. "It doesn't matter where we go, our issues always seem to follow us! It would be nice, though, to have this female companionship all the time. You ladies are so nice and funny. I am really enjoying our evening together."

Everyone agreed and shared sweet comments about each other, especially complimenting Isabella and Scarlett for the use of their spa. Elizabeth also thanked everyone for the best last single evening a girl could enjoy. They refilled their glasses, clinked them, and toasted themselves as well as the power of women gathered in unison anywhere. Sophie added a "woo" to the final statement, and it was amusingly echoed by the others throughout the room.

Julie rose from the massage chair that held her, and Sophie was then invited to plop herself down on it. Caroline replaced her mom on the chair where she had received her massage and Micheline joined Julie where she stood at the snack table. As conversations continued, Julie picked up one chip after another and slightly dunked each one into a bowl of dip that was sitting with others on a cart next to the table. "This dip is so amazingly delicious! Any chance whoever made it could share the recipe?"

Isabella and Scarlett looked over at Julie, alarm written all over their faces, before informing her that the dip she was enjoying was actually a massage cream. It was made up of a thinned skin lotion with powdered mint and a drizzle of baby oil added to it. Julie's face turned red with embarrassment. "Are you joking or am I just plain dumb?"

The owners and Elizabeth protested Julie's self-inflicted insult and told her that it was an understandable mistake and probably their fault for putting the massage-essentials cart right next to the table. Sophie exclaimed, "No! I have it! We will be millionaires, ladies, with our new product!

We can sell edible massage lotions and fill our purses with millions of dollars! Woo!"

"Sophie, that's not going to happen," said Scarlett. "It's already been invented and sold."

The young Eastern European woman asked, "Edible facials too?"

"Probably. I must say, though, that it doesn't make sense to me why someone would want to eat what has been detoxified from their face."

"Hmm. That is true," Sophie voiced with disappointment. "Well then, Ms. Julie, you can stop eating your plain-dumb dip. It's a no go."

"Sophie!" scolded Isabella. "You need to stop drinking!"

"No more Pink Panty Pulldowns for you. You are shut off, girl!" chided Scarlett.

"Shut down my drinks? But I didn't even pull anything down yet, and no one else did either. Wait! Sophie's next choice for Elizabeth's fun, everybody! Let's all pull down our panties and make another toast! Woo!"

The ladies declined. Elizabeth added that she loved Sophie better with her clothes on her body and that she appreciated all the hard work they did to prepare this evening for her.

Scarlett offered to make Julie feel better with a very funny and true story about a client they had in the past. Julie agreed, glad that the group was not as horrified as she was about her error. They were all being so kind in trying to make her feel better.

Scarlett continued. "A few years ago, I had a client who came in for a deluxe massage package. After she disrobed and covered herself with a towel, I had a hard time focusing on giving her the service she purchased because all I could smell was a strong fish odor! I discreetly shared this with

Isabella, and she suggested I use talcum powder on the client's private area to mask the smell. She advised that I make it look like part of the service so that no one would smell the strong odor and the client would not be embarrassed. So I kept shaking more and more talcum in that area under the towel and it ended up looking like a talcum snowstorm in the air! And it still smelled so fishy! Isabella and I couldn't think of what else to do. We were beside ourselves with the situation. That's when Penny quietly asked us what was wrong, because Scarlett wasn't doing what normally took place and poor Penny couldn't finish her lunch. Some of the talcum apparently was landing on her plate. We shared with her what was happening and she laughed so hard! When she could finally stop laughing, Penny shared with us that she was eating a double-stuffed tuna-fish sub!"

The group erupted in laughter.

Scarlett added, "We all laughed ourselves silly and let the client in on what had happened. Luckily she had the same great sense of humor as us. She has been a wonderful steady customer ever since, and to this day, we still enjoy a good chuckle over that one."

Isabella said, "That reminds me of another story! We once had someone working here named Lula. She went to some garage sale and bought a vibrator for fifty cents. She didn't know what it was at the time and was going to use it to give neck massages! Now Lula wanted to display it professionally, and she set it in a fake hand mannequin that she got from someone. So we had to explain it to her, especially when people walked in and saw that vibrator standing up long and tall in that hand mannequin!"

Bonnie interjected. "Any way you shake it, you had to hand it to her, though!"

The group roared with laughter once again.

"So see?" continued Isabella. "We all make honest mistakes that seem so logical to us at the time. You're in very good company, Julie!"

"We are all good company and such good friends now!" exclaimed Sophie. "We are having so much fun that I say we should do something extra fun together."

She looked around with a huge smile at everyone looking back at her and finished her statement. "Yes! I say . . . Brazilian waxes for everyone. I will do all of you right here, right now—my treat!" She clapped her hands together.

The women all looked at each other to gauge the overall reaction in the room. Caroline, Scarlett, and Isabella chimed in to say that they had already been privately waxed. Penny informed Sophie that she would pass on it this time. Julie and Micheline looked at each other, both slightly embarrassed that this topic was even being discussed and that such information was shared so easily. Micheline informed the ladies that she was not a Brazilian-cut type of woman. Elizabeth shared that she was a bride who was already prepared for her honeymoon with a private area that was nothing less than an enticing showpiece at this point. Julie blushed to hear this and covered her face. She just could not believe how open the younger women were being about such an intimate subject. *Pardon me? Yes, I shave down there. Please pass the chips.*

"So Ms. Julie, that leaves just you with me. You want to try it? C'mon! YOLO, William's mama, YOLO!"

"YOLO?" Julie asked.

"It stands for 'you only live once,'" Elizabeth offered. "Sophie, I don't think it's a good idea for you to give anyone a Brazilian wax right now. You should wait until you're sober. So let's wait for another day, okay?"

"Okay, Elizabeth, I will do that if it makes you happy, but what if your new mother-in-law wants one? I don't want to disappoint her, especially if it's her first one."

"Oh, I'm all set, Sophie," Julie jumped right in, "but I do want to thank you for giving me an idea of what the, um, fashion is these days."

"Any time, William's mama. We can turn you into a sexy senior on the prowl! You just say the word and we will take care of you any time! It is good to live a new day every day, no? C'mon! Let's dance like we're new!"

"Nude?" Penny asked.

"She said *new*," Bonnie explained in a louder voice.

"Hey! We can dance nude like we are new!" Sophie exclaimed.

Isabella and Scarlett shouted in unison, "NOT NUDE!"

Sophie replied, "Okay, but it's more exciting to try new things!"

She rose to change the music back to a satellite station with streaming dance-club tunes. She turned the volume up as well, and some of the ladies joined her in dancing. When the song was close to its finish, the group heard what they thought was a loud buzzing noise. They stopped the music altogether and listened closer until they heard what they confirmed to be the front doorbell. They all walked toward the front gathering space as Isabella unlocked and opened the front door. There at the entry way was a young uniformed man with an electronic tablet, a bouquet of flowers, and two rectangular gift boxes.

The ladies said hello to him and he returned their greeting before announcing to the ladies, amid giggles and smiles, that his name was LJ. He informed them that he had some flowers to deliver to the world's most beautiful bride, Elizabeth Leary, and boxes of candy for the world's two best mothers, Micheline Leary and Julie Morin.

Penny spoke first and gave the man a wink. "Sure you do, sweetie!"

"Ma'am?" LJ was a little confused by her response.

Sophie shouted, "We know why you're really here, Mr. LJ, so start the dance already! We've got a man stripper, ladies! Woo!"

Most of the group gave a collective cheer and started chanting, "Strip-o-gram! Strip-o-gram! Strip-o-gram!"

Elizabeth excitedly covered her mouth with her hands, partially laughing in disbelief. The poor man's face showed his growing panic.

"No, really! I'm LJ with After Hours Delivery, and it's *just* a delivery."

Sophie shouted, "See, ladies? He said After Hours, but Mr. LJ is still in his pants. C'mon, Mr. LJ man, Mr. Pants man, rip it off and dance for our Elizabeth!" She turned to the ladies and exclaimed, "Just look at him! He's so cute, and pretending to be so shy! He's going to bust out any minute now!"

"No! No! Look! Here are the flowers and the boxes of candy. Please! Where are Elizabeth, Micheline, and Julie?" the young man asked quickly. "I'm really—just really— here to deliver!"

"I bet he delivers!" Scarlett exclaimed with a growing smile.

Isabella replied, "Ooo, you really are all bad, Ms. Scarlett Allbad!"

"Why, thank you, Ms. Isabella Bella. We make a good pair!"

Sophie burst forward to grab the man's arms and started dancing with him. "Aiieee! He's going to strip for Elizabeth and the mamas too!"

Julie's and Micheline's eyes grew wide at the surprising thought. The younger ladies screamed with excitement. The

After Hours employee quickly dropped the flowers and candy on the floor and shouted, "Here you go! Thank you for using After Hours Delivery. My name's LJ, and I don't need a signature or a tip anymore!" With that, he abruptly turned and ran back to the white delivery van that was parked in front of the business. It indeed had a sign marked After Hours Delivery, with a website and phone number included.

Sophie looked at the ladies. "Oh! Oh! He really was just delivering and we scared him away, poor little LJ man! We were too much naughty and fun for him. Well, okay then! Who wants another Pink Panty Pulldown?"

The group roared as they picked up the gorgeous bouquet of flowers, the boxes of candy, and the messages that accompanied them. Each female there commented on how impressed she was with William's thoughtfulness. Julie secretly smiled to herself, basking in warm parental pride. Isabella called for two taxis so the visiting ladies could be delivered to their separate destinations. The cars that brought them could stay parked at the spa until someone could come the next day to get them.

Julie thought that it had been a great evening overall, with a mixed bag of sweet moments, great conversation, small challenges, and new things tried, but mostly lots of fun. Sophie turned out to be a true live wire, but Julie had learned a very important life lesson from this person. This young, energetic woman easily dared to be everything that Julie could only dream of from behind her self-imposed fear. She learned that fun puts the F in LIFE, and without it, a LIFE would only be a LIE to one's full happiness. She didn't need a lot of fun. After all, she and Mike were always loyal to their obligations. Somewhere, however, there had to be a little bit of fun for them so they could release the pressures and stresses that came with all their commitments. She and Mike needed a balanced journey instead of the roller-coaster ride it had been the last few years. There had to be a better formula for the sandwich generation, those supporting their children and their elderly parents simultaneously. The rest of the family was going to have to change a few things along with them. Many hands spending a couple hours helping out would surely be better than a couple pairs of hands spending many hours getting things done. Life wasn't about all work or all fun; it was about balancing both of them for a fuller life. It was the balance of yin and yang, him and her, give and take, and realigning it when necessary. If Mike and Julie were truly happier by better balancing their life's plate, the items life served them on that plate would not slip off and the home environment would improve. They definitely had to start trusting that other hands could help hold that plate when it became too heavy.

Thank you, Sophie! Lesson on how to make your own fun—check. Lesson on how to insist on your own happiness—check.

The taxis arrived and hugs were exchanged. Elizabeth thanked everyone again for such a nice and fun evening together on her last night as a bachelorette. After making comments about seeing each other tomorrow for the big day, Julie got into one taxi with the Learys while Penny and Bonnie entered the other taxi that was heading in the opposite direction. As the occupants were being driven away, Julie could see Sophie waving and yelling to them, "Next time, ladies, we do body painting and go skydiving. Woo!"

Woo, Sophie, woo!

Chapter 14

Julie woke to the sound of a siren careening down the highway outside their room. Opening one eye, she tried to read the bedside clock but her eyes just wouldn't focus. Fumbling for her glasses on the nightstand in the pitch-black room certainly was challenging, but the last thing she wanted to do was to turn the bedside lamp on and wake Mike. Three a.m. was now visible, though the numbers were still slightly blurred. *Sure glad I didn't consume any more of those Pink Panty Pulldowns. I'll just swallow a couple more aspirin and go back to sleep.*

She found the aspirin bottle in the light of the glowing numbers. When she reached for the glass of water she'd set on the nightstand, she overextended her arm and sent the glass crashing. *Broken glass leaves me no option. I have to turn on the light.*

Julie whispered, "I'm sorry, Mike. I didn't mean to wake you!" She flicked the light switch and turned to offer an apologetic smile, but he wasn't there! Julie did a double take. It was three o'clock in the morning, and the sheet on his side was still pulled tightly enough to bounce a quarter on it. She reached for her phone and called him, but it went straight to voicemail. *Where is he? Why isn't he here? Was there a car accident?*

A multitude of thoughts raced through Julie's mind as she quickly leaned over to retrieve the broken glass fragments. The hurried motion sent her head spinning, so she left the fragments on the carpet and retreated to her pillow. After way too many visions of accidents and emergency rooms, sleep finally came.

Five hours later Julie's eyes reopened. The rectangular numbers on the clock were no longer blurry, but she hesitated to roll out of bed, remembering the shards of glass on the carpet. Turning to face Mike's side of the bed, she was once again surprised. He still was not there. She reached for her phone and pressed the programmed number. *Come on, Mike, answer!*

Automatically connecting to voicemail once again caused Julie to worry for a moment. *Surely nothing serious happened; probably out all night with the boys. He's sure gonna pay the price for that today!*

She thought of calling William, but resisted the temptation. If he had the chance to get some additional rest after a night on the town, she certainly didn't want to be the one to wake him.

I'll just shower and head downstairs for breakfast. Mike's probably already there with the family. Julie rolled to her husband's side of the bed and reached for the notepad and pen by the room's telephone. After scrawling a warning for the maids about the broken glass fragments, she made her way to the bathroom. Her reflection was startling. Dark circles framed her eyes and half of her hair seemed to be programmed to remain at a forty-five-degree angle.

Thank God for shampoo, conditioner, mousse, and concealer.

The bachelorette party had definitely been a wonderfully fun-filled night, but not without consequences. The hot shower was refreshing and rejuvenated Julie's pink-tinged skin. Applying only a small amount of makeup, she slipped into her designated outfit for the pre-wedding festivities. There would be plenty of time to properly do her makeup once she joined the bridal party at the resort. After leaving her room, Julie took the elevator to the first floor of the hotel, where she headed to its restaurant.

Julie saw that almost all the tables and booths were filled. She immediately spotted her family sitting at a table near the front. They were happily chatting and browsing through their menus while sipping porcelain cups most likely filled with coffee and tea. Julie signaled to the hostess that she was all set and approached her family's table. Two nuns, one older than the other, sat at a table next to the partial Morin clan on one side, and an elderly couple sat near the opposite end. Julie was greeted with good mornings from her family as Kelly slid down one seat, allowing her a space to sit between GG and her niece.

"Where's Dad?" asked John.

"Well, he was gone when I woke up," replied Julie, "so I'm guessing he's with William."

The server arrived with impeccable timing, saving Julie from having to give any more details. She did not bother to mention that the same spot next to her in bed had been empty all night. There was no need to field a hundred questions. There would be enough discussion between Mike and her later, and she didn't want any disruptions to the harmony of William and Elizabeth's wedding day.

After placing their orders with the server, Kelly asked, "How did the ladies' night go?"

"The ladies might go? Where are we going?" GG chimed in to the conversation. Kelly explained to GG that she was asking about the ladies' party that had taken place the previous night. The grandmother shared that parties were a bit too much for her now and asked Kelly or Julie to politely decline for her.

"We will, GG, we will," Kelly replied, opting for the easier way out. John and Kelly traded opinions about people at the previous night's wedding rehearsal and the traditional Wisconsin fish fry that had followed it. Julie mostly listened to the commentaries and witty jabs being shared. She then zoned in on the conversation that GG had struck up with the religious sisters sitting at the table closest to her. Julie's mom introduced herself to them, and they in turn shared their names. The older one was Sr. Mary Margaret, and the younger one was Sr. Anita John.

"Don't worry, Sister, he's right here and he's going to help you, I'm sure," offered GG. Both sisters gave a mutual look of confusion as John spoke up and asked what was needed from him. The younger nun apologized and stated that his grandmother was introducing herself and that she was just sharing their names as well. GG countered, "Oh. Then why do you need John . . . Sister . . . Sister . . . what did you say your name was again?"

The sisters started to speak, but John interrupted and offered to handle it. He explained their names in a slower and clearer fashion to his grandmother.

"Ahh, okay. I'm sorry. I misunderstood," said GG.

"Mom, you're fine. Don't worry about it," Julie comforted her elderly mother.

Kelly, John, and the nuns all chimed in with their agreement to Julie's words. GG smiled with renewed clarity.

"Yes, it's an honest mistake but I understand now. You don't need *our* John. You need *a* john. I used it just before we sat down for breakfast. It's straight across from here and then take the first door on your left. Once again, I'm sorry, but I'm not used to nuns referring to restrooms in this way."

Sr. Anita John explained that they were not in need of a bathroom and that John was actually her last name.

"Oh! I see," GG nodded. "You know, Sr. John, you should probably say that first so you can avoid lots of confusion."

Both religious women tilted their heads until Julie politely spoke. "My mom's hearing is not always the best and so we have to deal with misunderstandings from time to time."

The nuns smiled kindly.

"Speaking of confusion," added GG, "I just helped the sisters through theirs. You know, as I always say, we're all here to help each other, right?"

Julie closed her eyes for a moment and shook her head slightly while the other members of her family reacted similarly.

"Yes, we are," Sr. Mary Margaret said, showing a gracious understanding of the elderly woman's issues.

Julie changed the subject. "We're in town for a family wedding. Do you two sisters live here or are you visiting as well?"

Sr. Mary Margaret hesitantly gave Julie a second look before the pair explained that they were in Madison to evaluate the needs of a new convent for their community. Julie asked for the name of their religious order, and Sr. Anita John informed her that they were the Sisters of Vocation, otherwise known as the Vocationist Sisters.

"So is that all you do? Vacation and pray? That sounds like fun!" GG exclaimed.

"It feels that way sometimes, but we actually dedicate ourselves to living our vocation to its fullest and to propagating our faith," Sr. Mary Margaret explained.

The elderly woman pushed further. "That's nice, but how do you do your work and vacation at the same time?"

Confusion settled in once again as people tried to understand why GG would be asking this question. Kelly piped up to complain that she couldn't hear everything from her end of the table.

"That's okay. Neither can GG," replied John with a smirk. There were chuckles among the younger Morins.

"What nuns are you again?" asked Kelly.

"They're vacationists, honey," GG offered before the religious women could respond.

"Oh, no, no, no! We're—" the sisters started before Julie jumped into the conversation.

"Mom, they're not vacationists, they're *vo*cationists. It's vocation, not vacation."

GG replied, "Ohhh. Okay then, that's nice, but do they still need John for something?"

As breakfast arrived at their table, Julie said to the nuns, "Well, I hope you like Madison enough that you come back often. It's a wonderful city."

"Yes, it is," Sr. Mary Margaret answered with a smile. "I'm originally from here, so I couldn't agree with you more. If I do take my final vows within the next year, I'll look forward to visiting again. I'm just struggling with that decision right now, especially after recent events. I must say though that it's nice to mix convent work with personal time visiting friends."

"Yes, it's nice when one can do that. Good for you!" Julie replied.

"Thank you. I even enjoyed a surprise visit and shared a coffee with an old friend that I ran into unexpectedly, someone from my younger, single days. So it was a very blessed and rewarding trip. Now Sister Anita John and I are returning today to our mother house back in New York, and speaking of that, we really have to get going if we're going to catch our flight."

Everyone at the table commented that it was nice to meet the sisters and that they hoped the nuns would have a safe return trip. The sisters thanked them and told GG that she was a lovely woman with a wonderful family and that they would pray for God to continue to shower them with an abundance of blessings.

GG interjected, "Good luck, and if you ever need John, I'll make sure he heads over to the new convent to help."

"We can't help out if the convent is here in Madison and we all live in Georgia!" John explained. "Our grandmother's geography is definitely interesting."

Sr. Mary Margaret acknowledged GG's thoughtful offer while the two religious women picked up their bags and rose from their chairs. At that moment, Julie spotted Mike entering the room carrying a beautiful, oversized bouquet bursting with lilies and hydrangeas. Julie immediately knew something must have happened last night and that it was not good.

Okay. Judging by the size of that bouquet, it must have been colossal and guilt ridden. Or does he have weddings on the mind? Hmm. Maybe he bought my favorite flowers seeing today is our firstborn's wedding? Yeah, right. Well, this should be interesting, at the least. I can barely see him behind that giant display!

As Mike approached the table he extended his arms to offer the bouquet to Julie. She put on her best practiced smile, guessing the reason for the flowers had something to do with Mike's peculiar absence from their hotel bed. As Mike handed the arrangement to his wife, everyone heard Sr. Mary Margaret gasp and turned in her direction.

"Mike?" the nun asked in disbelief.

Julie turned back toward Mike. "You two know each other?"

Mike was stunned. She could tell by the look on his face. He stammered, "Susan? I mean, Sr. Mary Margaret?"

"Sr. Mary Margaret is Susan to you? Mike, you two know each other?" Julie repeated her question, searching her husband's face for an answer. Everyone at the table watched like spectators at a tennis match.

"This is getting very interesting," John added like a commentator to the group.

Julie ignored her son's comment. "Mike? Care to explain?"

Sr. Mary Margaret motioned to Sr. Anita John as she started walking away. "I don't want to cause any problems. It was nice meeting all of you and it was nice seeing you again, Mike. Unfortunately, we have to catch a plane. I will leave you with your wonderful family. Thank you again for last night. It was truly special."

"Last night was special for you, Mike?" Julie started a slow boil as she watched the sisters leaving. The older nun's back porch offered quite a swing as the sisters exited the restaurant.

"What's the special?" asked GG. "Maybe someone else wants to order it too. I know I'm full, though."

Kelly chimed in. "Trust me, GG, you can't order a special like this!"

"You can't?" asked GG. "Then you shouldn't offer it if it's not on the menu."

"My thoughts exactly," Julie stated, her lips curling and eyes welling up as she stared directly into Mike's eyes.

"There you go jumping to incorrect emotional conclusions again," Mike chided her.

"Well, here's another emotional conclusion for you," Julie stated as she rose from the table. She dumped the bouquet and left her family behind as she crossed the dining area. The strength she used to hold back her tears matched the increasing speed of her steps as she searched for a destination that was anywhere but there. She needed to process what had just happened before she could talk with anyone, especially Mike.

The hotel's lobby was dotted with people coming and going in different directions while taking care of various tasks and errands. An observant hotel bellboy noticed Julie during her frantic search for a temporary haven.

"Is everything okay? Can I help you, ma'am?" the hotel worker offered.

At that moment Julie spotted a ladies' restroom to her left in an opposite corner of the lobby. "All set, thanks," Julie responded almost absentmindedly to the bellhop as she rushed off to her selected shelter. Her eyes had just enough time to catch his quick shrug and questioning look, but she didn't care. She instead focused on the door to the restroom and hoped that she would have the place to herself. She needed to figure out what to do next and how to avoid ruining William and Elizabeth's wedding day! However, she just couldn't ignore the fresh pain of her heartbreak!

Is Mike a cheating husband? And with a nun of all people? Or did I jump to the wrong conclusion like Mike suggested? Has he lost interest in me? Why do these things always happen on or just before days when something special is going on in our lives?

Julie pushed the door open and was relieved to see she was indeed alone in the restroom. She locked herself in the middle of three stalls. A flood of tears burst forth, breaking through the dam of composure she had been plugging with her very last finger of self-control. Julie managed to manipulate the last few sheets of toilet paper from the stall's container and dabbed her face. Her sobs came to a stop just as abruptly as they had started when she heard the restroom door swing open.

"Hey, Aunt Julie, quite the exit you made there! It was like a scene right out of a movie! Where are you? I know you're in here," Kelly barked.

"Kelly! You don't just start shouting things out without checking to see who's in here!" Julie scolded her niece in a loud whisper.

"Uh, okay. Anybody in here besides my ridiculous aunt who ridiculously thinks her husband would ever ridiculously cheat on her? No? All right, we're all set, so come on out."

"How did you even know I was in here?" Julie asked.

Kelly explained, "As I searched in the lobby to see which way you went, a hotel worker came up to me and said that the lady I was probably looking for went into this restroom. I asked him what the lady looked like, and he described you! When I asked him how he knew who I was looking for, he said it was just a pretty good guess. So here I am. C'mon. Let's get out of here and talk about all the *crazy* that just happened."

Julie refused to open her stall door. "Kelly, I just want to stay here for a bit and figure things out for myself. I don't want to talk to anyone right now. I'm going to gather my thoughts here so I know exactly what I want to say, just between me and your uncle, and it's going to be logical. I'm also going to get down to the bottom of what just happened." Julie began to sob again before continuing. "Kelly, just go. Thanks, but this isn't your problem."

"All right, you're making me do this, seeing you insist on staying in your ridiculous stall," Kelly warned before lifting herself up to hang over the top of the door in order to see her aunt. "You need to listen. If you two are fighting, it's the whole family's problem—if there is a problem—but there isn't! You've got something wrong somewhere. So let's get out of here, and we'll figure out who messed up where."

The door to the restroom opened and a lady walking in was very surprised to see Kelly hanging at the top of the middle stall door. Kelly snapped, "Yeah, it's that kind of restroom. Do what you need to do and move on, please!"

The lady balked at first and then said, "Well, I really do need to go." She headed to an adjacent stall and, before entering, stopped and asked, "You're not going to hang on my door too, are you?"

Kelly shot back, "Of course not! Don't be ridiculous! Do I look like a weirdo peeper to you?" The lady opened her mouth to answer, but Kelly quickly added, "Keep moving!" The woman obediently entered her stall.

"Kelly, please, don't make matters worse," Julie pleaded.

"Is this a heated lovers' quarrel?" the lady asked nervously.

"Yes, it is!" Julie wept between words. "There's a third person and I can't believe it!"

"I'm sure you two, um, significant partners will work it out if you stay calm," stated the woman in the stall.

"Rrr! It's not the two of us! Gross!" Kelly fired back. "She's my aunt, so butt out!"

Julie spoke up. "I'm not gross, but maybe I'm not—I'm not—oh, I don't know what I'm not compared to that woman." Her tears began again. "I need a tissue for my nose and there's nothing left in here."

The toilet flushed in the adjacent stall. Kelly readjusted herself at the top of the door and stretched her neck toward the other woman.

"Hey, lady." Kelly boldly took charge to correct the problem. "Now that you're finished, can you pass some toilet paper under to my aunt? She's all out."

"I have a packet of tissues in my purse, if you prefer," the woman offered.

"No, thanks, I don't want to trouble anyone. Toilet paper is fine," Julie replied between sniffs.

"I could just give you the pack, though, and—" she began.

"Please just pass the toilet paper, or I'm going to come down in there to get it myself!" Kelly demanded.

"I will do just that, but please don't threaten me. It makes me very nervous and scared and . . . well, there you go. Now I dropped the paper. Hold on. I have to pick it up and throw it out, and then I'll get some more."

"Shirley, are you still in there? Oh my gosh!" an older woman exclaimed as she entered the restroom and saw Kelly hanging on the middle stall door.

"Oh, great. Shirley has a friend," Kelly complained. "Aunt Julie! Open the darn door!"

Julie replied, "Kelly, you don't need to be here. Oh. Thanks for the paper, ma'am."

"What did you do with Shirley?" the friend asked in confrontation after taking a few steps closer.

"Nothing," answered Kelly turning her head and looking downward toward the lady while readjusting her arms over the top of the door.

"She threatened me," Shirley called out from her stall. "I'm not sure if I should come out with her hanging there."

Kelly argued, "I didn't threaten anyone, and I'm hanging here because my ridiculous aunt won't let me in her stall to talk and fix things!"

The woman questioning her was confused. "Your aunt?"

Julie started to cry again as she pushed her words out from behind the stall door. "That's me, and it's because I don't want to talk about my husband spending the night with a nu-u-u-n!" Her words turned into sobs.

"Marian, everything okay in here with Shirley and you?" another voice sounded. Two additional women, both husky and well dressed, popped their heads into the restroom to check on their friends. Their eyes grew larger as they were surprised by the scene in front of them.

Kelly hopped down from the middle stall door and placed her hands on her hips. "Where the heck are you all coming from? Does Shirley have a posse or an entourage or something?"

One of the husky women asked, "Why were you hanging on the stall door?"

"She was threatening Shirley for some reason. That's what I'm trying to find out right now, but the young lady's aunt is really upset because her husband cheated on her," Marian, the lady who confronted Kelly, explained.

"With a nun," added Shirley from within her stall, "and the niece threatened me, so I don't feel comfortable coming out. Sorry for the delay, ladies."

"Oh my gosh! I can't take this anymore!" Kelly shouted. "I didn't threaten you, Shirley! Aunt Julie, just open the darn door and let's get out of here before there's a whole box of these crazy cotton swabs. I promise we don't have to talk, but we do have to get to the venue soon so we can get ready for the wedding. Plus, you'll have a lot more privacy than you have right now. That's for sure!" Julie opened her stall door while dabbing a tissue to her eyes and sniffling. The two reached out to each other and hugged.

Marian asked, "So there's a wedding? Your uncle is marrying the nun and you're both going? What a strange family!"

Shirley chimed in. "I knew that as soon as I saw the niece hanging on the outside of the stall!"

"No. No. I'm sorry, but you don't understand. I'm—" Julie started to say before Kelly interrupted her.

"Nope. That's fine. You've got it. We're crazy, so just step aside and let us get out of here."

The restroom door opened and a male security guard cautiously entered. He looked around at the ladies. "Someone in here call for security? Everything okay?"

"Are you kidding me?" Kelly shot out with anger. "Which one of you saggy biscuits called for nothing?"

"I did," Shirley replied meekly from behind her door. "You scared me with your threat and my friends were waiting for me, so I called my cousin at the hotel's front desk and she called security for me."

"Aarr! I didn't threaten you!" Kelly growled.

"You seem like a threatener to me," offered Marian.

The security officer spoke next. "Let's everyone just stay calm until we can figure this out."

Julie offered an explanation. "I was upset and my niece was just trying to help. Then when I needed some tissue paper, Shirley in the other stall, who was kind to offer me a travel pack of tissues, misunderstood my niece's impatience. No one is going to hurt anyone, though, I can assure you of that. Oh, I'm so embarrassed."

Shirley unlocked her stall door and spoke to Julie. "I'm sorry about your husband, and I hope it all works out. Your niece must really care about you if she's willing to hang on a stall door just to talk to you."

The timid elderly woman then turned to Kelly. "You do come off as kind of scary when you talk to people. I just want you to know that."

"Yeah, well . . ." Kelly began.

Julie squeezed Kelly's arm and whispered, "Let's go. We'll talk."

"Fine, Aunt Julie. Okay, Shirley, sorry about that. We need to go, though, so is everybody good?" Kelly asked in partial resignation so they could quickly make their departure.

"I guess so, because your aunt seems so sweet. She doesn't need any more problems today," replied Shirley. Julie exchanged polite smiles with the woman and then hugged Kelly again. Her niece squeezed her back in return as the others in the room chimed in with their sounds of approval.

"Okay. Well, if I'm not needed then," the security guard stated, "I'm a guy and this is a ladies' room, so there is nothing I would like more right now than to leave. That is, as long as everything is okay."

The older ladies chuckled and some of them began to wash their hands while Julie and Kelly made their exit behind the guard. The last thing the two could hear as the restroom door slowly closed behind them was someone making the statement, "That's so weird that the husband cheated with some nun and now those two are going to their wedding! I know I wouldn't!"

Julie and Kelly went up to their hotel rooms to get their dresses and other items for the wedding. They didn't talk at all about the scene that took place in the restaurant. The only thing Kelly discussed was having a few shots at the venue with the other ladies before the wedding. That way Julie could sort her thoughts and loosen up from the stress before having a serious discussion with Mike. This seemed like a great idea to Julie, and the sooner she downed some liquid courage, the better prepared she would be. She didn't want to chance ruining the special day for others, so the air had to be cleared and repaired before the big event. They put their items into the back of Kelly's rental car and seated themselves up front.

The drive to the venue was filled with music from the radio, as Kelly drove and Julie quietly sorted through her thoughts. At one point, Kelly did ask about her uncle, and Julie let her know that his suit and things were gone, so he must have left with the boys, and they would meet up at the venue. Julie decided to share with Kelly just the basics about Mike not being in their hotel bed during the night.

Kelly suggested that perhaps there was a good reason for that, and wouldn't Julie like a chance to explain before being judged if the roles had been reversed?

"Touché," Julie agreed in resignation. "I kind of know that already, but things just happened so fast and everything just looked so bad. It got the best of me. I don't want you to worry. I'll talk with your uncle and hopefully we'll fix everything. There's just other things that need fixing too, so we'll see."

Not long after leaving the hotel, Julie and Kelly arrived at Hopa Akigle Place. They gathered their bagged dresses and other items and brought them inside. A young lady greeted them and escorted them up a winding grand staircase to the bridal room. Even before the employee opened the door for them, the Morins could hear the loud chatter and laughter that was coming from the room, sending vibes of happiness and excitement.

Okay. Please don't let me bring these ladies down with my problems!

It was as if her niece could hear her very thoughts when Kelly said in a lowered voice for only Julie to hear, "See? Listen to them! It's a whole bunch of happy, and that's exactly what you need! We'll get dressed, put on our makeup, have a few shots, and loosen up! Okay?"

Julie nodded as she entered the room with Kelly to a loud cheer from the gathered group. Sophie bounded forward first and generously hugged the two women while saying, "It's the mother of the groom and the cousin of the groom! You must get dressed, and then Sophie chooses shots for everyone!"

"I'm surprised you're not hungover this morning," Julie commented with a smile. "You were quite a party girl last night."

"I am what you call the hungover," explained Sophie, "but no one said it cannot be a happy hungover. I am so happy for the Morins today, all the many, many Morins!"

Kelly jumped in with her two cents worth. "See? A person can even be hungover and happy!"

Julie smiled her polite acknowledgement of Kelly's statement.

"Only if you're Sophie!" quipped Penny.

All the ladies laughed while Julie and Kelly made their way through the crowd, first chatting with Erin, Elizabeth, and Grace. Julie drew in her breath with admiration at the sight of her future daughter-in-law dressed in her bridal gown. The teamwork of Bella and Allbad was at their usual level of perfection. They had created a simply stunning lace angel–crown braid with Elizabeth's hair, and then added softly woven touches of baby's breath within it. The rest of her hair was arranged to fall in ornately woven tresses that highlighted Elizabeth's beauty. Seeing the bride's glow of hope and happiness suddenly struck Julie, reminding herself of her own wedding day. She and Mike had been ready to conquer the world together, for better or worse, because nothing could possibly be stronger than their love for each other.

For better or worse indeed! No one ever says how much better or how much worse a marriage will be, yet youth, with all its eagerness, assumes the two will be balanced. When is "better" going to happen again for Mike and me? The past few years have only brought us the "worse," and each "worse" gets, well, worse! I'm angry and I'm hurt, and he was with a nun of all people!

After a quick chat with everyone, Julie and Kelly changed into their dresses at Sophie's encouragement. This way the ladies could have time to make their toasts and enjoy their shots all together. The last two Morin ladies were ready to join the crowd after Isabella and Scarlett quickly touched up their hair and applied their makeup.

"Sophie's choice is to have the Morins' favorite tradition of Rooty Bombs, ladies! Drink up your shots!" Sophie bubbly exclaimed.

Everyone in the room, except for Erin and Grace, did so obediently and the shot glasses were refilled. Erin spoke next as she gave a beautiful toast for Elizabeth. "My brother may not always be perfect, but he will always be perfectly himself. Being in love, as I have learned, doesn't mean just staring at each other with rapidly beating hearts. It means facing forward in the same direction together, looking toward your tomorrow together, or as I think it should be spelled, t-w-o-gether. Here's to Elizabeth and William *two*gether!"

Everyone drank their second Rooty Bomb. Julie noticed Kelly texting and asked her, "What's so important to text while we're all enjoying a special moment together?"

"It's just a quick text. Don't worry about me. I know what's happening," Kelly replied.

"I just don't know how you can do all of it at the same time," explained Julie.

"Not only can I do it all at the same time, I can even make things happen! There you go!" Kelly said, showing that she was quite pleased with herself.

"There you go? What are you talking about? Am I going somewhere?" Julie looked around the room. Then she spotted Mike. He must have just entered the room because she hadn't noticed him there before that moment. He was heading her way with Jake.

Don't look! Turn around like you didn't notice him! Please, please, please don't let anything embarrassing happen!

"Hi, honey. You had an idea you wanted to share with me?" Mike said as he came up to her.

"An idea? I don't have an idea for anyone. By the way, are we all going somewhere that no one shared with me?" Julie asked.

"That's new to me," Mike joined Julie in her confusion.

Jake handed his father an empty shot glass while Kelly interrupted the conversation. "I'll tell you two crazy kids what's new—another toast! Sophie's coming around with the last shot before the ceremony. It's about time you're finally together today!"

Sophie arrived to refill Julie's glass and filled Mike's new glass. As the group turned to wait for the next toast, Mike gently took Julie by the elbow. He placed his finger up to his mouth as if he had a secret and he signaled her to follow him. Julie reluctantly obeyed. They placed their shots down on a side table and exited through a door to the hallway. Julie was not sure where Mike was leading the two of them, but she knew she didn't want any drama right now. She also didn't want to cause a scene or start crying just before the wedding. Julie decided she would simply study the parquet floor so their eyes would not meet. Oddly enough, it diverted her thoughts to the Boston Garden and the Celtics. Thanks to a basketball trivia night, she had learned that after years of use, the parquet flooring was officially retired and replaced.

Is that what happened last night? Was I replaced for a one-night stand? That's not the Mike I've lived with for all these years!

Julie had finally remembered this was the Susan from years ago who had once been quite a diversion. Perhaps a simple name change had not really changed Susan at all. As they turned the corner, Mike stepped into an alcove and Julie reluctantly followed. It was a moment of total role reversal, as he was the one pursuing conversation.

"Well?" he asked.

"Well what? I don't want to talk."

"I know you have questions. Let's just get this out in the open and be done with it."

"I don't want it out in the open right now, and it would take a miracle for us to be done with it before the ceremony starts."

"Come on, Julie, I know you. Just ask the question."

She needed diversion; she did not want to cry. Julie instinctively began pinching the skin between her thumb and forefinger, hoping the discomfort would work its magic as it had previous times.

"Just ask the question."

The pain in her hand was intensifying and the tears weren't coming. *Stay strong. Don't give in to his questioning.*

"Julie, just ask the question."

"No."

"Then let me ask it for you. Why didn't you come back to the hotel last night?"

"That's right! Why didn't you come back to the hotel last night?" Julie bit her lip with disdain. She had played right into his hand, and now everything was open for discussion. Julie found herself exactly where she didn't want to be.

"It was an innocent, unexpected meeting. That is all it was."

"Unexpected, perhaps. Innocent, not too sure. I have never forgotten about Susan."

"Here we go . . ."

"That's right, Mike. Here we go. You were the one who wanted to talk. You were the one that pursued this conversation now. We could have had this discussion a lot earlier, this morning for example, or even last night if you would have come back to our room. You could have even called me last night. In fact, why didn't you call me?"

"Because I knew this would be your reaction."

"And because you knew this would be my reaction, you pushed me to discuss this with you right before our son's wedding?"

"Absolutely! I want to make sure we clear everything up between the two of us before the ceremony."

"Oh, like it's just that easy!" Julie felt her eyes start watering and fought back the urge to cry.

"Why not? Does everything always have to be difficult to solve with us?" Mike asked.

"You tell me. You're the one who felt humiliated about the less-than-ten score at Notel Motel and then decided to try his luck with Susan Sister Mary Make-Me-a-Lucky-Man Margaret! Were you trying to score a ten with a nun, Mike? Trying to go big? Would that bring your coveted pride back to you?" Julie asked sarcastically.

"I can't believe you don't trust me after all these years! You're not even being reasonable right now," Mike stated.

"I'll tell you what's reasonable. Not having this discussion right now is reasonable! This whole talk needs to continue at a later time, just like I said at the beginning," Julie complained.

"I guess at this point you're probably right," Mike agreed. "I just wanted to—"

"There you two are!" Brett interrupted as he came rushing down the hallway. "We're all waiting for you. The ceremony's about to start!"

"We thought everyone was still doing toasts, so I guess we lost track of the time. We'll be right there. Give us a couple seconds," Mike answered for the two of them.

Brett started to leave. "Okay, but a couple seconds is all you have before the whole Morin army comes to get you!"

Julie replied, "Thanks, Brett."

Once Brett left, Mike looked Julie in the eyes for a long moment. "I guess we'll finish this conversation later. Right now we have a son that's getting married, so we can at least get this right for him. Shall we?" Mike offered his arm to his wife. Julie dutifully wrapped her arm around his and they walked down the hall to the stairway.

At the bottom of the stairs, they turned and exited the building. They were glad that people were sitting and facing the lake so that not many would notice their slightly late arrival. Everything looked spectacular, and even nature offered the bride and groom the gift of a gorgeous day. Everyone was in their place and ready for the ceremony to begin. The Morins smiled proudly as they were escorted down the aisle and took their seats. They were followed by the mother of the bride, who had been patiently waiting at the back of the gathering.

The ambient music faded and a string quartet began to play as the wedding attendants took their turns walking down the white runner. There were big smiles and camera clicks throughout the small gathered crowd as Grace tossed rose petals here and there on her way down the aisle. She was the perfectly cute and irresistible flower girl! After Grace arrived at her seat, the music fully stopped for a moment. The bridal march began, and the groom's parents looked at their son gazing down the aisle and beaming brightly. It was quite obvious that he was anxious to begin the journey of marriage with his beloved bride. Julie turned with Mike to watch Elizabeth walking down the aisle. She was escorted by her father and looked stunning in her bridal gown. It was touching to see Elizabeth's father hand her to William with his blessing. Together they turned and faced the justice as he began the ceremony. The young couple was ready to commit themselves to each other. Julie felt as if Mike was ready to commit himself to anyone but her.

Chapter 15

"Family and friends, welcome to Hopa Akigle Place for the marriage of Elizabeth Leary and William Morin. I'm Justice Nelson, and it is an honor and a pleasure for me to officiate this ceremony.

"Elizabeth and William thank each of you for coming this afternoon. It means so much to them to be surrounded by family and close friends. Here today are their parents, Micheline and Stan, and Julie and Mike, and their two grandmothers, GG and Edith. Joining us also are many siblings, an exceptional wedding party, and other important people who have come from far and near to be here for this celebration.

"Before I agree to officiate a wedding ceremony, I meet with the bride and groom because I first like to get to know them. Before planning the ceremony, I make sure that they have great potential in being part of a successful marriage. I personally do not like to officiate at a marriage that I feel will not last.

"Let me share with you what I learned about William and Elizabeth. William Morin was born in Portage. He grew up in Wisconsin and Texas, returning to Wisconsin to graduate from Wisconsin Dells High School, where he excelled in football and an active social life. After graduation he joined the Marine Corps Reserve. Along his life's path, he attended UW at Stevens Point, worked at Gagnon's Electronics, and then joined IDK. William was so successful in his work that he was able to build his own home by the age of twenty-six.

"He lost an aunt in the September eleventh tragedy, and that influenced him to enlist in the Wisconsin National Guard. Today he is an officer training in Alabama to fly Blackhawk helicopters, and he expects to be deployed to the Middle East next year. We thank you, William, for your service and dedication to our country.

"Elizabeth was born in Sun Prairie, where she became an enthusiastic football and basketball cheerleader. She was also dubbed 'Dr. Dill' by fellow classmates because of her sound advice that was given freely to those who sought it from their makeshift therapist. Elizabeth was also active in DECA, an association for those preparing for business careers. She earned a degree in marketing from MATC. She worked for Houle's Rentals, as well as the Wisconsin Department of Revenue, while in high school, and went on to a full-time position at John Ray & Associates. This past year, she has been working in a management position at In-SPA-ration.

"Now, Elizabeth once had a roommate named Lisa from the Dells, and Lisa knew a gal named Bonnie. At some point back a few years ago, in a beer tent somewhere, Bonnie said to Elizabeth, 'I should set you up with my cousin.' Her cousin was none other than William Morin. 'You'll love him,' she offered. 'He's strong, he's tall, and he's rich!'

"Elizabeth inquired, 'With qualities like those, what's wrong with him that he doesn't have a girlfriend already?' Bonnie's reply was, 'No time. He is totally devoted to IDK Delivery Express.'

"Bonnie called William after that, and he strategically set up a pontoon boating party on Lake Monona and invited a number of people. This way he could distance himself from Elizabeth if she wasn't 'a keeper,' so to speak. Elizabeth came to the party as a guest of Bonnie, so she had some distance too. She came a bit reluctantly because Bonnie was the only person she knew at this party. After all, who else would she talk to if William didn't turn out to be her type?

"Well, William turned out to be, and I quote, 'a great guy.' He was tall and muscular as advertised, very social, and very giving. What really impressed Elizabeth was that William had gone out of his way to buy pink lemonade for her instead of beer.

"William noticed that she didn't talk much to people she did not know, as he had been warned, but, ah, she was cute! Before the afternoon was half over, he asked her for a date. Thus began the courtship of William and Elizabeth that would eventually lead up to this ceremony.

"This couple has made a commitment to each other. They know each other well. They have consistent, reasonable expectations and shared goals. Elizabeth and William always speak about each other with a glow. They speak about their similarities and contrasts, their common values and goals, and of their desire to grow old together, with trust, love, and an abundance of good humor!

"Having listened carefully to their testimonies about the amazing qualities of each other, and having witnessed the sparkling and inspiring electricity between them, I find unusual compatibility, mutual trust, and love beyond a reasonable doubt, and so am satisfied that this marriage is something very special.

"A wedding ceremony can be very elaborate, or it can be very simple. Our law requires only a declaration that the two parties take each other as husband and wife in the presence of witnesses and of some person who is authorized by the state to perform a marriage. Once these simple requirements have been met, the community must recognize, respect, and protect the new relationship. Marriage is actually one of the most important institutions in our social order. It should not be taken lightly or thoughtlessly. It should be entered with reverence, deep purpose, and in the spirit of enduring love.

"A good and happy marriage requires effort. It has to be consciously created and sustained. In building this, it is often and truly the little things that become the big things. For example, holding hands should never fade away. It is the basic sense of touch and connection that sustains communication and affection. Other little things that become big things are saying 'I love you' at least once a day and never going to sleep angry. This saying has become cliché because it works with great success! Now here is the rest of the list: never taking each other for granted and living life as if the honeymoon has never ended; growing mutual values and common goals together so that you can stand united as one in facing the world—after all, unity breeds strength; forming a circle of love that includes the whole extended family so that you will have support during the challenging times and not stand alone; doing things for each other—not out of duty or sacrifice, but instead out of love and thoughtfulness; and speaking and showing appreciation and gratitude.

"Partners in a good marriage do not demand perfection from each other. Instead, they learn and encourage patience, flexibility, understanding, and a helpful surplus of good humor! They have a very important and endless capacity to forgive and forget. They encourage growth for each other and together.

"A good marriage establishes a relationship in which independence is equal, dependence is mutual, and obligation is reciprocal. It involves not only marrying the right partner, but also *being* the right partner. Now, with that being said, William, please hold Elizabeth's hands.

"William, these are the hands of your wife that are holding yours on your wedding day, as she pledges her love and commitment to you all the days of her life. These are the hands that will hold your children with tender love, soothing them through illness and hurt, supporting and encouraging them along the way, and knowing when it is time to let go.

"These are the hands that will hold you tight as you struggle through difficult times. These are the hands that will comfort you when you are sick, or console you when you are grieving. These are the hands that will passionately love you and cherish you for a lifetime of happiness. These are the hands that will hold you in joy and excitement and hope. These are the hands that will give you support as your wife encourages you to chase down your dreams. Together everything you wish for can be realized.

"Elizabeth, please face William and hold his hands. These are the hands of your husband, the ones that are holding yours on your wedding day, as he promises to love you all the days of his life. These are the hands that will work alongside yours as together you build your future, as you laugh and cry, as you share your innermost secrets and dreams. These are the hands you will place with expectant joy against your stomach one day until he too feels his child stir within you. These are the hands that look so large and strong, yet will be so gentle as he holds your baby for the first time. These are the hands that will work long hours for you and your new family. These are the hands that will passionately love you and cherish you for a lifetime of happiness. These are the hands that will lift your chin and brush your cheek as they raise your face to look into his eyes, which will be filled completely with his overwhelming love for you.

"God bless these hands that you see before you. May they always be held by one another. Give these hands the strength to hold on during the storms of stress and the dark of disillusionment. Keep them tender and gentle as they nurture each other in their love. Help these hands to continue building a relationship founded in your grace, rich in caring, and devoted in reaching for your perfection. We ask this in God's name. Amen."

Justice Nelson turned and faced William. "William, will you accept this woman, whose hands you hold, choosing her alone to be your wedded wife? Will you love her, comfort her, through good times and bad, in sickness and in health, as long as you both shall live?"

William gazed into Elizabeth's eyes. "I will."

Justice Nelson then turned to face Elizabeth. "Elizabeth, will you accept this man, whose hands you hold, choosing him alone to be your wedded husband? Will you love him, comfort him, through good times and bad, in sickness and in health, as long as you both shall live?"

Elizabeth returned William's gaze. "I will."

The justice of the peace continued. "As you take these vows, William and Elizabeth, I would ask you to remember that to love is to come together from the pathways of the past and to move forward, hand in hand, along the uncharted roads of your future. You must be ready to risk, to dream, and to dare, and always to believe that all things are possible with faith and love in God, and in each other. Together your lights will burn much brighter as one united light from this point forward. William and Elizabeth, you may now kiss as you begin your life together as one."

Justice Nelson introduced the newlyweds as Mr. and Mrs. William Morin to those gathered around them. Applause erupted as the bride and groom held hands and flashed smiles of true joy. Everyone was then invited to head over to the reception as the bride and groom planned to linger behind to sign papers and pose for a few photos. The guests slowly proceeded toward the building that was overlooking the same lakefront that served as the background for the wedding. As people left, there was an abundance of compliments regarding the beautiful words and touching moments of the ceremony. Once everyone crossed the neatly manicured lawn, they entered the door to the large reception room of Hopa Akigle Place, with the parents of the bride and groom at the back of the crowd. Mike held the door for Stan and Micheline. He motioned for them to go on ahead and also let them know that he and Julie would join them in a few moments. Once alone, Mike took his wife aside to speak privately. He pressed her back against the building.

"It's time to get this straightened out so let's just get to the point."

Julie could not believe Mike's ill-chosen timing. She refused to be vulnerable at this moment to any hurt feelings, upset tears, or angry words. She knew it would be too hard to regain her composure for the reception. She wouldn't forgive herself if they had an argument and it ruined William's and Elizabeth's perfect day. "No, Mike. No straightening. No points. We are not doing this right before the reception!"

"Well, if not now, then when? I mean, we're waiting for the bride and groom anyway."

"I don't want to talk until after this celebration and we are alone. I am not going to ruin this day for our son and new daughter-in-law, and that could happen if we talk right now. Let's just go inside, play happy, and do our part. Agreed?"

Mike shot back, "Fine. Whatever." Julie could tell Mike was not thrilled, but that didn't matter at this moment. She walked past him and he followed her inside.

Within a half hour the bride and groom were back, along with their bridal party. After each attendant was announced, William and Elizabeth were then introduced as Mr. and Mrs. Morin. They walked together to the center of the floor and enjoyed their first dance together as newlyweds. Julie wistfully smiled and watched her son dance with his new wife. She recalled that very moment for her and Mike.

They're dancing the same way we did at our wedding, as if no one else is in the room with them. William can't take his eyes off of Elizabeth, and Mike was exactly like that too. Now look at us. We're performing our parts like puppets for this wedding, and I'm barely sure of how we got to this point. Did he cheat on me with that Susan nun lady? I can't believe that I can't tell whether he did or not! We can't even have a private discussion right now without raising our voices or hurting each other's feelings! This reception will be good for us to settle down and collect our thoughts. Please, Lord, let me figure out what to do!

"Mom?" someone asked. It was William, and he was taking her hand amid the sound of clapping. Julie had been so lost in her thoughts that she didn't realize the newlywed's first dance was done and the mother-and-son dance had been announced by the DJ. She rose from her seat, kissed her son, and danced beautifully with him. Julie now remembered that a few of the important dances were going to be done before the meal was served. Indeed it was good to have all these things happening right now, and

Julie was going to stay focused on them. The rest of the reception went off without a hitch. After the meal was finished, a few more announcements were made and the last of the special dances were announced. People ate and drank and danced the time away. There were toasts dotted with memories, jokes, beautiful words, and good wishes. Family and friends enjoyed themselves, and throughout it all, no one even noticed the dark cloud that hung over Mike and Julie's own marriage. After the newlyweds were sent off in grand style and the guests all left Hopa Akigle Place, there were just Mike and Julie left on the lakeshore. They had gotten in their car to leave with the last of the bridal party, but then decided to talk things out down by the lake. A cleaning crew was just finishing removing the setup for the wedding ceremony. The Morins thanked the workers as they walked past them toward two of the Adirondack chairs sitting by the shoreline.

Julie attempted to be the first to begin the difficult conversation. She opened her mouth to speak but, after a few false starts, could only say, "Mike, I don't know what to say to you. I don't even know how we got to this point! All I know is that I do love you and I'm really hurt. I'm not sure what we need to fix, but I do feel like there's something broken about us."

"I'll tell you, Jules," Mike began. "The first thing I've realized today is that this trip has painted some pretty perfect examples of our marriage."

"Really? How did you come up with that?" Julie inquired.

"Well, this is how I see it," he stated.

"So I suppose this is all going to be according to Mike?" she asked.

"Yes, and it's a whole other story."

About the Authors

Mary Becker

In fifth-grade English class, Mary (Leary) Becker discovered her love of writing, and even though it was her favorite of all classes, she never imagined that as an adult, she would be an author. Along the way, she's been fortunate to have many opportunities in different career fields, but her favorite will always be her role of wife and mother. Mary is presently living happily ever after with her high school sweetheart/husband in a storybook cottage, which includes a revolving door that is always open to their children, their children's spouses, and grandchildren.

Diane St.Cyr Janelle

Diane St.Cyr Janelle grew up in New Hampshire with her parents, who gave her and her four brothers the gifts of love, laughter, and resourcefulness. Diane always dreamed of becoming an elementary school teacher and an author. She taught for many years in Manchester, New Hampshire, and now she is blessed to pursue her passion for writing. She dabbles in all things creative, likes to honor her French and Abenaki ancestries, and thoroughly enjoys her time spent living and laughing with family and friends! Diane currently resides in Georgia with her wonderful husband, Marc, and their two beautiful children, Emilie and Mathieu. She continues to chase her dreams and delights in sharing her humor with others for the joy it brings to life's journey.